the
puzzle
of
you

the puzzle of you

LEAH MERCER

LAKE UNION
PUBLISHING

Text copyright © 2019 by Leah Mercer

Published by Lake Union Publishing, Seattle

www.apub.com

Amazon, the Amazon logo, and Lake Union Publishing are trademarks of Amazon.com, Inc., or its affiliates.

ISBN-13: 9781503959804
ISBN-10: 1503959805

Cover design by whittakerbookdesign.com

Printed in the United States of America

the
puzzle
of
you

CHAPTER ONE

The first thing Charlotte McKay hears is the distant sound of a child crying.

She groans as the wails break through the thick layer of fog shrouding her brain. She wishes the noise would stop . . . wishes she could sink back into silence. The cries grow louder and she strains against them, trying to escape, but something holds her tightly in place.

'Are you all right in there?'

A loud banging replaces the child's screams, and Charlotte forces her eyes open. Nausea churns inside as the pain in her head swells. She puts a hand to her forehead, her eyes widening when she discovers blood coating her fingers. *What the hell?* She blinks and scans her surroundings, trying to piece things together.

A steering wheel. An airbag, limp and lifeless. A seatbelt, gleaming like a snake in the sharp sunshine, biting her skin as she shifts in the seat.

She's in a car. She's in a car in the driver's seat, and there must have been an accident. *Please God, may it not have been her fault.* What is she doing driving, anyway?

'*Hey!* Are you okay?'

Before she can even try to respond, the car door swings open. Gentle hands unlatch the seatbelt, pull her from the car and strap her on to a hard board. Voices hammer into her head, asking for her name, where she lives, where it hurts, if she can move her legs. But everything is blurry and unclear, and the questions wash over her before draining away. She can barely understand the words, let alone answer.

The brilliant blue sky above her gives way to the scratched metallic roof of an ambulance. The doors slam shut, and a blissful silence fills the small space. No demands for information, no shouting . . . no crying. Charlotte winces, remembering the howling child. Did she hit another car – another car with a baby inside? She tries to remember what happened, but a hot wave of pain sears her brain, blunting any memory.

Tears fill her eyes, one spilling on to her cheek. She wants David. She wants David to hold her hand and tell her that everything will be okay; to touch her head and ease the pain. He's always been there for her, keeping everything ticking over when she works long hours – or disappears for weeks – trying to close million-pound deals for work. She may wear the trousers in their marriage, but he is the solid, grounded one keeping her tethered to reality.

Memories of their recent trip to Rome filter into her head, and she grasps on to the sun-dappled images, clutching them close like a comfort blanket. The lemon ice cream they loved so much that they had three cones a day. The pizza they scoffed, the opera she dragged him to where they sat so close to the stage they got sprayed with spit each time the soprano sang, the buzz of the square outside their hotel at night . . . and the sex. Oh, God, the *sex*. There must have been something in that ice cream, because after almost five years together, making love with her husband was better than ever.

The ambulance lurches around a corner then comes to a stop. The doors open, and Charlotte screws her eyes shut against the light and noise. The stretcher rattles beneath her, its wheels squeaking as it carries her down a corridor. Finally it stops, and she hears the scrape of rings on metal as a curtain is pulled around her.

'Hello.' A voice fills the space and Charlotte opens her eyes, gasping at the pain in her head. A woman with large brown eyes and curly dark hair stands over her, gazing down with the detached, brisk expression of what could only be a busy A&E consultant . . . not that Charlotte has any first-hand experience. She can't remember the last time she was in A&E – or even a hospital, for that matter. David always jokes that her body wouldn't dare defy her. So far, it hasn't. She wouldn't let it.

'I'm Dr Bhatt. Can you tell me your name? What's your date of birth?'

'Charlotte.' Her voice is creaky, like she hasn't spoken in years. 'My name is Charlotte McKay.' Her head pounds with every syllable, and for a second, she's sure she's going to be sick.

'Okay, Charlotte. Great.' Charlotte flinches as the doctor shines a light into her eyes. 'Sorry to strap you on to such an uncomfortable board, but we had to make sure your neck and back are all right. You were unresponsive at the scene, so we're going to do a CT scan of your head, okay? Just to check that the knock to your brain didn't cause any swelling or other injuries.'

'Okay.' Charlotte doesn't care what they do to her right now. She can barely even understand what the doctor is saying through the throbbing of her brain. She hasn't had a headache this bad since uni, when she and her best friend Lily consumed a massive bowl of vodka jelly in one sitting. 'Please can you call my David? My husband, I mean. David McKay.' His number is buried so deeply in her head that the numbers emerge from her mouth automatically.

'We'll get in touch with him straight away,' Dr Bhatt says. 'And I'm sure you're worried, so I wanted to let you know that your daughter is fine. We'll give her a good check-over just to be on the safe side, but she seems perfectly all right. She certainly has a good set of lungs on her.' She grins, patting Charlotte's arm.

Charlotte blinks, trying to process the doctor's words. *Daughter?*

'My name is Charlotte,' she forces out. It's agony to talk, but she has to clear this up now. Whoever that child belongs to, it needs its mum. 'Charlotte McKay. And I don't—' Her stomach clenches and bile rises in her throat before she can explain that the child isn't hers.

'Call my husband,' she manages to say. He'll make everything clear. He'll tell the doctor that they don't have children.

Dr Bhatt nods. And the last thing Charlotte hears as she's wheeled up to be scanned is that child still crying, calling frantically for her mummy.

Poor thing, Charlotte thinks as the howling thankfully recedes into the distance. Wherever – *whoever* – the mother is, Charlotte hopes she's all right, because her child desperately needs her.

Then she closes her eyes as the stretcher carries her away.

CHAPTER TWO

'Charlotte. *Charlotte*. God, are you okay?'

Charlotte opens her eyes, relief flooding into her at the sound of David's voice. Finally her husband is here. She'd felt so alone as she'd waited to be scanned, staring at the ceiling with her head hammering, cold spreading up her bare arms until every inch of her was shivering.

David takes her hand, his warmth seeping into her frozen fingers. She can tell by his voice that he's shaken but trying to stay calm, and tears fill her eyes again.

'David.' Her lips are dry and cracked, but just saying his name makes her anxious thoughts quieten. He's always had that calming effect, slowing the frantic spinning that winds her so tightly she feels like she might break. David's the one person she doesn't have to prove anything to – someone who loves her as she is, workaholic tendencies and all. He might tell her to slow down, but he's never tried to change that . . . or her.

She grips his hand now, shifting her gaze towards him and smiling. Christ, he looks *awful*, as if his worry has aged him. Skin sags under his eyes, the furrow in his brow is even deeper than usual, and his normally neat hair is messy and unkempt. Charlotte makes a mental note to drag him to the ridiculously expensive barber just down their street this weekend. You could buy a small country for the price of a shave and trim there, but David is definitely worth it.

'The doctors said you were unresponsive when the paramedics first got to you. They had to drag you from the car, they said.' David runs a hand through his hair, an agonised expression on his face. 'Char, I'm so sorry. I'm sorry I didn't tell you sooner. I just, well . . . I felt like it was my fault. And I didn't know you wanted— I hadn't realised—'

'It's fine,' she interrupts, unable to bear the tension in his voice. She hasn't seen him look so worried since his mother rang to say she was having a heart attack, only to find out it was heartburn from her lunchtime cocktails. '*I'm* fine.'

She has no idea why he's apologising, but it can't be anything too serious. When it comes to the big things in life, they've always been perfectly in tune. She squeezes his hand and the side of his wedding ring bites into her fingers, just as it has since he first slid it on five years earlier in a huge ceremony in the Orangery at Kensington Gardens. Charlotte had always said that when she tied the knot, she was going to go all out. And although it had practically wiped out her savings, she'd done just that.

Okay, so the ten-piece band, the caricature artist and the cocktail bar in an old Routemaster bus might have been a *bit* excessive, not to mention the hot-air balloon Lily had convinced her to hire. David had been as delighted with it all as she'd anticipated, though, and everyone had had an amazing time. If you didn't make a big fuss of the man you loved on your wedding day, when would you? Anyway, it wasn't like she and David needed to spend the money elsewhere. Thanks to their generous salaries, they already owned a one-bedroom flat in an idyllic location off the King's Road in Chelsea. Sure, it was tiny, with no room for even a dining table, but it was enough for the two of them. Someday they might need to go bigger, but for now – and for the foreseeable future – it was perfect. Besides, she'd rather spend any extra cash on romantic holidays than on boring property.

'I have a killer headache, but apart from that I'll be fine.' She tries to turn towards him, but the neck brace holds her firmly in place. 'Or at least I will be when I can get back home.' She draws in a shuddery breath and David smiles, but his face is still pinched and white.

'Try to relax,' David says, even though he looks like he's doing anything but. Something about him seems . . . *off*, although Charlotte can't quite put her finger on it. *He's had a shock, too*, she reminds herself. *It's not every day your wife is in a car accident.*

'I know you're worried,' he continues, 'but Anabelle is with my mum now, and she's perfectly fine.'

He pushes a lock of hair back from her forehead, and Charlotte winces as strands trapped in dried blood pull at her skin. Who the hell is Anabelle? And why would Charlotte worry about David's mum? She tries to piece together her husband's words, but thinking hurts like hell.

'Anyway, we should have the results from your scan soon,' David says. 'If everything is all right, the doctor says you'll be able to go home.' He shakes his head. 'You're lucky the driver who hit you wasn't going any faster. The police said he missed a red light and ploughed straight into your side of the car. They reckon the side airbag must have pushed you up against the window, and that's how you hit your head. When I think about how things could have gone . . .' David's shoulders hunch, and he rolls his neck in a gesture so familiar it's comforting.

So that's what happened. Charlotte tries to tease the accident from her brain, but everything is fuzzy and indistinct. His mention of another driver reminds her of the crying child, but before she can ask if the little girl found her mother, David's mobile rings.

He fishes it out of his pocket. 'It's Mum,' he says, glancing at the screen. 'Better get this.'

Her mother-in-law, of course. Who else would David talk to when his wife is lying on a gurney in A&E? Charlotte rolls her eyes, wincing at the pain – just moving her eyeballs feels like an ice pick hacking her skull. She can't count the number of times she's told David to let his mother Miriam's calls go to voicemail, but David reacts as if she's suggested gagging her . . . wishful thinking. The only time he doesn't answer his mother's missives is when he and Charlotte are making love, an excellent incentive to shag as much as they can – not that they need an incentive. She closes her eyes as David updates his mother on Charlotte's condition, his voice fading away as the pounding in her head takes over.

'Anabelle wants to talk to us,' he whispers, reaching out to touch Charlotte's arm. Her eyes fly open and she blinks at the name, trying once again to place it. *Anabelle. Anabelle.* It doesn't seem familiar, but then she was never great at names. Still, the way David's looking at her, it's clear that whoever this person is, she's someone important.

Has Miriam finally taken that lesbian lover Charlotte always jokes with David about? Charlotte's lips twitch, despite her aching head. Miriam hasn't been with a man since David's father left her ages ago, and Charlotte often teases him that maybe she'll switch sides in her advancing years.

No, surely she would remember that. Christ, it would be the best thing to happen all year! At the very least, it might get Miriam off her back about having kids. If she needs to explain yet again why she's not ready, she's going to lose it. Thank God David hasn't jumped on that bandwagon . . . yet, anyway.

'Okay, Anabelle,' David says in a louder voice, flicking the phone on to 'Speaker'. 'Mummy can hear you now.'

'Mummy!' A child's voice bursts through the handset. 'Why are you still in hospital? When will you be home?'

Mummy? What the—? Charlotte's eyes lock on to David's face, as if his familiar features will help her make sense of what's happening. Has her husband gone mad? Or has she fallen through to a parallel universe? Because in this life, she and David haven't even started trying for children, despite the longing in her husband's eyes every time he spots something baby-related. He's the only man she's ever known to get broody over nappy adverts on the telly, and sometimes the desire on his face is so much she needs to turn away.

Like most couples, they'd mused about what their child might look like, but the notion of offspring was always more theoretical than real . . . a pleasant way to spin dreams together after making love. David would wax lyrical about the benefits of stay-at-home dads, saying he'd be only too happy to give up his insurance job to raise their child. Charlotte would laugh, pushing aside the pang of guilt at the thought that he might be waiting a very long time. David would never pressure her, but she knew he was keen to have a family of his own one day – anxious to be the father his own dad had never been to him. And maybe, one day, she'd be ready. Maybe.

Just not now.

'David,' she says slowly, trying to get her brain in gear enough to form a question – enough to ask if *he's* the one who bumped his head. But her husband's nodding at her encouragingly, as if it's normal that a phantom child should address her as its mother – as if she should recognise this voice. An incredulous laugh bubbles up inside her at the ridiculousness of it all.

David's still waving the phone at her, deep creases lodged even more firmly in his forehead. 'Anabelle, Mummy's not feeling well just now,' he says, once it becomes obvious she can't talk. 'She sends her love and a big, big cuddle. Now—'

'Sir, you shouldn't be using your mobile in here.' A nurse with a steel-grey bob pokes her head into the room, her face wreathed in disapproval.

David jumps. 'Sorry,' he says, and despite her bewilderment, Charlotte can't help smiling at his guilty flush, as if he's been caught cheating on a school spelling test. He's always been one to follow the rules, whereas she's more likely to push them – or break them, if it suits her. 'I'll just take this outside,' he says. 'Back in a sec.'

He scuttles from the room. Charlotte watches him go, confusion muddling her brain even more. Yes, she had a knock on the head. A big one, if the pain is anything to go by. But . . . a *daughter*?

Charlotte takes a deep breath as the child's voice rings in her ears. *Mummy.* It's ludicrous. It's not possible, and yet . . . She goes cold, recalling the mix-up about that crying child: a mix-up where the doctor thought the child belonged to her. Everything about the accident and its aftermath is so hazy, but is it possible those seemingly distant cries were coming from inside her car – that there was a child in the back seat when she crashed?

Is it possible that that child is *hers*?

Panic scrabbles at her gut and she wills herself to focus, to cut through the screaming agony of her brain and try to remember anything about getting pregnant, having a baby and whatever else that entails. She lets out a snort as she realises she doesn't even *know* what that entails.

There must be a logical explanation, she thinks – something she's missing at the moment. Maybe that conversation with David wasn't real. It *feels* real, but maybe hitting her head confused things a bit. Maybe she's hallucinating. Maybe—

'Right, your scan came back all clear, so I'm going to take you off the board now,' the nurse says. 'You'll be much more comfortable.'

'Great.' Relief floods through her that there's no lasting damage. Perhaps the strange scenario that just played out was her brain's way of unwinding, like the nightmares she has after stressful work days . . . or something. The nurse loosens the straps, and Charlotte gingerly moves her legs and arms. Everything aches, like she's been encased in cement for days.

'We'll get someone in to have a look at the wound on your head,' the nurse says, peering closer. 'You might need some stitches. Just sit tight for the time being, all right?'

'Okay,' Charlotte responds automatically. If she escapes with just stitches, she's more than lucky – maybe she can even be back at work tomorrow. She has an important pitch she really needs to prepare for.

Now, where on earth has her husband disappeared to? She needs to see him to dispel this crazy notion her mad brain has dreamed up; this idea that she has a daughter. She shakes her head. *Anabelle.* That's how she knows this whole thing can't be real – they'd never give their daughter such a prissy, girly name.

God, what she wouldn't give for some water. Charlotte slowly manoeuvres her legs over the side of the bed. The room swings around her and nausea pokes through the blinding pain in her skull, but somehow, she makes it to the sink. With no cups in sight, she bends down, sighing in relief as she gulps cold water from her cupped hands. She splashes some on her face then straightens up, jerking back as she spots a reflection in the mirror.

The person in the mirror is her . . . but not; it's like looking into a warped mirror at a funfair. Her edgy black pixie cut is gone and has been replaced by a softer, layered chestnut-brown style that falls around her shoulders. She leans closer, heart pounding now in time to the throbbing of her head. She looks so tired: lines criss-cross the skin around her eyes and mouth – lines that definitely weren't there before.

What the hell is going on? There's no way she could delete more than a few hours from her memory, is there? The scan said she was fine, after all.

Charlotte closes her eyes and grips the sink as one word bleats in her brain. *Mummy. Mummy. Mummy.*

No. She shakes her head. It's one thing to forget a new hairstyle or bury your head in the sand about the state of your ageing skin. But there's no way she could forget a child . . . *her* child. That kind of connection cannot be erased, no matter how hard you smack your skull.

She slides a hand down to her stomach, jerking her fingers away like they're scalded. It's not the flat, smooth belly she's so proud of, honed over years of running a good 10k each night – even more when she's training for marathons. It's soft and cushiony, a band of fat protruding from under her bellybutton. She forces herself to breathe in and out, in and out, as thoughts chug through her sluggish brain. Perhaps she's just bloated. Perhaps she had a huge lunch – eating too much bread always does that to her. Perhaps . . .

She takes a deep breath and moves back from the mirror. Her arms shake as she lifts a bright red sweater she doesn't recognise. She glances down to take in – horror of horror – *jeggings*, complete with an elasticated waist. Her waist is thicker than it used to be, but there's no obvious sign . . . She pushes the waistband down and squints at a faint line crossing her abdomen. What is that? It kind of looks like a scar, but she's never—

Oh, God. She sinks on to the floor as the knowledge filters in. It *is* a scar. It's exactly like a scar from a Caesarean section; one of her friends proudly showed off hers not long ago. Charlotte remembers shuddering at the thought of having a baby ripped from her body.

And now she has. She's had a baby ripped from her body. A baby she doesn't recall – a young child, by the sound of things. She is a mother, after all. And she doesn't remember any of it. She doesn't remember *wanting* any of it.

Fuck.

CHAPTER THREE

Four years earlier
20 March

Oh, *fuck*.

Oh my fucking fuck. Seriously, there aren't enough fucks in the world to express how I'm feeling right now.

I'm pregnant. Pregnant. *Pregnant*. I feel like throwing up, and I can't even blame it on morning sickness – surely it's too early for that? I watch my pen form the letters as I write them here, unable to believe that this word relates to the state I'm in.

Preggers.

Knocked up.

With child.

Up the duff.

No matter how you say it, I still can't get my head around it.

How? How did this happen? I mean, I know *how*. David and I have a thorough understanding of the mechanics of it all . . . a very thorough, few-times-a-week understanding that thankfully hasn't abated since we married. In fact, on our holiday to Rome a few months ago, we actually set a personal record for the most times in one night: three (almost four, but we both fell asleep in the middle of . . . well, I don't need to spell it out here).

So I know how it happened, of course, but I don't know when. I remember Lily saying there are two or three days each month when you're the most fertile, but I can't recall when exactly during the cycle that might be. To be honest, I've never really cared enough to learn more. Was it that time David and I were both squiffy on champagne – well, more like sloshed – after Lily's thirty-fifth birthday party? I still can't believe how drunk she was, but I suppose if I'd been through the same as her these past two years, I'd get off my face, too.

The sex that night was *incredible*. So incredible, maybe, that David's sperm managed to beat the pill I swallow every night at ten on the dot, saying a little prayer that it'll work – ninety-nine per cent effective, when taken as it should be, according to the nurse.

Leave it to me to be the one per cent for whom it fails.

I still remember the rictus smile on that nurse's face when she told me the odds, then asked if it would *really* be a disaster if I fell pregnant. After all, I was over thirty-five now, and married. Wasn't it just the natural course of events? (Okay, she didn't say the last two bits, but I could see she was thinking that.)

The thing is, it is a disaster. Not for David: every year that goes by, he muses more and more about our 'future child' – and I'm not even sure he knows he's doing it. I once caught him looking online at our local primary school, visions of chubby, cherubic children clearly dancing through his head. No, for David having a child isn't a disaster, not at all. But for me . . .

I finally got that promotion I'd been working my arse off for – the one my boss Vivek promised me if I managed to exceed this year's target. And I more than exceeded it; I blew it away. I'm a senior account director in business development now, team lead and the top performer when it comes to securing new clients. I know everything there is to know about pitching companies to run their pharmaceutical trials, and I love that feeling. People come to me for answers, for advice and for strategies. After years of hard graft and words of wisdom from Vivek,

I'm exactly where I want to be (well, vice-president would be nice, but I'll save that until Vivek retires), and I don't want anything to throw me off track. For me, pregnancy *is* a disaster.

Okay, so maybe 'disaster' is too strong a word. If David's serious about staying at home, maybe it's more like 'disruption' . . . a bit of time off, then I'm back in the office. But the thing is, I don't want time off, not even for a month or two. How will I manage my work – the long days, the late-night conference calls with our teams in Asia, travelling around the world for pitches – while heavily pregnant, never mind with a screaming baby at home? Because even if David does the lion's share of work, I'm still the mother . . . a mother I can't even fathom being; a mother I don't *want* to fathom being. I worked hard to make my way up the ladder; to prove myself and my commitment. Am I going to compromise all that by having a child?

I know lots of women manage. My mum, for example, who worked full-time at a busy public relations agency all through my childhood. Who *still* works full-time, despite approaching her seventies. But it wasn't easy, even with Dad's help – she barely slept, and she was always on the go. I remember creeping out of bed for the loo late at night, and she'd be tapping away on her computer. And to be honest, I don't want to *manage*. I want to thrive: to work every hour, as hard as I can, and see how far I can go.

And I'm just . . . I'm just not ready to have a child. I like my life right now. I *love* my life right now – how David and I can take off to anywhere at the drop of a hat, from an island in Croatia to an art gallery in Dalston (my ideas) but how we're equally happy just lounging at home in the sanctuary of our flat (his idea). Our world is perfectly balanced, and a baby will change all of that. Friends keep telling me my clock will start ticking so loudly it drowns out everything else. But so far, the only clock that's ticking is the countdown to wine at the end of each day.

And there's something I've never told David, something I'm afraid to say out loud. And that's that, although I *want* to believe I'll want children one day, I'm just not sure I'll ever be ready. Ready for someone to need me, all of the time – to be there not just physically, but emotionally, too. Ready for a lifelong commitment of worry, of fear. Ready to be divided, always, between myself and another being – another being I've created – for whom I am everything, and who means the world to me.

Ready to be a *mum*.

All this sounds terrible, I know. Thank God no one will read what I'm writing. I can see their thoughts now: *Cares more about a career and nights out than bringing a child into a loving family? Doesn't want to give her all to someone else, for a greater cause? God, she's missing out. Missing out on a lifetime of happiness and love that makes every sacrifice worthwhile.*

But . . . does it? I've seen how stressful having a baby can be. I've seen how my friends who are new mums slug back booze on rare nights out as if the world's alcohol supply will dry up the next day. I've heard them snipe at their husbands; seen them suddenly be made part-time or even redundant during maternity leave.

Having a baby isn't a magic happy-pill. To me, it seems the opposite.

I wish I could talk to someone about all this and tell them how I feel, but most of my friends have children now, and those who don't are scattered across the globe in various exotic locations, taking full advantage of their child-free status. And Lily, well . . . we've drifted apart. She's desperate for a baby, and even though I was miles from understanding, I tried my best to be there for her as she struggled to get pregnant. I listened to her talk about ovulation, fertility and all that for hours, and when a baby still didn't appear after a year or two, I even helped her research IVF clinics. I held her hand during procedures when Joseph couldn't be there, telling funny stories from uni to distract her (although I don't think the nurse appreciated hearing about the Chunder Chart and our epic nights out).

And when that very first round of IVF was successful, I celebrated with her and Joseph, toasting their family's future with elderflower tonic, soaking up the happiness that was pouring from them. I was going to be the baby's 'mad auntie', like we'd always joked, and I couldn't wait to get started spoiling their child. I even bought the cutest little rattle and squeaky soft toy, wrapping it up in blue-and-pink stripy paper.

Then, one week later, Lily lost the baby. She withdrew from the world, not returning my phone calls or even answering the door when I went round. I understood – I'd been the same after my father died when I was in uni – but I was determined to drag her out, the same way she had when grief had engulfed me. She'd sit and study with me for hours back then, then close my books and haul me to the nearest bar, where we'd dance all night. I would have drowned if it wasn't for her.

We were over dancing all night now, but I just wanted to get her to talk to me. And eventually she did, but it wasn't the same. Whereas before I knew every little detail of her reproductive journey (sometimes a bit too much, if I'm honest), now she barely told me anything. It was like she was afraid to hope again; afraid to let me back into her family's future.

We still meet up every once in a while, but there's a distance now that wasn't there before. It's as if she's filtering everything she says . . . holding herself tightly in case she cracks. I miss the Lily who laughed at herself, whose bubbliness and energy made anything fun. I miss the friends we used to be.

The old Lily would help me make sense of all this, but how can I tell her that I'm pregnant and not ready? How can I say that, when she's just the reverse: ready, but not pregnant? If I could switch places with her, I would in a heartbeat. But it's too late now. I can't switch places with her, because I *am* pregnant. There's a baby inside me . . . Christ, I still can't believe it.

The one person I *could* talk to is David. It's amazing how different we are, yet how we understand each other without needing to have complicated conversations. He'd soothe my worries and convince me that having this child will be the best thing ever – for me, for *us*. But the thing is, I'm not ready to be convinced. I'm not ready to accept that this is real.

Because once I tell him, we won't be just a married couple. We'll be a married couple with a baby on the way.

I'll be a mother – well, almost.

Fuck.

CHAPTER FOUR

'Sorry about that.' David edges his slim body back through the half-open door. Charlotte studies her husband's face, the bags under his eyes and the shaggy hair now making sense. If that's all he's changed in these past couple of years, then he's got off much lighter than her. She thinks of her soft stomach and the network of lines scoring her skin, her heart sinking as she touches the craggy ends of her long hair. *God*.

'Mum couldn't find Zebby,' David says, sitting down on a chair in the corner. 'And you know what Anabelle's like without that thing.'

Charlotte nods slowly, although she hasn't the slightest clue what he's talking about. Who's Zebby? And just what is their daughter like without it?

Their *daughter*. Even if her head didn't feel like she'd downed ten tequilas in quick succession, she'd still be struggling to absorb that she and David have a child. A child they named Anabelle, for some unknown reason. God, what a princessy name. Her mouth twitches as she recalls David joking that if they had a baby girl, they should call her Miriam, after his mother. Suddenly Anabelle doesn't seem so bad.

How could she not remember choosing her daughter's name? How could she forget wanting a baby, then getting pregnant, giving birth and raising the bloody thing for the past few years?

I haven't, Charlotte decides now. She couldn't have. No one forgets becoming a mother . . . being a mother. No one forgets their own child.

The scans have shown there's nothing wrong with her head, so it must just be the shock of the accident. Once she's back with her daughter, she's sure the memories will all return. The past few years will swoop into her, knocking away the confusion, the panic . . . and, if she's honest, something approaching dread.

But there's no reason to feel that way, she tells herself. Even if the idea of her as a mother feels completely foreign, she and David wouldn't have had children unless they were more than ready – and unless she'd felt it wouldn't have an impact on her job. God knows she's worked too hard to let anything knock her off track, and David must be that stay-at-home dad he always joked of becoming. She rakes her eyes over his familiar features, love swelling inside as she pictures him rocking his daughter to sleep, getting up at night to give her a bottle, tenderly changing her nappy . . . He'd be a brilliant father, she knows that for sure, and he'd love every minute of it. Their child couldn't be in better hands, and she'd be able to work hard – and play hard, too. Kind of like her life now, only with a baby in tow. She could actually enjoy motherhood rather than become a giant stressball trying to fit everything in, like some of the working mums she knows.

She squints, trying to place where she'd be on the workplace ladder at Cellbril, the pharmaceutical research company where she's worked in business development for well over a decade. If their child is two or three, Charlotte's probably well on her way to taking over the VP of business development position from Vivek when he retires . . . if he hasn't already. Excitement flashes through her. Maybe she's VP now!

'Everything all right?' David asks, and she realises she's still staring at him. Worry pinches his features, making him seem more anxious and aloof than she's used to.

Charlotte draws in a breath, picturing David's concern when she tells him she can't remember having their baby . . . and that the very thought of it is like something from a bad science fiction film. There's no reason to upset him by telling the truth – a truth that is only temporary, anyway. He's already worried enough, and the last thing she needs is for him to ask for more tests, prolonging her stay in this dreary hospital. Right now, she's desperate to go home – to be with her husband and to absorb this new reality. If anyone can make her feel better about it, he can.

'Oh, yes. Fine.' She raises a hand to her head. 'Just hurting, that's all.' It feels odd keeping something from him, but it won't be for long.

'I can imagine.' David winces. 'Thank goodness it's nothing more than a flesh wound.'

Charlotte tries her best to smile reassuringly, but her lips tremble, sticking to her teeth. 'Can I have some water, please?'

'Sure.' David jumps off the chair. 'There aren't any cups here. I'll grab some from the cooler down the hallway. Be right back.'

He returns as the nurse is finishing up the last few stitches in Charlotte's forehead.

'Sorry, sorry,' he says, out of breath. 'There weren't any cups there either, so I had to—

Oh, God.' Colour drains from his face as the nurse manoeuvres the thread through Charlotte's skin. 'Almost as bad as childbirth! Remember how I just about fainted? And I didn't even see the worst of it. Thank goodness for that partition.'

Childbirth, ugh. Charlotte shudders, thinking that at least she managed to have a Caesarean and keep her nether regions intact. She's always thought it the best option, anyway: you can plan around it. The idea of simply waiting for your body to surprise you with the indignities of labour never really appealed. Horrified, more like.

'Sorry, honey,' the nurse says, perhaps thinking that Charlotte is responding to the pain. 'Right, all done. You should be fine, but if you start to feel dizzy or if you're sick, you may have a concussion.' She hands Charlotte an information pamphlet. 'Have a read through this. Any symptoms, come back straight away. All right?'

'All right,' Charlotte croaks. Maybe that's why she doesn't remember: she has a concussion? Would that block out the past few years' memory, though?

'I'll keep an eye on her,' David says, taking Charlotte's arm and helping her off the bed. She catches sight of her feet, clad in Converse trainers, the kind she always shunned. In fact, she can't remember the last time she wore flat shoes. At only five foot three, heels are compulsory. The trainers are bloody comfortable, though, she has to admit.

But trainers and jeggings? Why isn't she at work? It's a weekday, clearly: David is wearing his usual suit and tie. Whatever happened to his plan to stay at home . . . ? Or maybe their daughter is old enough for nursery or school now? But why is she dressed in this get-up?

Alarm rises within her, and she bats it away. There must be a reason. Perhaps her office has implemented casual days? Vivek always said he'd rather retire than watch his team turn up in ripped jeans and stained T-shirts, but even he kowtows to HR policies.

What had Vivek made of Charlotte's pregnancy announcement? He wouldn't have been pleased, that much she knows for sure. He was always whingeing about having to fill maternity leaves, as if the women were doing him a personal disservice. But as the top contract winner, she was sure that he – and she – wouldn't have let it interfere with her career path. Vivek understood economics, if not compassion.

She leans against David as they make their way along the labyrinth of hospital corridors and out through the door. His body is warm and solid against hers – even more solid than she remembers; he must have put on a few extra pounds. But then again, so has she. The first thing she's going to do when she's better is get back out and run. Goodbye, Mum Tum. She shudders. God! *Mum* tum!

'David?' She glances up at him, waiting for his trademark grin and squeeze that were guaranteed to make her feel better. Instead he glances down at her, his face set and body stiff like he's protecting himself from invasion. Finally he pats her elbow, but the gesture feels foreign and strange.

'Yes? Everything okay?'

Charlotte nods mutely, uncertainty zinging through her at his stone-like façade. Why is he being so odd? *He'll be fine once we get home*, she tells herself. *Everything will be fine*. More than fine, actually. Maybe she'll love her life even more now than before! A wonderful husband, an amazing daughter, a job she loves . . . she'll be one of those women who has it all.

The cold air hits her flushed cheeks and she blinks in surprise at the winter-bare trees, the warmth of the Italian sun still lodged in her mind. David unlocks the door of the trusty Volkswagen he's had since uni, and Charlotte raises her eyebrows. He still has this thing? He always claimed it could run on fumes alone, a distinct advantage when the sky-high fuel prices threatened to bankrupt him as a poor student. She smiles, remembering the time they'd decided on a whim to drive to Oxford, only to break down on the A40. Lorries and cars had whizzed past them for hours as they'd awaited the recovery truck, but they'd never got bored. The eventual silence that had fallen between them was a comfortable blanket, wrapping them in its warm folds. Sitting in the car as rain hammered the roof, she'd never felt so contented. Despite the fond memories, though, she'd always assumed that when they became 'proper grown-ups' (i.e., parents), they'd ditch this clunker and get a family car. Why didn't they? Was *she* driving the grown-up car?

Charlotte leans against the battered bonnet, trying to recall the last time she actually drove. She's a dedicated Tube and bus girl, shunning London's traffic at all costs. But all that changes when you have a child, she guesses. God, imagine hauling a buggy up and down the Tube station stairs, or on to a packed bus. She's always pitied the poor mothers who had to do that, stopping to help whenever she could spare a second.

David unlocks her door and Charlotte climbs inside, grimacing as she takes in the grubby interior. David has always been on the more 'relaxed' side of cleanliness – his habit of leaving items strewn across the flat like a snake shedding its skin is the only thing they argue about. But the state of this car has surpassed relaxed and gone straight to filthy. Rubbish litters the footwells, a black banana skin peeps out of the seat pocket, toys are crammed in the back window. And the car seat – well, the less said about the state of that, the better.

Wow. If one child can wreak such havoc in a confined space, what does their flat look like?

She leans back on the headrest as David starts the engine, praying this car isn't a reflection of their home. Their place may be small, but thanks to her constant nagging of David and the efforts of their cleaner, it's immaculate: she hadn't spent hours poring over magazines to choose the right furnishings only for it to be permanently fit for a pig. God, she can't wait to flop down on the comfy goose-down duvet; to pull the thick turquoise curtains over the large sash window and let sleep wash over her.

Charlotte sucks in air as a thought hits. They *do* still live in the same flat, right? Would their small space fit a toddler, along with two adults? Her eyes drift closed and she tries her best to place a child in the midst of their home.

What does their daughter look like? Does she have David's wavy dark locks or her mother's straight-as-a-pin hair? Are her eyes dark blue like Charlotte's or brown like David's? Is she strong willed, like they'd always joked she would be? Does her gentle easy-going father struggle to control her? Charlotte strains to fit together the pieces but they refuse to slot into place, one tumbling away as soon as her consciousness grips another. It's hard to believe that this isn't some post-coital imagining and that this little person actually exists. That she belongs to them . . . to their life.

That she's at their home now, awaiting their arrival.

Waiting for her mother.

Every muscle in Charlotte's body stiffens – stiffens even more, because her muscles already feel like they've been lashed so tightly to her bones that she can barely even twitch. As the car travels through the London streets, she wants to scream at her husband to stop . . . to freeze this moment in time, just the two of them together, before a child plunges into their lives. She wants to throw her arms around David and pull him close, to breathe in the comfort of his body against hers and to let the shock, the pain and the strangeness of the day wash away. She's not ready to face a new reality – a reality she doesn't even remember choosing – and she needs him now more than ever.

She turns towards him, conjuring up the right way to tell him she has no memory of their daughter. But one glance at his tired face – the crows' feet by his eyes underlining the passage of time – and those words fade away. Unlike that day in their broken-down car, the silence between them now feels like a barrier, the missing years creating a huge space she can't even fathom how to cross.

It will be fine, she tells herself. It has to be, because she is a mother, whether she remembers it or not. And she did choose this, after all – she and David. This is the life they've forged together, as a family. She *will* remember, and when she does, it will all make sense again.

Charlotte takes a deep breath to quell the growing fear, and braces for impact.

CHAPTER FIVE

24 March

I told him tonight. I told David I'm pregnant – or, rather, *we're* pregnant. I know, I know. Saying 'we' heightens the cheese factor of this whole thing, and I'm regretting how I used to roll my eyes every time a couple uttered those words. But the truth is, that's how I feel. It's how I need to feel, and thankfully David agrees: we're both in this. I won't be alone, and even though it's my body that will nurture this child – my milk that will sustain it for the first bit of its life – we'll do this together. Thank goodness, because whenever doubts start to seep in, telling me I'm not exactly mother material – I've never cooed over babies, and I can barely keep a plant alive, let alone a human being – I remind myself I'll have David by my side . . . and he *has* cooed over babies. He'll be an amazing father, filling any gaps my own lack of abilities may leave. We'll be the perfect team to build a world for our child. This baby will add to us and make us stronger, not divide us, like I've seen happen to so many of my friends.

The last few days have passed in a daze. I've made my way from home to work to home again, running miles in the evening, still knocked sideways by the news that I'm knocked up. It felt so strange, keeping something from David . . . something so important and something I knew would make him so happy. But I needed time to understand what was happening; time to let it sink in. And after a few days, my head at least had absorbed the state of my body, even if my heart didn't quite feel ready. But it would, I was sure. It would, once I told my husband. Once I made it real.

I got home from work before David for once, and was tapping away on my laptop when he returned ashen-faced from the litany of human horrors that parades before him at the insurance office. I'll never understand how someone as empathetic as David can bear to work there, but I guess coming face to face with such woes makes you realise that even though the worst can happen, you're still doing okay. In typical David fashion, he manages to calmly and efficiently find the best possible outcome for these poor people, working against the corporate machine to make sure they get the compensation they need. It's not a job he loves, though, and I suspect that's part of the reason he always jokes about being the stay-at-home dad.

I guessed I'd soon find out how serious he actually was.

As soon as his key turned in the lock, my pulse picked up pace. He gave me his usual hug and kiss, then went into the bedroom to slough off his suit . . . and the day. The first thing he does when he comes home is get changed; not that I blame him. If I had to wear stiffly creased suits and silk ties like nooses around my neck, I'd change as soon as I got home, too.

Thank God I love my job. I'm practically glued to my work email – by choice. It's not just an extension of my life. It *is* my life . . . besides David, that is. And now, besides this baby. Because although I may not feel it now, I'm sure there's room in my heart for someone else – someone I'll love so instinctively it's not even questionable.

'How was your day?' I asked, my voice shaky and tense. This was a big moment, the moment you see in adverts on telly: an excited, happy wife about to tell her husband the best news of their lives. So why did I feel so *empty* inside? Ironic, really, given I was harbouring another human being.

'Oh, you know. The same,' he called from the bedroom. He hates to talk about work, unlike me, who can babble on for hours. I plucked a loose thread on the sofa as I waited for him to come back to the lounge. My heart pounded and I gulped in air, wondering why I was so nervous. This was my husband, the man I'd shared my life with for the past five years. But I knew that once I told him, there was no backing out. We'd be on a new track to a new life; a life I couldn't yet see. I longed to tighten my arms around him and savour *us*, for the very last time.

He sat down beside me and grabbed my legs, swinging them over his lap. He looked for the bottle of wine I usually had on the side table, then turned towards me. 'What's going on? Don't tell me we've run out of wine?'

He couldn't have given me a better intro if he'd tried.

'Actually . . .' My pulse whooshed in my ears. This was it.

I took a deep breath.

'I'm pregnant.'

There. It was done. I could feel the past falling away behind me and something new opening up ahead.

Parenthood. Motherhood.

A family.

David's eyebrows flew up and he couldn't get his arms around me fast enough – a little difficult when someone's legs are in your lap, so we ended up a tangled jumble of limbs. Finally, he managed to kiss me, and when he pulled back, I don't think I've ever seen him so joyous, so delighted.

'But how?' he asked, looking like I'd handed him the world. 'I thought you were on the pill?'

'I am,' I said. 'But I guess it didn't work.' I shook my head, still unable to believe I'd been so unlucky. No, *lucky*. I had to get my head around that. 'And I'm sure. I must have done about ten tests.'

'I can't believe it.' He drew me even closer, his hand cradling my stomach. 'I can't believe we're having a baby.' He leaned back. 'Are you okay? I mean, are you feeling sick or anything? Do you think you should maybe stop running? Until we know it's safe, anyway?'

My stomach clenched – I hadn't even questioned whether or not it was safe to run. I hadn't even thought that I'd need to stop. I mean, thinking about it now, of course I won't be lumbering through parks at seven or eight months' pregnant.

But now? When our baby is barely bigger than a grain of rice (or something like that; I've yet to start reading baby books)? There can't be any reason to stop so soon in my pregnancy, can there? I need to run to work off my restless energy and the adrenaline of the day. Far from pumping me up, it calms me down enough to sleep.

'I'll check with the doctor, but I'm sure it's fine,' I said. Something twisted inside me at his words, seeping away before I could identify it. I've always been the strong one in our relationship, both mentally and physically. It was weird to see him being protective of me.

'Look, I know this wasn't expected,' David said, pulling me close again. 'But honestly, I don't think it could have happened better if we'd planned it. We're stable financially, and, well . . . it's *time*, isn't it?'

I nodded and forced a smile. Looking into my husband's glowing face, I couldn't tell him that even though I'd got my head (mostly) around this pregnancy, I still wasn't sure there ever would be a right time . . . for me, anyway. I couldn't tell him that, actually, if I was being honest, I wanted to be a VP more than I wanted to be a mother.

'And Charlotte, I want to be there for our child,' David said. 'I *need* to be there for our child, in a way my dad never was for me.' His lips tightened and anger flashed across his face, and I remembered him telling me how dreadful it was when his dad abandoned the family on David's seventh birthday, leaving Miriam with three children and a cake on the table that no one could touch until he came home again. It sat there until it rotted. 'I really would love to stay at home with the baby, for the first year, at least . . . if you're okay with that. It's so important to me to be a part of its daily life; to be there to change nappies, do nap-times and whatever else . . . hell, if I could breastfeed, I'd do that, too.'

I couldn't help smiling at the image, and relief buoyed me up. I was hoping he'd say that; hoping he'd be all in, like my father was. This baby would be our ultimate project, and we'd work as well together raising it as we always had in our marriage. And while I'm still struggling to imagine a child in our world, with David at home maybe a child will be a 'disruption' after all, not the disaster I feared. I can be VP and a mother; they don't have to be mutually exclusive. And there are such things as babysitters, so David and I can have our fun nights out, too.

We will love this baby with all our hearts, but it won't engulf us. It won't change who we are, or what's important.

Everything will be just fine.

CHAPTER SIX

Charlotte heaves a sigh of relief when their car turns on to a familiar side street just off the King's Road. *Thank God, thank God, thank God* – they haven't given up their flat. She turns to smile at David, gulping back the shock that hits each time she spots the extra few years on his face. No matter what else may have changed, she should have known they'd hold on to the place where they had built their life together . . . not to mention its brilliant location in stylish Chelsea. They have so many wonderful memories there, and she can't picture them anywhere else.

Warmth rushes over her, and she reaches out to touch David's hand on the gearstick. Living in a one-bedroom flat with a toddler can't be easy, but if anyone can work it out and still manage to have a love life, they can. She smiles, remembering the first time they made love. They'd both been slightly tipsy from the gin and tonic shooters at an experimental cocktail bar and they'd rolled right off the bed, landing on the hard floor with a thump. They'd lain there and laughed, but then the *sex* . . . It was as if that thump had knocked any 'getting to know you' nerves out of them both, because they'd instantly gelled, and it had only got better from there. Sex connects them in a way that words can't, and they rarely go a day or two without making love.

Parenthood wouldn't have changed that, she's sure. Maybe they've partitioned the lounge area to create a small bedroom? Whatever they've done, she has every confidence it looks fantastic. She wouldn't settle for anything less, and David always gives her free rein over any decorating decisions, claiming that whatever makes her happy makes him happy, too.

Clever man.

'Right.' David expertly jemmies the car into a space outside their front door, and Charlotte tries not to groan as the movement jerks her head. 'Just wait there – I'll come around and help you.'

He slams his door then hurries over to her side, taking her arm. Every muscle protests as she unravels her body from the seat. God, she feels like she's aged forty years, never mind . . . however long it's been.

She stands for a minute on the pavement, heart sinking as she stares up at their first-floor flat. Where are the turquoise curtains she paid an absolute fortune for? They may have been a little overpriced, but they had a lifetime guarantee! David used to laugh that he could spot them from the top of the street. You could, if you peered closely, and she'd always prided herself on the small splash of colour in the otherwise brilliant-white façade of their terrace.

But now . . . now the curtains are gone, replaced by hideous blackout curtains that look like they're straight from an Argos catalogue. Ugh, she can see the plastic backing from here. *They're just curtains*, she tells herself, beating back the fear that she's capitulated on other, more important matters, too. *Fabric quality is hardly a matter of life or death*.

David takes her arm and together they head up the walkway. The front door clicks open, and Charlotte breathes in the familiar scent: a hint of damp mixed with something like chicken soup. She smiles as they start up the stairs, remembering the first time David carried her over the threshold after their wedding, laughingly scooping her up in his arms despite her protests that after consuming almost all the champagne at the head table, she was going to be sick on his shoes.

'A little vomit is a small price to pay for matrimonial bliss,' he'd said, although he'd set her back down when she started to gag.

As her husband fits a key in the lock, a wave of certainty sweeps over her. Small changes like curtains are bound to happen when you have kids. But when it comes to the big things – relationships, work, *life* – she's sure they've kept things the same. This child is the icing on top of their wonderfully delicious cake. And once Charlotte sees her daughter and is back in her familiar environment again, her memory will surely return. The strange in-between place she's in right now will vanish, and her world will be right again.

Right, here we go. David opens the door and Charlotte steps gingerly into the flat, ready to embrace a tidal wave of emotion.

Ready to embrace what her life is now.

'Mummy!' A little girl streaks into her arms, throwing her body against Charlotte with such force that she struggles to stay upright. She sways back and forth, tightening her grip on the child so they both don't fall over. The girl is warm and wiry, and it's as if she's trying to attach herself to her mother . . . as if she wants to be an extra appendage.

Charlotte breathes in the toddler's fresh, soapy scent, and waits. Waits, for that fierce protective love mothers always rave about. For the all-consuming emotion, the connection unlike any other, the instant recognition of flesh and blood.

Waits to become a mother . . . to remember wanting to be a mother.

Silence hums in her ears – silence inside and out. Because even as the child wraps herself closer, Charlotte just feels *empty*, as if this girl belongs to someone else. She closes her eyes and tries her best to conjure up memories and emotions. But everything stays blank, a metallic deflector lobbing back the last thing she remembers about children: she's not ready. Panic and fear rise inside, and she glances up at David for help.

'Whoa,' David says, reaching out to steady their daughter. 'Go easy on Mummy, Anabelle. She's got a rather big lump on her head.'

The child pulls back and reaches out to touch the bandages on Charlotte's forehead. Charlotte's eyes trace her daughter's face, and she tells herself to stay calm. She's been through a lot in the last few hours, and perhaps it's too much to expect memories to just rush back in. But they will return. They have to. She *must* remember her very own child – remember wanting her, loving her. This girl in front of her now is half her DNA, for God's sake.

And taking in the face before her, it's obvious that this *is* her daughter, unmistakably so. She has the same dark blue eyes, fringed by lashes so long they won't need mascara. The same straight thick chestnut hair, already showing its annoying tendency to escape from any ponytail, any time. And the same nose with the slight upturn that Charlotte hated as a child, and still does. It's like looking at a picture of herself from thirty-odd years ago. The only bit of David she can spot is the high, wide forehead . . . and perhaps the bow shape of Anabelle's top lip.

Charlotte shakes her head. It's so bizarre to see their features mirrored in a child – *their* child. Will she ever get used to that?

Of course I will, she tells herself again. *Just relax. Just give it time, and everything will come back.*

'Does it hurt, Mummy?' Anabelle asks, her finger prodding the tender spot on Charlotte's head.

'Shit!' The word slips out before Charlotte can stop it, but Christ, 'hurt' is an understatement. 'Sorry,' she mutters through the blinding pain, glancing sidelong at David. He's looking at her as if she just killed a kitten rather than let a swear word loose.

'Do you want to go and lie down?' he asks tentatively, as if he expects her to protest. 'I can take Anabelle to the park, if you're okay with that.'

Of course she's okay with that! Entertaining a toddler with a head like this is impossible, and David's more than capable of taking Anabelle out on his own. Her head is throbbing even more now, and she needs to rest and give the memories space to start filling up the empty spot inside her.

'Thanks, babe.' Charlotte leans into her husband, desperate for something solid in this strange world. He's still for a second before putting his arms loosely around her, as if he's afraid she'll break. She lays her head on his chest, breathing in his scent as her arms tighten around him. He's still using the cologne she got him last Christmas – or whenever it was – and she remembers how he sprayed it on, then hugged her so close that she pulled away, laughing that she couldn't breathe. The cologne clung to her for the rest of the day, and even now, when she smells it she feels the strength of that hug – the strength of their love.

'Would you look at the state of you!' Miriam comes into the corridor, a look of horror on her face as she examines the bandage on Charlotte's head. 'I can't believe they let you out of hospital. They should have at least kept you in for observation. In my day . . .'

Charlotte nods numbly as Miriam's voice drifts over her. A few years may have passed, but her mother-in-law hasn't changed. She's still going on about 'her day' and she looks remarkably the same, although she always did appear older than her age. Charlotte remembers her surprise when, a few months after they'd met, David announced he was organising his mother's fifty-fifth birthday party. With deep lines scoring Miriam's face and wispy grey hair in a no-nonsense short style, Charlotte had reckoned her to be at least ten years older. Raising three young boys on her own had clearly taken its toll. But instead of relaxing and enjoying life now that they'd grown up, Miriam remained as focused on them as ever, as if her happiness was solely dependent on theirs. Her sons still worshipped her, despite the constant stream of advice and phone calls, doing everything they could to make her life easier.

Sometimes too much, Charlotte often thought, after David was summoned yet again to change a light bulb in his mother's cavernous home in suburban Surbiton. Even so, she couldn't help but think that Miriam must have done something right to have such devoted sons.

'The doctor said everything looks fine,' Charlotte says to Miriam now, aware that everyone seems to be awaiting her response. Just saying the words calms the fear prickling inside her. The doctors wouldn't let her out if things weren't right. All she needs is rest, and then everything will come back. 'Thanks for staying with Anabelle.'

Miriam nods, drawing Charlotte in for a hug. Charlotte's eyebrows rise in surprise as she's engulfed in her mother-in-law's soft embrace, and she resists the urge to pull away. She never hugs Miriam! The most warmth her mother-in-law has ever shown her was letting her turn on the boiler early for a hot shower during a rare overnight visit to her house. Right from their very first meeting, things between them were strained. Knowing how important Miriam was to David, Charlotte had launched a campaign to make a great first impression, picking David's brain for hours on what she could do. They'd settled on inviting Miriam out to a posh restaurant Charlotte had spent ages choosing. They'd had a lovely meal, but within seconds of ordering after-dinner espresso, David had turned green and rushed to the loo to be violently ill. Miriam and Charlotte had bundled him into a taxi back to the flat and Miriam had stayed the night to take care of her son, pronouncing him poorly from food poisoning. Charlotte had tried everything to help, but Miriam had only shaken her head and brushed her off brusquely, as if she was trying to intrude on Miriam's rightful place.

Things hadn't gone any better since. Miriam had never really warmed to her, despite her constant efforts over those first couple of years, as if she was never truly convinced Charlotte was the right woman to make her son happy . . . as if she somehow knew she wasn't up for producing the clutch of grandkids Miriam so desperately desired. Any suspicions certainly hadn't put her off talking about it every ten seconds, though.

'Thank goodness you and Anabelle are all right. I can't bear thinking about the alternative.' Miriam dabs her eyes, and David pats her arm.

'Oh, Mum. It's okay, don't worry,' he says.

'I'll feel much better when you're all within shouting distance,' Miriam says, fishing a tissue from her cardigan sleeve. 'Then I'll know where everyone is, all the time.'

Charlotte forces a smile through the rising dread. What does Miriam mean, 'within shouting distance'? Is she planning to move to Chelsea? Perish the thought. The only way Charlotte can cope with Miriam now is by pretending that she doesn't exist . . . or that she lives on another planet, only dropping by for intergalactic visits to criticise the way others live. Then she's gone, disappearing into a black hole that sometimes sucks David in, too.

It couldn't be more different to Charlotte's relationship with her own mother, whose life is too busy and full to provide her daughter with endless opinions on inane topics . . . thank goodness. *Is she still working just as hard?* Charlotte wonders. After all, her mum would be . . . how old, exactly? Even with however many additional years, it's hard to picture her mother slowing down. The last she remembers, her mum still worked full-time as the chief operating officer for a London public relations firm, having climbed up the corporate ladder quickly during Charlotte's childhood. She may not have always made it home for bath and bedtime or out to the endless school concerts and activities, but Charlotte never doubted that her mum loved her. She didn't need her to dash across the city for a ten-minute school assembly to prove that; she felt it in every cuddle. Anyway, she had her father, who had more than made up for any gap her mother's crazy work schedule had created.

Charlotte smiles through the pain in her heart, thinking of her kind, good-natured dad. He'd been the ultimate father figure, even if he'd often played more of a maternal role. With her mum gone most of the time, he'd thrown himself into raising his only child, working part-time so he could be there when she needed him. It was him she'd turned to when she'd broken her tooth by tripping into the door, and him she'd first cried to when Tom Baxter had broken up with her in Year Eight.

When her dad died of a heart attack in her second year at uni, Charlotte had felt like she'd lost the centre of her world. At his funeral, both she and her mum had stood like statues, unable to hug or even speak. Without her dad to connect them, their grief kept them apart. Charlotte had thrown herself into her studies, emerging from her books only when Lily insisted. Her mum had done the same, getting promoted that year. After graduation, Charlotte had followed her mother's example, using work as a convenient way to block out the sadness that ambushed her whenever she had a free moment . . . and had discovered along the way that she loved the rush of success and pride that came with every pitch she won. The burst of emotion inside would never erase the pain her father's death had left, but for just a split second, it filled her up once more. Over time, she and her mother had bridged the chasm her father had left, although they'd never had a close relationship. Lily, then David, were the ones she'd learned to turn to.

Charlotte was proud of her mum, though, and she'd always regarded her as the kind of parent she wanted to be: having a successful career to set an example for her child, yet loving and present whenever possible. Like mother, like daughter . . . hopefully, anyway.

Please may I be exactly like my mother.

Charlotte glances down at her jeggings and trainers, wondering again why she's dressed like this. And where had she been going with Anabelle in the car? Had she left work early? Nausea swirls inside and she puts a hand to her mouth, hoping she won't be sick.

'Go and lie down.' David nudges her into the bedroom. 'Have a rest, like the doctors said. Anabelle and I will walk Mum to her car, and then we'll go to the park. Can you just tell me where her jacket is? And maybe her wellies, too? Do you think she'll need them? And her mittens?'

His questions barely penetrate Charlotte's pounding head, rebounding off her as she pads into the bedroom. She clamps her lips closed to stop a moan from escaping as she takes in the interior. The tranquil bedroom she'd designed in shades of turquoise and cream has been totally transformed into something infinitely less desirable, and much less relaxing. Hideous grey blackout curtains hang from the window, a small chest of drawers has been shoved into the tiny space by the bed, and nestled in the corner of the room is a toddler bed with a menagerie of soft toys on top of a garish dinosaur duvet. Anabelle's name is printed on the headboard in pink (pink!) stickers, along with a huge number '3' beneath it.

Okay, then. Her child is three – that's not so bad. At least Anabelle can talk, and she must be able to do most things for herself, right? She must be past the phase of needing her mother for everything. Thank goodness Charlotte doesn't need to change nappies. *Ugh.*

She sinks on to the bed – thankfully the mattress is still the same – and pulls the now-stained duvet cover over her. She knew it would be difficult squeezing everyone into a one-bed flat, but . . . bloody hell, how do she and David ever have sex? Not to mention a lie-in or one of their infamous 'bed parties', where they cart wine, cheese and those horrible smelly nacho chips David loves to the bedroom, then burrow under the duvet for hours, just enjoying each other and their life together?

Because as much as she must love her daughter, Charlotte's certain she can't want to be by her side every hour, every day – and night. Motherhood doesn't have to be the total surrender of your time, your space, your *life*.

It can't, because she'd be certifiably crazy by now if it was.

This much she knows for sure.

CHAPTER SEVEN

14 April

I'm about two months in now – two months of growing this tiny human inside me. And no matter how many times David tenderly touches my belly, the fact that there's a baby there still feels so theoretical. A very small part of me worries that I'll show up for my ultrasound in a few weeks' time and the sonographer will turn to me with a furrowed brow, asking why on earth I thought I was pregnant, since my stomach is empty.

Not that I'm complaining about my lack of symptoms so far. Oh God, no. I've heard horror stories from friends who were practically bedridden with nausea from day one, or those who kept falling asleep on the job. I *could* do without the extra cup size – I'm curvy enough without adding more – but I suppose you can't pick and choose.

Apart from my blossoming bosom and David's occasional reminder to eat more and work less, life is carrying on as usual. I'm still running every night after presenting David with my exhaustive research showing that it is indeed safe, and I'm still planning our weekend forays to markets, pubs and theatres. I'm working as hard as ever, taking on new projects and pitches. When I tell Vivek I'm pregnant – and I will, once I pass three months – there will be no room for him to doubt my commitment.

I could wait to tell him until my belly is big . . . Hell, I could probably wait until the month before giving birth, for all the notice he takes
of my physical appearance (once I dyed my hair red, and it took him
two months to realise I'd changed something). But I've heard Vivek
grumble about women waiting until the last moment to say they'll
need cover, leaving him and the team scrambling. I can't do that to
him, and I want time to show him that this pregnancy doesn't mean
anything different. I don't need any special considerations, and I don't
need any concessions. I'll still be the one he can count on to deliver; the
one drinking in every extra bit of knowledge and experience he shares.
Impending motherhood won't distract me from my job.

The only thing in my life that *has* changed is the appearance of baby
books in our flat. I've been doing everything possible to prepare for a
newborn, right down to understanding the mechanics of breastfeeding
(although, to be honest, the word 'lactate' will always gross me out). I've
stuffed my mind so quickly with so many facts, I feel like I'm cramming
for an exam I only remembered I was doing at the last minute.

Even though that's not the case, the clock *is* ticking, and I need to
do everything possible to ace this. Ace motherhood, ace being a working
mother, ace adding a new little person to our world. Already, I know
everything you can about pregnancy to year one . . . although I'm planning to go back to work after two months.

Or maybe six weeks, just like my mum. Or maybe even a month?
We'll see.

I was surprised at David's shock when I told him how soon I want
to return to the office. He knows how I feel about work – although he
may not understand it, given how much he detests his job. But surely he
wouldn't expect me to kick back at home with the baby for more than
that? What the hell would I *do* all day? I'm many things, but a kicking-
back-at-home kind of person isn't one of them. God, I'd go crazy!

And it's not just that, of course. If I take more than two months
off, Vivek will have my head. I can kiss any chance of ever making it to

VP goodbye, and I don't want to have worked like a demon these past few years for nothing.

Thankfully David's ready to take over whenever I want him to . . . he's itching to, in fact. This baby belongs to both of us, so why does the mother always need to be the one to stay at home? All that nonsense about 'mother knows best' is so old-school. Why would I know more than David, just because I gave birth? At this point, we know as much as each other, all based on the plethora of books we devour every night.

We've plenty of time to prepare. That's what I tell myself when the thought of the coming 'exam' makes my heart beat faster, and something like fear sweeps over me. For God's sake, we're not even at the hallowed three-month mark yet, the point when my ever-cautious husband will feel comfortable sharing our big news with friends and family.

I wasn't fussed about waiting; this whole thing is so surreal that it feels on a par with telling people we're jetting off to Mars. But David asked how I'd cope if things went wrong and we had to tell people *that* news, too. I couldn't say that since I barely believed I was pregnant in the first place, it was hard to imagine how I'd feel if I lost it. Anyway, there's no reason for things to go awry. My body behaves like clockwork; I rarely even come down with a cold. This baby is safe while it's inside me. It's when it emerges that we really need to prepare for.

The one person I *did* tell was my mother. She's rarely someone I confide in, but I wanted her reassurance . . . to hear that I could be a mother and have a successful career, too. Her reaction wasn't exactly what I'd hoped for, though. She kept asking, 'Are you sure?', as if I'd somehow failed to read the test correctly. Or maybe she meant: am I sure this is what I want? Either way, she was stunned, saying she'd thought I didn't want any children. I barely stopped myself from answering that I *didn't* – not right now, anyway – and that this wasn't planned.

We didn't talk long. I couldn't bear the doubt her questions stirred up, the uncertainty I'd managed to clamp down on. I made an excuse to get off the phone, and we haven't spoken since. I'm sure she meant well, but it's a little late for questions. This is real . . . or so I keep telling myself.

And I *will* want this. I will feel something for the child inside me. I'll keep cramming in all that baby information, keep working hard so I can take time off without worry, keep telling myself everything will be okay and that I've got this all under control.

After all, it is just a baby. How hard can it be?

CHAPTER EIGHT

'Mummy, up!'

Charlotte's eyes barely open before a heavy weight lands on her midsection, knocking all the air from her. Her head still pounds, and she glances at the clock on the bedside table in disbelief: it's just gone 5 a.m. Even on the busiest of workdays, she rarely makes it out of bed before 5.30. She stares at the child on top of her, dismay flooding in as she realises that her mind, her *heart*, are still blank.

'Back to sleep, okay? It's not time to get up yet.' *Please, God, may it not be time to get up yet.* Despite lying down for most of the evening yesterday and all night, her body aches like she's run a marathon – and having run three of them, she knows exactly how bad that feels.

'Nope! Let's get up!' Anabelle shakes her head, her bed-head hair waving around her like a halo. With her rosy cheeks and long-lashed eyes she's the epitome of cute, but Charlotte can see by the set of the girl's face that she's not going to be pushed around. Well, two can play at that game, and Charlotte is the adult here. How difficult can it be to evict a child from your bed?

But before Charlotte can open her mouth, Anabelle dives under the duvet and burrows into her so closely it feels like she'll need surgical removal. Haven't three year olds heard of personal space? And where the *hell* is David?

Charlotte manages to lift her head just enough to make out that David's side of the bed is empty, the covers undisturbed. Has he even come to bed? She attempts to wriggle away from Anabelle's death grip, conscious that she's not wearing any pyjamas. She's never worn pyjamas, actually, but if she'd known she'd be cuddling with a three year old, she definitely would have put some on last night.

Ugh, last night. She grimaces as images flood into her throbbing head. Anabelle and David had returned from the park just in time for supper. David had turned on some telly channel from hell while cooking foul-smelling fish fingers he'd picked up from the off-licence down the road. Knocking up supper didn't sound that complicated, but given the number of questions he lobbed at her from the kitchen while she feigned sleep, it must have been in the realm of astrophysics. How come an intelligent man like him couldn't figure out how to work the oven?

Not that she has any clue – well, she never used to, anyway. She can't remember the last time they actually used that oven. Usually, one of them picked up a takeaway on the way home from work. Either that or they ordered from the thick stack of menus they'd collected over the years.

The telly kept blaring until David convinced Anabelle it was bedtime, then ushered the girl into their room without even brushing her teeth. She'd whined that she wanted Mummy to put her down, and Charlotte could tell David was caving in. But she kept her eyes firmly closed and her back turned away, even when David persisted in asking question after question. Where were the PJs? Did he need to brush Anabelle's hair? Did she wear a nappy at night?

Hadn't her husband ever put their daughter to bed, for goodness' sake? Even if he wasn't a stay-at-home dad now, he must do it on a regular basis – there's no way Charlotte would make it home from Cellbril this early, not in million years. It seemed like he was the one with amnesia, not her.

Not that she could blame him for faltering: Anabelle's bedtime appeared to be more complicated than directing a mission to Mars. From the endless stories David had to tell, to the holding of her hand a certain way, to singing a goodnight song while rocking back and forth just so . . . Charlotte couldn't believe it was so complex. Did they do this crazy dance every night? How on earth had they allowed that to happen? For God's sake, put the child into bed and get on with it.

Finally Anabelle was asleep, but she didn't stay that way. She woke up once for the loo, once because she couldn't find Zebby, and once because, well, Charlotte didn't even know why. Even if she hadn't already had a headache, she was sure she'd have one after such a broken night's sleep. No wonder she looked so bloody knackered.

'You need to go back to bed,' she says again, in what she hopes is an authoritative voice. She kicks her legs gently to try to dislodge Anabelle, but the little girl grips more tightly. How did such a small thing get so strong? 'Go back to bed and close your eyes.'

'But Mummy!' Anabelle lifts her head from where, unbeknown to her, she's currently squashing Charlotte's nipple. *God.* 'Look! It's light outside now.' She gestures to a tiny bit of light slicing through a crack in the blackout curtains, and Charlotte squints. What's the good of ugly curtains if they don't even do the job?

'It's just streetlight,' Charlotte mumbles, heart sinking as she realises there's no way her fully alert daughter will fall back asleep. She pulls the duvet against her, creating a shield between her nakedness and Anabelle. 'Right. Well, why don't you go get breakfast and turn on the telly?' She always turned her nose up at mums who shoved their kids in front of the TV, but right now she can't get her child there fast enough. 'I'll be up in a minute or two.' More like an hour – she needs more sleep for her brain to start functioning, let alone firing on all cylinders at the office.

Because she *is* going to the office today, even if her head feels like it's about to burst. There's no way she's staying home in this chaotic, cluttered flat. Her temporary memory loss might make this morning a little challenging, but she's sure she can get up to speed on everything quickly. She knows her job inside out, and right now she needs something familiar.

Does Anabelle go to nursery? Where does Charlotte drop her, and when does she pick her up . . . or does David do that? He must, since he always leaves work earlier, right? Confusion swarms over her, and she sits up in bed. She has to remember something soon, but right now, she's as clueless as ever. Thank God for David, wherever he is. He'll have things organised to a T. Then she remembers his five million questions last night, and doubt trickles in. Well, he'd better, because she sure doesn't.

Anabelle's eyes pop, and her mouth forms a round 'o'. 'Mummy, you never let me watch TV! You get me dressed, and then make my porridge, and then drink your coffee while your "brain gets started".' She scoots from the duvet, rolling with a thud on to the floor. 'Silly Mummy.'

'Okay, okay. Come on, then.' Charlotte groans, then swings her feet on to the floor, remembering too late that she's naked. Anabelle gives her a full-body scan and Charlotte sighs, grabbing her robe. The last thing she needs this morning is a three year old questioning why she hasn't waxed her bikini line in what looks like forever. 'Let's find David. Er, Daddy. Dad. Whoever.'

It's so weird to think of David as *Daddy* . . . but not as weird as thinking of herself as a mother. She really *must* remember today – she's not sure how much longer she can keep pretending. Charlotte opens the door to track down her husband, wondering if she should just tell him the truth now. There's no way she's dealing with this on her own. There's no way she *can* deal with this on her own.

Her eyes widen when she spots David curled up with a pillow and blankets on the sofa. Why did he sleep out here? Did he not want to disturb her when her head was so sore?

'David!' she hisses, wincing at the pain hammering her skull.

He lifts his head and wipes his mouth, and once again she's surprised at the bags under his eyes and the grey now colonising his hair. It *has* been a few years, she reminds herself. And – she sighs, remembering her pudgy tummy – she's changed, too. Well, her body has, anyway.

'What? What's wrong?'

Charlotte sits down, nestling into his body. He's as warm as ever, and she plasters herself against him, drawing in his strength. No matter how strange the last few hours since the accident have been, he is still here, and they are still them – Charlotte and David, as solid as ever. She tries not to flinch as Anabelle wiggles her way between them, separating them as neatly as a knife before hopping off the sofa again.

'I need a wee! I need a wee!' Anabelle is jumping from one foot to the other. 'Mummy, I need a wee!'

'Well, go on then,' Charlotte says, noticing David give her a funny look. Is that not what she says? She's hardly going to accompany the child to the loo. Is she?

'Come on. I'll take you.' David hauls himself off the sofa, and Charlotte raises an eyebrow at the state of his boxers. Saggy and faded, they're more fit for the rubbish than the bedroom. She used to buy David expensive new underwear twice a year, birthday and Christmas, like clockwork. What happened to that?

David takes Anabelle's hand as she keeps up a constant chatter on the way to the toilet. Charlotte closes her eyes as the two of them clatter around the kitchen then into the bedroom, where it sounds like David's wrestling Anabelle to get her dressed. They head back to the toilet and begin a tooth-brushing battle while Charlotte pads into the bedroom, her mouth stretching in a yawn. Despite her pounding head, she can't wait to get to work. She loves lurching on to the top deck of the bus each morning, watching from above as the city comes to life; feeling she's a part of the heaving, striving metropolis. She loves the ball of adrenaline that ping-pongs around her belly when she enters the office every morning, her brain revving up as she runs through the list of clients and projects awaiting her attention. And she absolutely loves pitching for new business, and the thrill of success when she signs yet another huge deal. Work makes her feel *alive*, in a way that nothing else can.

Charlotte opens the wardrobe, heart sinking as she takes in the jumbled collection of baggy shirts, jeans (and an impressive assortment of jeggings!) and jumpers. Where are the ten pairs of black trousers she owned, in every length and cut? David used to mock her when she bought yet another pair, but you can never have too many black trousers. She'd had a range of sharply cut blazers, too, and those are nowhere to be seen. Maybe she moved them somewhere else? Along with the sparkly tops for nights out on the razz . . . although those nights had been fewer and fewer as more of her friends had defected to Babyland.

What the hell does she wear to work every day? She *does* go to work every day, right? Her gut clenches and a cold dread seeps through her when she remembers the casual clothes she was wearing at the time of the accident, and the fact that she was nowhere near the office on a weekday. She can't be working part-time; Vivek always says that Cellbril 'isn't a place for slackers who can't get off their arse and into the office five days a week'. She wouldn't *want* to drop any days. Doing so would obliterate any hope of future progression, and there's no way she'd throw away what she's been working towards for years.

No, there must be another answer to this wardrobe conundrum.

David pushes past her, practically jumping into trousers, shirt and jacket.

'I've got to get going,' he says, gathering up his keys and wallet. 'I'll drop Anabelle at Mum's for the day. No arguments; she'll be absolutely fine, and you're not in any fit state to be supermum today. She'll bring her back around three. I'll be in and out of meetings all day, but call if you need anything, okay?' He meets her eyes. 'We'll talk tonight. About what happened at Lily's, and something else that's come up.' His face tightens and he takes a step towards the door. 'Okay?'

She nods, but she's still stuck on the word 'supermum'. Is that what she is? And what exactly does that entail? Nothing that affects her working life, right? You can be supermum and superworker at the same time. If anyone can do it, she can.

'Oh, and I talked to the mechanic last night,' David says, struggling to get Anabelle's wriggly arms into her anorak. 'He says your car will be sorted by the end of the week – just the side dent to fix and some paintwork. But you'll be around home as usual, right? You won't need the car for anything.'

Around home as usual? Charlotte recoils at the words. What the—? She draws in a breath, telling herself to stay calm. Maybe she works from home? There had been rumours about Cellbril's headquarters moving to Germany, leaving the UK office to work virtually, in a bid to cut costs. Vivek had told them it'd never happen, but . . . that might explain the absence of work clothes, although wouldn't she still need those for pitches and meetings?

'Right, Anabelle, give Mummy a kiss and let's make a move.' David jingles his keys.

Anabelle streaks over to her and places a crumby kiss on Charlotte's forehead, but Charlotte can't even force a smile over the fear and panic gathering inside her. She can't have given up her job – a job she adores, a job that's been her life – to simply stay at home. It's just not possible. She can't imagine the boredom of the daily grind, your world revolving solely around a child. Some people might be happy with that life, but she certainly wouldn't.

So where the *hell* are her clothes?

'David.' Charlotte's voice cuts across Anabelle's chatter, and David turns from doing up Anabelle's zip.

'Yes?'

Charlotte bites her lip, thinking now's the time to let him know that she has no idea what her world has become – that she's *praying* it's just as she left it, at least on the work front. But with 'supermum' ringing in her head, she can't release the words. She's always pushed herself to excel, and that clearly hasn't changed with motherhood. Telling David that not only is she miles from being a supermum, she can't even remember having a child, feels like admitting she's losing her grip . . . like she's out of control. And that's just not her – past or present, it seems.

'Just . . . well, is there anyone I should call? To say I won't be there? Or that I'm taking a sick day?' *Please may he say I need to call work.* She's desperate to know that she still has her job; her place in a company she's worked so hard for. 'I'm feeling a little, well, foggy this morning,' she mumbles, thinking that's the understatement of the year.

'You really did take a knock on the head, didn't you?' David's face softens. 'Well, I'm not exactly sure of your weekly schedule. You and Anabelle usually have some kind of playgroup or music class every day. Maybe check your calendar?'

'Okay.' She can barely get the word out as her heart crashes to the ground. Playgroup? Music class?

Shit.

The door closes, and Charlotte sinks to the floor. She wants to scream, to bang her fists on the walls and wail, but it feels like all her energy has drained away, leaving behind a lifeless shell. All those years . . . all that hard work, the long hours, the travel for weeks at a time . . . she loved it, yes, but she'd pushed herself for a reason. She'd wanted desperately to be VP, to be in a position that meant something.

And now that's gone.

She won't be going to the office today, or any day in the future. She won't be vice-president, an important voice in the company where she's worked for the past decade. Christ, she doesn't even have a job, full stop. She's not one of those women who has everything, after all. She's become someone she never dreamed of being.

Someone with nothing in their life but their kid.

Charlotte lets out a cry, cradling her aching head in her hands. How could this happen? Why would she give up everything she loves for a life she'd never be happy in? And while she's at it, how did she ever get to the point of actually wanting a child, anyway? Of being *ready* to have a child? Because of course Anabelle was wanted. Charlotte always took her pill religiously, and it's unlikely she'd be within the one per cent unlucky enough to fall pregnant. And even if she were . . . well, they'd obviously decided to go for it.

She strides over to the bookcase and peers at a large framed photo. It's a family portrait – quite recent by the looks of things – of all three of them. She and David are sitting on a wooden bench under a leafy tree with Anabelle squeezed in between them. Anabelle is grinning brightly at the camera, while she and David are smiling down at their daughter as if she's the most important thing in the world. Charlotte looks so happy, as if she's glowing with love from the inside out.

She closes her eyes, begging her brain to explain how she ended up in this strange, foreign place . . . shoved into the body of a person who's torn the only future she'd ever wanted away from her. But her head just pounds with pain, and she's left as clueless as ever. Fury flares inside as she stares at this woman gazing tenderly at her child, and she has to clench her fists to stop herself from smashing the glass. *How can you be happy?* she wants to yell. *How can you be happy when you've thrown everything away? How can you smile with the huge, inescapable responsibility of motherhood on your shoulders . . . forever?*

Charlotte sinks on to the sofa and shuts her eyes again. It will all be okay. Soon, she'll remember. It hasn't even been a day since the accident, and whatever tricks her brain is playing, it'll sort itself out.

It better had, anyway. How else can she cope with this disbelief and blinding anger that everything she's worked for has gone? How can she live this life when she can't even remember wanting it?

And even worse . . . how can she be a mother when she doesn't even love her own daughter?

CHAPTER NINE

16 May

I made it past the three-month mark this week.

David is ecstatic. This date has given him permission to fully open the emotional floodgates, and I've never seen him so happy. In fact, it was him who marked the occasion with fake champagne and the teeniest, tiniest Babygro I've ever seen. He wrapped it up and handed it over with a huge grin on his face, and for a split second, I thought he might have bought me something to wear (although I'm glad he didn't, as he has terrible taste when it comes to women's fashion).

Opening the package and finding something for a baby – for our baby – was a very strange feeling, like I'd stepped into an alternative universe. Probation period might be over for my husband and my body, but in my mind, it still feels like I'm treading in a foreign land, despite all my reading.

It's a strange place, a world where my husband fends off my sexual advances (God, I'm horny), saying he's afraid he'll hurt the baby. It's a place where, all of a sudden, it feels like he has a say over my body, too: what I should eat ('Is this bite going to benefit the baby?'); in what position I should sleep; and what vitamins I should take. I'm not just his wife; not just Charlotte any longer – I'm the caretaker of his child, too. That trumps everything, even me. It makes me feel . . . smaller, somehow.

I suppose it's part of the reason I haven't told Lily that I'm pregnant, although I mostly don't want to upset her. And how can she not be upset when the 'mad auntie' will soon become the mother she longs to be? Her journey to get pregnant has been filled with struggle and grief, whereas mine . . . well, mine wasn't a journey at all. It wasn't even *wanted*. Her journey is continuing, full of uncertainty and hope, and mine will be ending in six months at the destination she's desperate to reach: parenthood. I can't help feeling that my news will put even more distance between us, and there's already enough as it is.

And if I'm really being honest, I don't want my oldest friend to think of me as anything other than the woman she knows now. I don't want her to ask how I'm feeling, if I'm going to breastfeed, when I'm going back to work . . . I don't want to default to baby talk, if there's a chance she's even up for that. Not yet, anyway.

This all sounds terrible, doesn't it? So self-absorbed, I know, and I wouldn't dream of saying any of it out loud. I should be lifted up by giving birth to a new life. I should feel exalted by this shift in my world, finally 'fulfilling my role as a woman' – as Miriam so helpfully pointed out when we told her the news. But instead I feel unsettled and unstable, like I'm trying to grip something that's sliding from my grasp.

Like the harder I grab, the more slippery it becomes.

Because despite my determination that things won't change, they already have – and this baby isn't even born yet. It's not just David, either. It's worse than that, or at least it feels that way: it's my boss, too. I mean, I knew he wouldn't be happy when I told him the news. The few women in our department who'd dared to go off on maternity leave got plenty of stick . . . and even more when they tried to return on reduced hours. And I have to admit, I hadn't exactly been supportive of that. Why should I need to put in more time so they could work at home? Because we all know what 'working from home' really means – faffing around in your pyjamas while answering the odd email to show you're actually there. It's part of the reason Vivek is so keen to keep our UK base open, despite plans to become a virtual office.

But I wasn't just your run-of-the-mill employee. This was me: 'pitch perfect', Vivek calls me, a dedicated professional who's proven her worth time and again. Surely he wouldn't let a minor detour like a baby cloud his judgement of my value, especially when I was planning to return so soon after giving birth?

I was nervous when I went to tell him, but not too worried. I took a few deep breaths, knocked on his door, then delivered the news quickly (he hates it when you waste his time). And his response? 'That's a shame.'

A shame that I'd opted out, I guess. A shame that my future was no longer what he'd envisioned. And even as I assured him I was coming back full-time within six weeks, I could tell by his dubious expression that he didn't believe me.

I could tell that things had changed.

I wasn't his successor, the one who'd knock him off his throne, like he'd joked. I was a woman having a baby . . . a woman who'd disappear soon into the same black hole that had swallowed so many other women in our workforce.

His phone rang and he waved me out, like I was damaged goods now. I left the office with a cold, hard knot in my stomach, the terrible sense that having this baby *was* going to affect my career. I sat down at my desk and stared with unseeing eyes at the screen, the noise of the office fading away.

I'm pregnant. I'm going to be a mum. But I'm also a damn good worker, and even if my boss sees me differently now, I'll show him I'm not. I love this job, and I won't let it slip away. I won't let my *future* slip away.

I'll prove him wrong, no matter what.

CHAPTER TEN

By mid-afternoon, Charlotte is practically climbing the walls. She hasn't been home on a weekday for ages, not since a spectacular case of food poisoning a few years ago turned her off sushi for life. She's not used to the silence of the flat – well, silent now that she's muted the annoying WhatsApp group that dinged every few minutes, offering some new kiddie activity. She's examined the huge array of family photos in forensic detail, riffled through the bookcases, and even flicked through her wardrobe so many times she could probably itemise its contents . . . as if by memorising the material items of her life, she'll slide seamlessly back into the present. Every muscle longs to relax, but each time she glimpses herself in the mirror, disbelief and confusion at where she's ended up propels her back and forth across the flat, like she's seeking a foothold in this new life. David's face flashes into her mind and she sighs. Maybe she should just tell him the truth. He'll be stunned and concerned, but at least they can get through this together.

She glances out of the window, thinking that now her head has stopped pounding – at least it no longer feels like it will lift itself right off her shoulders – maybe some fresh air would do her good. It's stuffy and warm in this flat, and just being here makes her feel so close yet so far from the life she knows . . . the only life she remembers.

Hell, the only life she *wants*. Right now, anyway.

She's about to grab her coat when she spies Miriam and Anabelle coming up the road. Anabelle is holding Miriam's hand, practically skipping as Miriam corrals her down the pavement. Her mouth is moving a mile a minute and Miriam nods, then scoops the little girl up in her arms and swings her around. Charlotte can hear Anabelle's delighted shriek from here, and Miriam's positively beaming. Charlotte blinks, thinking Miriam looks a good twenty years younger. She's never seen her mother-in-law so *happy*.

Charlotte studies her daughter's animated face as Miriam sets her back on the ground. She looks clever – well, she's definitely a talker; must have got that from her mum. She certainly seems to have plenty of energy, and she looks strong and healthy. *Please God may she not be a fussy eater*, Charlotte thinks, making a face. She always rolls her eyes when she sees parents cajoling their children to take 'just one more bite, there's a good girl'. In her opinion, they should eat or go hungry. God knows her own mother hadn't any time for that. In fact, there were times Charlotte *had* starved after refusing to eat something her mum had cobbled together after a long day at the office . . . if she made it home in time for supper, that was.

Charlotte starts, thinking of her mother. What does she think of her daughter giving up work to be a stay-at-home mum? Her mum is never one to comment on Charlotte's life unless asked, but Charlotte's sure she has some choice thoughts about her daughter's life path.

Miriam's key scratches in the lock, and Charlotte takes a deep breath, bracing herself for her daughter's arrival. Okay, she can do this. She may not feel like a mother, but at least she can act like one . . . although God knows what kind of parent she is. Is she like her own mum, about as maternal as a potted plant? Or is she more like Miriam, the ultimate mothering role model? Either way, she'll have to fake it until her memory – and emotions – kick in.

'Mummy!' The door opens and Anabelle hurtles into her arms.

Despite the mud coating her daughter's jeans and trousers, Charlotte forces herself to hug Anabelle tightly, trying not to think about the damp seeping through her own clothes. It *is* nice that someone's so happy to see her, despite the added layer of dirt.

But . . . Charlotte draws back, wiping her cheek and trying to keep the expression of disgust from her face as she examines some goo that's transferred on to her cheek. What is *that*?

'Oh dear, Anabelle.' Miriam pulls a tissue from her pocket. 'Your nose is running again!' She swipes at the child's nose as Charlotte inwardly shudders. 'Now don't you worry,' Miriam says, patting Charlotte's shoulder. 'I had her coat on all the time, and she didn't get too wet. She'll be fine.'

Charlotte nods, thinking that she's not worried at all. Should she be? Okay, so it's winter, but London is hardly the Antarctic. Surely she's not one of those neurotic mums who freaks out if their child so much as coughs.

She watches as Miriam peels off Anabelle's jacket to reveal a lurid pink sweatshirt emblazoned with Peppa Pig paired with spotty red trousers. Charlotte raises her eyebrows, thinking that as much as she admires creative flair, she'd envisioned her hypothetical child decked out in a cute pinafore with a bow in her hair. God, she must have been really out of it this morning not to notice this fetching ensemble. As Anabelle kicks off her wellies, a handful of sand tumbles out on to the floor. Charlotte cringes, thinking there's nothing worse than sand underfoot.

'You go sit with your mother while I tidy this up,' Miriam says, propelling the two of them towards the sofa. 'How's your head? Better?'

Charlotte nods. 'Yes, thanks. Still a little painful, but getting there.'

If only she could remember the little girl now tugging her hands so hard she almost falls over. She lets herself be pulled on to the sofa and Anabelle snuggles into her, clutching Zebby in one hand and a fistful of

Charlotte's jumper in the other. It's as if she can't get close enough; like she wants to burrow inside her mother and bury herself there.

'So what did you do today?' Charlotte asks, wondering what she's supposed to say to a three year old. The last time she was alone with a child had been years ago, when David and his eldest brother had popped out to the shops during a brief visit. Charlotte had entertained his brother's five year old by practising an upcoming sales pitch, adding the word 'poo' to the end of every sentence to keep him laughing. It'd been a great short-term strategy, but somehow she didn't think it'd work in the long term.

She needn't have worried, though, because Anabelle launches into a detailed description of what they did at Granny's house, the sand cake she made, who she met at the play area, the puddle in front of the fountain . . . Charlotte leans back, fighting the urge to close her eyes and have a little sleep. The niggling pain in her head is flaring again, but she's not sure if that's down to the accident or her daughter.

'I'll just pop off now.' Miriam runs a hand over her granddaughter's head, and Anabelle smiles up at her. *It's wonderful that the two of them have such a close relationship*, Charlotte thinks. Does her own mother come round much? Although her mum lives practically around the corner, in Kensington, Charlotte can't imagine her playing doting grandma.

'Will you be okay for tomorrow?' Miriam asks. 'I'm happy to help if you need me to, but I'll have John's three to deal with as well. It might be a very full house! The more the merrier, though.'

Charlotte raises an eyebrow. John is David's youngest brother, and the last thing she remembers is him having their first child. And now they have *three* kids? They've certainly been busy.

'That's all right,' Charlotte says. 'I'm sure it will be fine.' David can stay home tomorrow, if need be. He seems a little clueless, but he must help out when she's ill or has something else she needs to do. What the *hell* happened to make her give up work rather than him? He was the one who was chomping at the bit to quit his job, not her.

'Charlotte . . .' Miriam puts a hand on her arm. 'It was wonderful having Anabelle today. We had great fun, and it's good for her to get used to the house before you all move in with me. Oh, I know it's not for some time yet, but we need to plan these things.'

The words flow over Charlotte and it's all she can do to nod with a nailed-on smile as she tries to process everything. They're moving into Miriam's house? *While she's still living there?* It was bad enough when she thought Miriam might come to Chelsea, but to actually move in with her mother-in-law?

Charlotte takes two or three quick breaths, forcing air into her lungs as she struggles to believe what's happening. How on earth has she agreed to this? Has she had a brain transplant? She hates that house; hates it with every fibre of her being. It's everything she detests in a place: knick-knacks on every surface, and heavy drapes covering net curtains, blocking out what little light makes it through the dusty windows. The bedrooms are a riot of mismatched colours, from the hideous blue carpets to the fading floral wallpaper.

But forget that. She can deal with it – she can renovate the hell out of it.

What she can't change is her mother-in-law. Although she seems a bit warmer than Charlotte remembers – and although she and Anabelle clearly adore each other – Miriam is still *Miriam*. Charlotte may have produced a grandchild, but she'd bet her laptop that hasn't stopped Miriam asking when the next one is coming along. Why would Charlotte want to subject herself to that 24/7? Not to mention Miriam's infuriating belief that she – and only she – knows best . . . especially when it comes to her son's happiness.

And why would she and David leave Chelsea? They're cramped here, sure, but it's manageable. It has been for three years, anyway. They always swore they'd never leave the city, laughingly repeating that when you're tired of London, you're tired of life. Christ, have they somehow morphed into the exhausted couple fleeing the city for the space of the suburbs? Not bloody likely. But then . . . she doesn't even know who she is any more, and every new piece of information makes her feel further away from herself.

Charlotte thinks back to a conversation over lunch with Miriam one day, when David had proudly told his mother about his wife's promotion to senior account director. Miriam had congratulated her, but then had gone on to say that no success in the workplace could compare to the joy of holding a child in your arms, and that her fondest wish was that, one day, Charlotte would experience that.

David had squeezed Charlotte's hand in silent support, but he hadn't been able to keep the hopeful expression off his face. Charlotte had swallowed, feeling the walls closing in as frustration swirled inside. *How the hell did Miriam know that?* she'd wanted to retort. Had Miriam ever been promoted? Hell, had she ever had a job? What gave her the right to diminish Charlotte's success, to reduce her to someone who would only *really* be fulfilled through procreation?

Her heart sinks as she thinks about her life now: how she doesn't work, how she stays at home, how her world revolves around her child. Is there a chance Miriam was right? That once she had a baby, the happiness and love blotted out everything else . . . even the person she used to be?

Maybe she *has* had a brain transplant, after all – or a personality one. How else could she not only have quit her job, but also agreed to move in with her mother-in-law? Somehow, though, she can't believe it. People don't turn into someone else just because they've had a child . . . do they? Charlotte glances at the family photo on the bookcase once again, studying her image, as if she can read there what's going on inside her. The beaming face stares back, taunting her with its smile.

Charlotte closes her eyes as Anabelle crawls even further on to her lap. She can't wait any longer. Supermum or not, she needs to talk to David and tell him she can't remember . . . that she doesn't recognise anything about the present. She needs him to fill in the blanks and explain how she ended up here; to reassure her that even though she is a mother, she's still *her*.

CHAPTER ELEVEN

30 May

I saw her today. I saw our daughter. Because we're having a girl . . . or at least the sonographer thinks so. I may only be fifteen weeks along, but she is quite sure our baby has no 'willy' (her cutesy word, not mine. I can't think of a *less* cute appendage, to be honest). David's thrilled, telling me that secretly he was hoping for a girl. When he asked if I was happy too – if that was what I wanted – I nodded. But the truth is, despite the sonographer's confirmation that there *is* actually a baby inside me, I've been trying to carry on the same as always . . . and that hasn't left a lot of spare time to think about genders.

Actually, I'm wrong. I haven't been carrying on the same as always. I've been working longer hours than ever before, developing new presentation templates, liaising with old clients to see if they have anything in the pipeline, and working on a list of new clients to pitch to. David gets at me to slow down and put my feet up, but as long as the baby is all right, why shouldn't I work as hard as I can? Pregnancy isn't a disability, and mine has been one hundred per cent normal. Aren't there women in Africa who carry on working while in labour? Not that I'd take it *that* far, of course. But I do plan on bringing my laptop into the hospital with me, just so I can keep track of everything going on.

I'd be lying if I said I wasn't worried, though . . . if I said that all my extra work is simply for the thrill of a job well done. Because even though I *do* love my job – and believe me, I do it well – it's not just that. It's the gnawing feeling that sat in my gut as I left Vivek's office after telling him I was pregnant. I was right to be concerned, much as I hate to admit it.

It's only been a few weeks since my pregnancy announcement, and already there's been a shift in attitude: not just from Vivek, but from my team, both male and female. Where once I'd always got first shot at bid meetings and strategic accounts, suddenly I didn't seem to be on the list at all, despite the fact I'd *developed* the bloody list! And while I could understand if I'd been within weeks of my due date – or if I'd been planning to take an extended maternity leave – it didn't make sense when I wasn't yet four months gone. I was the company's most experienced account director, but now it felt like there was a sign on me saying I'd already checked out.

Like I was being walled off, brick by brick, until it was too late to do anything.

And I wasn't not going to let that happen. I wasn't going to be pushed aside just because of some biological function. Pregnancy shouldn't be a punishment, for God's sake.

So last week, I marched straight into Vivek's office. Family photos ringed his desk, and anger swept through me that *he* hasn't been penalised for having children.

'Charlotte!' Vivek beckoned me in. 'Please, sit down. How are you feeling?'

'I'm fine, thanks,' I replied. I'd pondered getting that tattooed on my forehead, just to save people from having to ask. God knows they certainly weren't interested in my internal workings before I got pregnant.

'Any heartburn? You know, my wife suffered terribly with that with our eldest. It got so bad she used to be sick, and—'

'No, no heartburn.' I cut him off. I wasn't here to talk about pregnancy, or his wife. I was here to talk about my *job*. I stayed on my feet, even though my heels were killing me. 'Look, I just want to make it clear that I'm able to handle a full workload, as usual. There's no reason to ask others to take on proposals and organise bid meetings.'

'Of course, of course.' Vivek nodded, but I recognised that tone. It was the gentle, placating one he used to soothe irrational clients. Since when had I – the person he always said has airtight logic and reason – become irrational? Did being pregnant somehow signal that my brain wasn't functioning?

'And you know that even when I am off on leave' – for some reason, I resisted the word 'maternity'; I don't know why – 'I still want to be kept in the loop, so I can hit the ground running when I'm back.'

'Sure, yes.' Vivek was still nodding, and I felt the urge to knock his head just like I used to do with those nodding dogs. 'You're a valuable asset to the company, Charlotte, and I do hope you'll come back to us.'

'I will.' The response came out between gritted teeth. Just what did I have to do to convince him? Give birth under my desk? 'And I don't want any favours right now, all right? Nothing has changed. Okay?'

'Okay.' Vivek was already looking away from me, reading something on his laptop screen.

I had to reschedule this ultrasound appointment twice because of clashes with work meetings. If I said I didn't want any special consideration, how could I duck out at such critical times? In my pre-pregnant life, I'd never dream of making doctor's appointments during the day . . . in fact, I rarely even saw the doctor, often leading to last-minute dashes to the sexual health clinic when I discovered I'd run out of pills, or a call to the emergency dental line when my loose filling fell out. Sure, this is a baby and not a dental appointment (and I have to admit, I did whisper a little 'sorry' to my belly when I couldn't make the ultrasound), but my presence at work is crucial right now. Just because I'm pregnant, I'm hardly going to morph into a different person – a person who no longer cares about my job. I'm having a baby, not a personality transplant.

I was a few minutes late this time, but I made it. David was there before me, as usual. I swear, he's more excited about all of this than me . . . which makes me feel a little guilty, as if I should be super-amped up about my body performing its biological function. My mind was full of preparations for the client meeting later that day. I was excited to see my baby, of course – to confirm that there's a person actually inside me – but it's so hard to switch my mind from work to baby to work again, like I'm existing in two separate universes. Thankfully one is safely tucked inside me with few demands . . . unlike my job. Part of me wishes I could stay pregnant forever.

They called my name and I hauled myself on to the table and pulled up my top, my stomach as smooth and flat as usual. David clutched my hand and we both chit-chatted with the sonographer about the weather – behaving like spring, for once, with the streak of sun and balmy temperatures, so unlike London – and football, and the coming elections. The sonographer moved the probe against my belly and I tried my best not to squirm away from the pressure on my bladder. I'd really taken those instructions to drink plenty of water to heart.

'Here she is,' the sonographer said, tilting the screen towards us, and David drew in a breath.

'*She?*' he asked. The sonographer nodded and smiled, and I turned from the blurry black and white image on the screen to meet David's eyes. They were glowing with love and excitement, and I tried hard to reflect that back. A *girl*. I was going to have a daughter. A little girl, and she was right there on the screen in front of me.

I stared at the screen again like it was a window into my soul . . . as if by focusing on that image long enough, I could somehow grip the future, hold it tightly in my grasp and make everything all right.

Because everything will be all right. My job will be fine once things settle down; we'll be more than prepared when our baby comes, and together, David and I will smash parenting. I grasped David's hand as the sonographer did the measurements, breathing deeply and staring at our baby on the screen.

'Everything looks perfect at this stage,' the sonographer said, and I let out a breath I didn't even know I was holding. David smiled at me and helped me sit up. His face dropped when I couldn't stick around for the sonographer to print off a strip of photos for us, but I had to hurry back to the office, where Vivek was waiting to discuss a potential new client. I grabbed my handbag and caught a taxi, my mind swinging back to the day ahead. I'd barely enough time to register the fact we're having a daughter before sliding into work mode.

I'm living in two worlds now: pregnant woman with a daughter on the way, and senior account director with an eye to vice-president. The past few weeks have shown me these two places aren't exactly compatible. I'll need to keep doing everything in my power to make sure they don't collide. But why should they?

Everything is perfect, the sonographer said, and I know she's right. It will be that, and more.

CHAPTER TWELVE

After Miriam leaves, Charlotte and Anabelle settle down for what Charlotte hopes is a few placid hours of TV until supper. Surely her daughter must be tired after being out all day? But after a few minutes Anabelle slides off the sofa and grabs Charlotte's hand, dragging her over to the pile of toys in the corner.

'Mummy! Come and play with me!' The little girl's nose is running again, but before Charlotte can tell her to get a tissue, Anabelle's wiped it on her sleeve. Charlotte makes a face. God, kids can be disgusting.

Charlotte manages to break free, plopping down on the sofa again. Judging from the avalanche of brightly coloured plastic in the corner, the child has enough toys to entertain her until the apocalypse. She doesn't need someone to play with her. How do you play with a toddler, anyway? Charlotte would rather sit through a million PowerPoint presentations than manipulate googly-eyed farm animals covered with God knows how many germs.

'You go ahead,' she says. 'I'll watch from here.'

Anabelle's mouth droops and her forehead wrinkles, and for a split second, Charlotte recognises her own disgruntled expression on the little girl's face. Anabelle marches over to the sofa, takes Charlotte's hand again and pulls.

'Mummy, you have to play with me. Mummy. Plays. *Now.*' She gives a final tug on the last word and Charlotte, surprised at the girl's strength, tumbles off the sofa and lands with a thud on the floor.

'Christ!' she bellows, as pain radiates from her bottom up to her very sore head. 'What the—'

She stops as she realises Anabelle is crying, tears running in rivers down her cheeks. *Oh, shit.* 'Look, I'm sorry. I didn't mean to scare you. It hurt when I fell on the floor, that's all.'

Anabelle scoots over and climbs on to Charlotte's lap. 'You always laugh when you fall down. You say your bottom is your cushion!'

Ugh, well, that much is true. Unfortunately. 'Come on.' Charlotte sighs, getting to her feet. 'Let's play.'

Charlotte tries her best to engage, but apparently dressing up a dolly or running Thomas the train around an imaginary track isn't enough. Anabelle is like a mini playtime dictator, ordering Charlotte to follow her elaborate instructions and chastising her when she gets them wrong. How is Charlotte to know what the old elf from Ben and Holly sounds like? Who *are* Ben and Holly, anyway? And can she help it if the critical piece for the Lego tower is missing? When she glances at the clock, she's stunned to see only twenty minutes have passed. How does she do this all day, every day? Doesn't she miss her job . . . doing something important?

It must be different when you *feel* for your child, when you're full of love, pride and appreciation for them. It must be more fulfilling . . . and definitely less boring. It would have to be, surely: if parenting really is this dull, why would anyone choose to do it? If Anabelle asks her to 'put baby to bed' one more time, Charlotte's going to scream.

With every creak of the stairs and bang of the outside door, Charlotte's heart jumps in hope that it's David so she can relinquish her domestic responsibilities and get in the bath, or grab some fresh air, or just relax without 'Mummy!' being bleated in her ear. She's missed him, too. He's the only thing she still recognises in this strange world, and she's desperate now to talk to him and have him fill in the gaps in her memory . . . to end the confusion those missing years have created. But suppertime comes and goes – she manages to present Anabelle with an unappetising concoction of ham and jam, reminiscent of her child-hood suppers – and there's still no sign of her husband.

Remembering the complicated bedtime routine from the previous night, Charlotte prays David will be here by seven. He did say he'd be home early, right? If he doesn't usually make it back before bedtime, when on earth does he see his daughter? Even if he does work full-time, he *is* still a father. Finally, just as the bedtime song blares from CBeebies and the channel flicks off-air, the door swings open and her husband appears.

'You're home!' Both Charlotte and Anabelle throw themselves at David, and Charlotte doesn't know who's more delighted to see him. A surprised expression flits across her husband's face before he kisses her cheek (what's up with that? Lips, please) then bends down to kiss Anabelle.

'How are you feeling?' he asks Charlotte, taking off his shoes. 'I managed to get away early for once, thank goodness.'

Charlotte's eyebrows fly up. Seven o'clock is early? Back in the day, he'd routinely make it home by five-thirty, escaping the office as soon as possible. 'I'm . . . well, I'm okay, I guess. My head feels better, anyway.'

'Oh, good. Do you want me to order some takeaway tonight, or have you made something?'

Made something? Has hell frozen over? 'Takeaway's good, thanks. I'll order while you put Anabelle to bed.' She's been with their daughter for the past few hours, and it's his turn now. Besides, there's no way she's going to even attempt the bedtime routine.

'Um . . . sure, okay.' David ushers Anabelle into the bathroom and Charlotte slumps on the sofa as the Battle of Toothbrushing begins.

One hour later, the takeaway is cold on the table, and she's still waiting for David to reappear from the bedroom. Afraid to turn on the telly in case it disturbs Anabelle, Charlotte stretches out on the sofa, listening to the hum of traffic outside the window. It's just after eight, and normally she'd be getting off the bus and making her way down the pavement after a crazy day at work, thinking about what to order for supper and anticipating her first sip of wine. Then she and David would turn on Netflix and she'd sink into his arms, revelling in the comfort and peace of home – and her husband – after the madness of the day. God knows she needs that even more right now.

'Hey,' David whispers, his mouth stretching in a yawn. 'I fell asleep in there. The food's here?'

'Yes, it came a while ago. Hopefully it's not cold.' She responds in her normal tone before noticing David wincing and placing a finger to his lips. 'Sorry,' she says in a whisper. Christ, will they need to whisper all night?

He plops on the other end of the sofa and stretches out his legs. Charlotte moves closer, drops a kiss on his lips, then lays her head on his chest. As she breathes in his scent, her eyes fill. She felt so alone today – so adrift in this bizarre new world – and so *angry* at how she'd thrown away her life. David is a bridge between the past and the present, and she needs his optimism and reassurance now more than ever.

She's always loved his calm, positive outlook. It's a running joke between them that, no matter how heavily it might be raining or how threatening the sky may be, David can be relied upon to say that it'll be fine; it should clear up soon. He might be a touch *too* easy-going sometimes, but if something ever did go wrong then he'd be certain to keep his head and try to find the best outcome.

His positive outlook drew her to him when they'd first met. She'd been at a hotel in York after a client meeting, and David was there for an insurance convention. In the middle of a bitingly cold, clear winter's night, the bloody fire alarm had gone off, and all the guests had been evacuated into the car park. Heart pounding, Charlotte had wrapped a duvet around her and stumbled down the stairs, then out into the darkness. It was mass chaos with people crashing into each other, so she pushed her way through the crowd and towards the edge of the car park, right next to a grassy field.

'Nice night, huh?'

A voice from beside her made her turn, and she spotted a man about her age. Normally she'd just grunt and move away, but there was something about his warm, friendly face that made her stay put.

'Not sure I'd call it *nice*,' she said, her voice raspy with sleep. 'Bloody freezing, more like.'

'Well, yes.' The man smiled. 'But look.' He pointed into the sky, where a million stars were winking down on them. 'You don't get that in London.'

'No, you definitely don't.' Even as tired and cold as she was, Charlotte had to admire them. The sky looked like a giant blanket shot through with sparkly thread.

'I'm David.' He held out a hand, and Charlotte grasped it, loving how his fingers closed firmly around hers. There was nothing worse than a limp handshake.

'Charlotte.' She moved a bit closer, and for the next thirty minutes or so – until they were given the all-clear to go back inside – David pointed out the different constellations. Charlotte couldn't have cared less, to be honest, but she loved the sound of his voice and how it felt like it was just the two of them, alone in the night. Somehow, he had transformed a rude awakening into something magical.

And when they were both back in London, things just went on from there. They balanced each other out, and even though she was more forceful and outgoing – urging him off the sofa and across the city to explore new sights – she relied on his quiet strength and positivity. She could tell him anything and he'd make her feel better about it. In that way, he reminded Charlotte a bit of her father.

'I'll just grab the plates.' David's voice cuts into her thoughts now and she nods, pushing aside the strange feeling that, despite their bodies being so close, they feel miles apart. Is he still upset about the accident? He manoeuvres himself out of her embrace and into the kitchen, returning seconds later with some cutlery.

'You do look more yourself,' he says, forking out some noodles on to her plate before tucking into the remainder of the dish straight from its box.

Charlotte meets his eyes, her mind whirling as his words ring in her ears. *More yourself,* whoever that is. Someone who wears jeggings, with a flabby belly and a cushiony bottom? Who's shunned her beloved, satisfying job to stay at home, and who's packing up their city flat to move to the wilds of Surbiton?

Someone who apparently *cooks*, for God's sake?

'Look, I know you're still recovering,' David says, winding some noodles around his fork. 'But—'

'David.' Charlotte can't let him go any further. She's *not* recovering from the accident, and she needs his help. Please God, may he be able to help. 'I . . .' She pauses, hoping he won't try to convince her to go to A&E. That's the last thing she needs right now. 'Well, I'm having some problems remembering things. Since the accident, I mean.'

'Hmm?' David swings around to face her. 'What do you mean?'

Charlotte takes a breath. 'I mean, when I was in hospital and you mentioned Anabelle . . . I didn't know who she was. I didn't remember having her.'

'What?' David drops his fork, and his eyes widen. 'But you remember now, right?'

Charlotte shakes her head. 'That's just it. I *don't.*' She pauses, meeting her husband's incredulous stare. 'I don't remember having her, or raising her, or even trying to get pregnant. The last thing I recall is coming back from Italy, right after our anniversary . . . four years ago.' God, four *years.* She reaches out to take David's hand, waiting to feel a squeeze in return, but it stays limp in her grip. Silence stretches between them, and she can almost see her husband's brain working to take in her words.

'So you . . .' He tilts his head, exhaling. 'You don't remember anything? Getting pregnant, giving birth, and . . .' His face twists. 'None of that?'

'No. Nothing.' Charlotte tries for the millionth time to conjure up some memory, but it's like trying to break through a brick wall.

'*Wow.*' David gawps at her like she's landed from Mars. 'But why didn't you tell me? In hospital, I mean. Why didn't you say that you couldn't remember?'

Charlotte glances down at their hands. 'Well, I . . . you looked so worried, and I didn't want to upset you.' She meets his gaze again. 'I thought it was just the shock of the accident, and that everything would come back after a good night's sleep. I mean, who can forget their own child?' She forces a laugh through the fear flaring inside. She can't have forgotten – it's impossible. 'I'm sure I will remember. It *has* only been a day since the accident.' God, it feels like an eternity.

'You're right, of course. It will come back,' David says, and Charlotte squeezes his hand again, pleased that he's finally giving her some reassurance. The way he was staring at her was unnerving. 'But even so, I think we should take you back to the hospital. Better safe than sorry, right?'

'No!' She surprises herself with the vehemence of her reaction. She's not sure why, but just thinking of the hospital makes her hair stand on end. 'There's no need for that. They did all the scans and everything, and they said nothing is wrong. Let's give it another day or two, okay? If I don't start remembering, then we can book an appointment with a consultant or something.' It *will* come back in another day or two. It has to, because she's not sure how long she can stay in this strange state before going crazy.

'All right.' David nods slowly.

'And in the meantime, can you help fill me in? Help me understand . . . *this*.' She gestures around the lounge to the toys dotted on the floor. 'It's so surreal. I'm a mother. A *stay-at-home* mum. How on earth did that happen? We always joked about you quitting work. I mean, I'm sure I love it,' she adds as his lips pinch together. 'It's just so unexpected. Maybe you can tell me why we decided to have kids, what the birth was like – not too much detail, though, please.' She makes a face. 'How Anabelle was as a baby, what we're like as parents . . .' She shakes her head. 'It's still so hard to wrap my head around all this. It seems like only days since we were making love in Rome!' She caresses his fingers, a warm glow inside. 'Remember that? The time we—'

'You're a wonderful mum,' David says, and Charlotte pulls back at the interruption. So much for wandering down memory lane. 'I couldn't have asked for a better mother for our child. You'd do anything for Anabelle. And after she was born, you were just so strong. It was a very hard time, but you were incredible.' He smiles, but his eyes look sad instead of admiring.

Her brow furrows. *So strong? Incredible?* She's not about to reject such high praise, but is it possible he's being slightly over the top? Childbirth couldn't have been that traumatic. She *did* have a C-section, after all – it wasn't like she'd gone through hours of difficult labour. 'Why was it so hard?'

'You really don't remember?' His eyes laser into her, like he's trying to see inside her brain. 'None of this?'

Charlotte shakes her head, her heart beating faster. Did something go wrong during the operation? One of her work colleagues had once told a terrible tale of a doctor accidentally injuring his wife's bladder during a C-section, leaving her leaking urine and needing multiple surgeries. Charlotte's bladder seems fine at the moment, but what if something else inside her isn't working properly? Surely she would have noticed by now, but . . .

David pulls his hand from hers and stands. 'When Anabelle was born, the doctors discovered there was something wrong with her heart.' His voice is robotic, as if he's recounting something not connected to him.

Charlotte's hand flies to her mouth. 'Her heart?' Oh my God. She'd never thought that something might have been wrong with Anabelle. That must be every mother's worst nightmare: to have their child born with such a serious defect. And you couldn't get much more serious than the heart.

The poor baby. Poor *parents*. She jerks as she realises that she *is* one of the parents.

David nods. 'It's called transposition of the great arteries,' he says, turning away from her to look out the window. 'The arteries in the heart are flipped around the wrong way, and the only way to survive is through surgery within the first few days of life.'

'Shit.' Charlotte shakes her head, hunting for something to say. She can't begin to imagine living through that scenario – giving birth then having your child wrenched away from you to the operating room. Had she really been as strong as David says? Right now, she can only envision running away screaming.

'Did we know about it before she was born?' She hopes so. The thought that they might have been able to prepare for such a traumatic start makes her feel more positive about what they must have gone through.

But David shakes his head. 'No, we had no idea,' he says. 'Sometimes they can pick it up on scans, and sometimes not.' His shoulders lift, and he faces her again. 'But the important thing is that Anabelle's okay now. She needs to go to the specialist for check-ups every year, but she's fine.' He says the words with absolute certainty, and Charlotte sighs in relief.

'Thank God.' Just the thought of a child's bright future limited by illness is desperately sad, not to mention any physical suffering she might experience. And when that child is your own . . . Charlotte's gut twists, and for the first time she feels a thread of connection to the person she's become. She gets to her feet and reaches out for her husband, but he edges away. Her heart drops, and she bites her lip. Clearly they've been through hell – she can't even fathom what they must have felt – but they must have pulled together. There's no way she could have gone through all that without David's support and optimism providing a much-needed lift. So what is this distance between them all about?

'Look, I'm certain everything will come back to you soon,' David says. There's a heaviness to his words, almost as if he doesn't want her to remember. 'You love your life with Anabelle – you're constantly saying how lucky you are and how you wouldn't have it any other way.'

Charlotte winces, then tries to smooth out her expression. It's just so hard to believe that she felt like that.

'And in the meantime,' David continues, as if he hasn't noticed her response, 'I'll make sure I'm home early to do Anabelle's bedtime, and I'll ask Mum to help out during the day. You just rest and try to get better.'

'Okay.' Charlotte pulls her knees to her chest. She longs to curl up in her husband's arms and flick on the telly like they used to, but he's already grabbing the pile of blankets and pillows from beside the sofa.

'I'm turning in,' he says, yawning. 'We can talk more tomorrow, if you like.'

'But it's not even nine o'clock. And you haven't finished your food!' She'd really been looking forward to him coming home and helping to ease the anger and disquiet inside her.

'Sorry, I'm not hungry any more,' David says, clearing the remains of his supper from the table. 'I'll just take this to the kitchen. Good night.' He doesn't even wait for her response as he disappears around the corner.

Charlotte watches him go, her heart twisting. It's not just the shock of the accident or the confusion caused by her memory loss: something *is* weird between them. She'd always been so certain that nothing would affect their closeness, but there's a distance now that wasn't there before. What the hell happened?

She catches her breath as a thought enters her mind. Is it because she's not working any longer? David always said her ambition was a turn-on; that she had more than enough for both of them. He loved that she was so passionate about her job, sometimes getting her fired up about it then pulling her on to the bed to make love. She used to joke that her passion was good for them, too.

Has the spark gone out now that she stays home, just a mum and not 'Madam Vice-President', as David used to call her? Surely it would take more than that to pull apart their relationship, though.

She gets to her feet and heads into the dark bedroom, undresses and pulls on an old T-shirt, remembering Anabelle jumping into bed with her that morning. Then she tugs the duvet over her body. Anabelle's steady breathing fills her ears and she forces herself to focus on it, desperate to silence the questions in her head.

In and out. In and out. In and out.

Did she ever fear Anabelle would stop breathing; that her heart would stop beating? Did she lie here, night after night, praying for her daughter to be all right? The experiences that had shaped her – Anabelle's shocking condition, and the terror that must have accompanied it . . . well, how can she even *begin* to visualise such a desperate situation? If having a baby is the life-changing event everyone says it is, what must it be like to have a child who's critically ill – to have the dearest thing to you threatened and be unable to protect it? Charlotte can only think of one word: *horrific*. That must be why she didn't go back to work as quickly as she might have otherwise. Of course she'd want to make sure the baby was okay.

But Anabelle is fine now. So why is Charlotte still at home, three years later, with David on the edges of their life? For God's sake, he's even sleeping on the sofa! And yet, according to him and the picture she's seen, she's happy – saying over and over that she wouldn't change her world for anything. How could she even begin to think that, with a career she's chucked and a husband who prefers clearing the table to talking to her?

Charlotte freezes as the realisation filters in. She *must* have changed . . . must have had that personality transplant she'd wondered about earlier. 'Supermum', 'strong', 'incredible' . . . she winces as David's words ring in her ears. She sounds like a bloody saint, the kind of parent she could never – not in a million years – picture being. Who on earth *is* that person? And how can she ever get back there if she can't begin to recall what set her on the Supermum pathway in the first place? Right now it seems as impossible as a mission to Mars.

Panic rises and she takes a deep breath. There might be a strange distance between her and David, but he did say they could talk more tomorrow. He'll help her memories come back again.

He'll have to – he's the only one who was there.

He's the only one who knows what really happened.

CHAPTER THIRTEEN

5 July

I just got back from seeing Lily – and telling her I'm pregnant. I should have told her sooner, I know. For God's sake, I'm almost five months along now, although if I wear a loose-fitting top I can still get away with hiding my bump (the benefit of big boobs and loose tops . . . they just hang straight down). I would have told her sooner if we'd done one of those big Facebook announcements like David wanted to, complete with pink balloons and blurry ultrasound photos. But I'm not into that stuff, and since I privately vowed not to let my timeline be overtaken by baby photos and videos, I'm starting as I mean to go on. Anyway, why would two hundred acquaintances care about the state of my womb? Anyone I want to know, I've told in real life.

Except my best friend.

I was desperate not to hurt her with my news, but I knew it was impossible. I couldn't put it off any longer: I had to let her know before my baby actually exits the womb. And so I persisted with my texts and my voicemails, a mixture of relief and apprehension flooding through me when Lily finally called back. As I rushed from work to meet her, I wondered if she would treat me differently, like Vivek, David and even Miriam. Would she still see me as *me*? Or would I represent solely something she desires but still hasn't got: motherhood? And if she could only see me that way, were the weakening bonds of our friendship strong enough to sustain this load?

I prayed they were.

We met in Shepherd Market, a little street in Mayfair full of restaurants and cafés. It's our haunt, a place we used to go every night to discuss our big dreams back when we'd first started out: me in business development at the research company, Lily as a newbie secondary school teacher in Bethnal Green. She'd tell me horror stories of kids twice her size throwing chairs out the window, I'd rail on about sleazy colleagues who leered at my cleavage, and then we'd both drink a bottle or two.

But tonight, only a carafe of tap water graced our table. Oh, how times have changed. Lily shot me a smile when I asked for the jug, and for a second, I thought she might be pregnant, too. Then she reached out and touched my arm.

'Thank you for ordering water, my friend. After the day I've had with Year Eight, I'm dying for some booze, but with these new fertility drugs, it's a no-go. If you had some wine, I'm not sure I'd be able to stop myself. Although I'd be on the floor after one glass . . . IVF shoots my tolerance to hell. Still, you have to keep hoping, right?'

'Oh, um, right. Yeah, no problem,' I stuttered, my heart sinking. I knew this was going to be hard, but . . . I swallowed, thinking I should break the news sooner rather than later. Get it out of the way, and then we could hopefully move on. Fear shot through me at the thought of her reaction. *Please may she be okay.*

'Lily, I have something to tell you.' I forced the words out.

'Let me guess.' She smiled. 'You got another promotion? This time, you're going to rule the world? The universe, even? Sell meds to aliens?'

'Ha. I wish.' She couldn't have been further off if she'd tried. 'No, it's not that.' I drew in a breath, hoping once more that my news wouldn't tear her apart. 'I'm pregnant.'

The words floated in the air, almost visible. Lily sat back, the colour draining from her face as she stared at me. My heart sank as splotches of red appeared on her neck and cheeks, a sure sign she was upset. I wanted to apologise, but saying sorry sounded odd.

'You're pregnant,' she said at last, her voice oddly flat. '*You* are pregnant.'

'Well, yeah.' For some reason, I felt defensive all of a sudden. I didn't want to tell her it wasn't planned.

'You, the person who – what was it you said? "Couldn't care less about pushing a human being out of your body"? "Would rather drink wine every night of the week than breastfeed a baby"? You're pregnant?'

I cringed as she spewed my words back to me. I couldn't remember actually saying those things, but I must have at some point. Lily always did have an amazing memory. And although I can't recall the words, I *can* remember the sentiments.

But that's changed now. It has to. Because in about four months, I *will* be pushing a human out of my body, with all that that entails. And while I may still feel like drinking wine rather than breastfeeding, at least I know now that you can't do both within a good few hours of each other.

'I know it's probably a little surprising . . .'

'A little?' Lily shook her head. 'I'd be less surprised if you told me you were joining a nudist colony! I just thought . . . well, you never told me you were even trying.'

I ducked my head down. 'It's been so busy with work and all that . . .'

'You do know you're not going to be able to work your usual crazy hours with a baby, right?' she said. 'I mean, flying off to God knows where at the drop of a hat and staying at the office until ten every night.' She looked almost triumphant as she said the words, and unease flared inside me.

'It will be fine. David's going to help,' I said, for some reason not wanting to tell her that I'd be going back to work and David would stay home. Unease ballooned into panic, and I gulped in air. It *would* be fine. The worlds I'd been working so hard to keep apart would not collide. There had been a few near misses, like when I went last week for the anomaly scan to make sure the baby was developing properly. I'd sandwiched it into a busy day between client meetings – the only time David was unable to make it, since he had a meeting in Leeds – but the only time I could. And since I was the one who needed to be there . . . I turned up sweaty and stressed, but lay on the table and breathed deeply as the sonographer pulled up a picture of our daughter on-screen. She bounced around merrily inside me, and even with the clock ticking down to my next meeting – an important pitch I'd spent hours preparing for – I couldn't help but smile.

The sonographer did the measurements she needed to and was just saying she was almost finished when the screen went blank. Despite her best efforts (switching the machine off and on), she couldn't get it working again. She called her colleague while my heart raced. *Come on, come on*, I urged her. I was going to be late! Vivek would murder me, especially after I'd made such a big fuss about not wanting special considerations.

I couldn't wait any longer. I sat up, wiped the gel off my stomach and said I'd reschedule. Dashing out the door of the hospital, I only just made it to the meeting on time. Crisis averted.

I still haven't managed to reschedule the ultrasound, and to be honest, work is just too busy. The sonographer had completed ninety-nine per cent of what she needed to, and everything was fine – perfect, as the last scan had showed. David was annoyed I didn't have any printouts of it – I'd only told him the printer wasn't working – and he was constantly pushing to book into one of those Harley Street clinics that video the baby inside you. But who has time for that? We'll see our daughter soon enough.

'Sure, but David can't breastfeed.' Lily's voice jolted me back to the present. 'And you really should breastfeed for at least a year, to give the baby the maximum benefits. You could pump, I guess, but then what about bonding with your child? Please tell me you're not going to have the baby and go straight back to work.' She stared at me, and I hoped I kept my face neutral. 'God, I really can't understand why those people even bother to have children. Surely you'd *want* to stay home with your baby for as long as possible.'

'Er, well, we haven't sorted it all out yet,' I said, although we had. No baby died from having formula, and this child would have an amazing relationship with her father, like I'd had with my dad. I tried to stay calm, telling myself that all of this was coming from Lily's hurt and frustration. I knew she'd be angry that the person she'd least expected had got pregnant when she'd been trying so hard. It was hardly fair.

Lily grabbed the glass on the table and swigged her water in one go, as if it was the alcohol she'd been craving. When she put it down again, her face looked almost normal.

'When are you due, then?' she asked.

'Eighteenth of November.' I was almost afraid to talk. I didn't want to hurt her more.

'November?' Her face contorted again. 'But that's only a few months away! So you're already . . .' Her voice trails off and I can see her mind calculating. 'About five months along?'

I bit my lip. 'Well, yes, I—'

'You didn't want to tell your oldest friend your big news,' she said, her mouth twisting. 'You didn't think I could be happy for you? Or want to talk about being pregnant, being a mother, all the wonderful times ahead?' She tightened her lips. 'Well, I can. Of course I can. I want to hear all about it, and more.' She sat back and crossed her arms, almost as if she was protecting herself from our coming conversation.

Dismay flooded in as I met her gaze. How could I tell her it wasn't that at all? It was me – *I* didn't want to talk about baby stuff. I wanted to laugh, to joke, to trade stories about our jobs like we used to. But as the dinner limped on, Lily fired question after question at me, as if she was trying to prove to herself she could handle it. It was like taking that exam I'd been cramming for – or undergoing an interrogation – and my best friend was either going to pass or fail me, with our friendship under fire. And oh, how I wanted to pass. Even if I did understand why she might not be able to support me, I needed Lily now more than ever.

But when we finally hugged goodbye, my growing baby bump felt like a barrier between us. She told me to keep in touch and said we should catch up again soon, but I knew this would be the last time we'd meet – that our friendship *had* failed. Like I'd feared, she could only see me one way now – mother – and although I knew why that was, it didn't stop the sadness from swirling inside. We'd been through so much together, and even if we weren't as close as we used to be, I'd hoped that would see us through.

And maybe it will. Maybe, given time, she'll come around. Maybe she'll get pregnant and have a baby, too, and then we'll be past all of this. We can be cool mums together, sipping wine in pubs while our children quietly colour in pictures of pirates . . . or whatever they're into these days.

But right now, I just need to keep telling myself that I can't control other people. Lily, David, Vivek . . . I can't control how they see me now, how they think I should behave and what they believe is best for the baby. I *can* control myself, though. I can control what I do, who I am, and whether this baby will change me.

And I'm one hundred per cent sure that it won't.

CHAPTER FOURTEEN

Charlotte stretches on the sofa, the oversized metallic clock she and David bought on a trip to Berlin ticking loudly in the silent flat. It's been three days since the accident, and she's still not used to being here on a weekday. The flat is her territory only on weekends, when she and David lounge in bed until the need for caffeine gets the better of them. Then they crawl from the covers and head somewhere for brunch: down to Borough or the South Bank, lazing over their coffees and eggs while scanning *Time Out* to plan that night's adventure. Weekdays are for getting out of the flat and to work as quickly as possible.

Or they used to be, anyway. She rolls her neck to ease the tension clutching her shoulders; tension that comes every time she remembers that this *nothingness* is her life – but it's not, really, since Miriam's pitched in to take Anabelle every day, mostly exempting Charlotte from the whirlwind world of motherhood. Charlotte has pleaded with David to come back to their bed, but every time, he mutters something about his snoring then scurries away as if she's got the plague. It's not just to help when Anabelle has nightmares or loses her teddy; Charlotte really hates sleeping without him. Curling up beside him each night used to be one of her favourite times of the day, and every time he turns away from her is like a kick to the gut.

Despite saying they could talk, David barely utters more than a few sentences to her each night, never mind helping her plug the gaps in her memory. Three days later, and Charlotte is still no closer to remembering anything about her own child . . . or to recognising her life now.

David *has* helped with Anabelle, though, enduring marathon sessions to get her into bed each night. Although she's only three, the little girl somehow seems to sense that something isn't quite right these days, running from the bedroom to crawl on to Charlotte's lap time and again. Charlotte hugs her, silently begging her to please go to sleep so she can talk to her husband. But even as her own impatience rises, David manages to remain remarkably patient, tucking Anabelle back into her bed: he's been the hands-on father she'd always envisioned he would be, yet for some reason never was until now.

Had her focus on Anabelle left no room for him to parent? Had she become one of those mothers who believed only they could soothe their child, no one else? Is that why he's not more present in their lives; why he seems so removed? God, if only they could talk. If only she could remember.

She *will*, she tells herself yet again. She will, and this bizarre out-of-life experience will vanish; she'll slot back into her wonderful world once again. As Miriam said when Charlotte finally told her about the memory loss, such a 'devoted mother' couldn't forget her own child.

She shakes her head. For Miriam to utter those words, Charlotte really must be the world's greatest parent. Her mother-in-law doesn't give compliments easily – Charlotte can count on the fingers of one hand the number of times Miriam's said something nice to her – and being termed a devoted mother is one of the highest accolades Miriam can hand out.

Charlotte heads to the bathroom and turns on the water full-force. She lets it stream down her body, trying to find some – any – trace of that devoted mother. But all she can feel is sadness and anger at losing the life she knows, not happiness and joy in the one she has . . . a life in which she almost lost her child, a child she cherishes with everything she has.

A child she can't even remember having now.

Maybe I should book an appointment with a consultant, she thinks, scrubbing her skin. An expert might be able to help her, since her own brain doesn't seem to be doing the job. God knows how much longer she can carry on like this; and Anabelle needs her – needs a mother, a mother who knows what the hell she's doing – someone who wants this life. Yet a small part of Charlotte is resistant, as if the doctor might press a button and delete this version of herself . . . the version she's only regained by accident – quite literally. That's selfish, she knows. But despite David's words and Miriam's assertion that everything would be different once she had a child, Charlotte's still struggling to accept she really did love her life as a stay-at-home mum. Could she have changed *that* much – so much she's become a different person? And would David even know if she had been unhappy? After all, they didn't seem to communicate much, beyond what to eat for supper.

She's pulling on yet another pair of jeggings (she seems to have every colour under the sun, but they are comfortable), along with a sweater, when the door buzzer rings. She freezes, waiting for whoever it is to go away. But the buzzer keeps ringing and she's forced to pick up the handset.

'Hello?' Her voice is hoarse.

'Hi! Got time for a quick visit?' Her best friend's voice bites back, and Charlotte's eyebrows fly up. *Lily!* Relief sweeps through her. Oh, thank God. Someone who knew her before she magically morphed into this all-giving, all-sacrificing Madonna, and who can shed some light on the past three years . . . hopefully. They haven't really been close since Lily's miscarriage, and while Charlotte understands how grief can affect you, she misses her friend. After David, Lily knows her better than anyone else. Well, she used to, anyway.

Has having Anabelle affected their relationship? Charlotte bites her lip, thinking that it must have been torture for Lily to watch her best friend going through pregnancy. Lily had been to hell and back trying to have a child, while Charlotte couldn't have cared less. They must still talk, though, or Lily wouldn't be downstairs now.

'Come on up.' Charlotte hits the buzzer, running her fingers through her hair. She's definitely looked better, but it doesn't matter. Lily has seen her much worse. She smiles, recalling how they met during their first year at uni, up in Leeds. It was the most boring class ever; so boring, in fact, that Charlotte can't even remember its name. She *can* recall that it started at the ungodly hour of 8 a.m., and she'd dash from her student halls to the lecture room with messy hair, sporting wrinkly pyjama bottoms . . . not a far cry from today, actually.

She'd been drifting off to sleep in class one day when Lily had jostled her arm, jerking her back to consciousness.

'You're snoring!' Lily had said, then the two of them started to giggle. They giggled so much that, embarrassingly, the lecturer asked them to leave.

Outside the lecture room, they'd burst out laughing like two naughty schoolchildren.

'Want to go get some breakfast?' Lily had asked, and that had been it. They'd remained good friends all through university. Lily's carefree personality lifted Charlotte from her regimented study schedule, forcing her to have fun and develop a spontaneous streak that remains to this day – well, as much as she remembers, anyway. She'd gone through a difficult period when her dad had died, but Lily had always been there to help her through. Despite the upheaval, Charlotte had earned a first-class honours degree, studying through crashing hangover headaches, thanks to Lily's patented three-egg, double-cream cure. And Lily had managed to pull her own degree out of the bag at the last minute, thanks to some hard-core coaching by Charlotte, too.

They'd stayed firm friends through their first jobs in London, and through all their horrific dates and car-crash relationships . . . until Lily hooked up with Joseph, and then just a few months later, Charlotte met David. They'd always done everything together, but when Lily proclaimed she was ready for a baby, Charlotte, on the other hand . . .

'Hi!' Charlotte swings open the door, and the two of them do a mutual double-take: Lily's eyes widening at the bruise still evident on Charlotte's head, and Charlotte staring at the tiny infant nestled against Lily's chest in a sling. So Lily had a baby! Happiness rushes through her for her friend – happiness, and relief that Lily's treacherous journey did have a positive outcome, after all. And maybe now they can be friends again – real friends, like they used to be. Charlotte had tried not to dwell on it, but she's really missed Lily: the belly laughs, the crazy nights out until morning and the long lunches that stretched on for hours. But then, Lily wouldn't be able to do that now. Not with what looks like a very young baby in tow.

'What happened to you?' Lily asks, pushing inside and up the stairs. She plonks down on the sofa and removes the baby from the sling, shrugging her shoulders and rolling her neck. 'First time I've used this sling – actually, it's my first time out of the flat since the baby was born. Joseph had to come this way to pick up something, and I managed to convince him to drop me off here. He'll be back in a few minutes.' She plops the baby on her lap, shoves down her sweatshirt, and plucks out a breast. 'There we are,' she says, easing it into the baby's already open mouth. Charlotte tries not to stare, but there's something about seeing her friend breastfeed that feels so *bizarre*.

'I thought this would be really strange,' Lily says, staring down at the baby as if it's everything in the world. 'But actually, it feels incredibly natural. It's amazing to have such a connection with your child.' She starts. 'Oh, God, I'm so sorry. I forgot you weren't able to breastfeed Anabelle.' She glances around the room. 'Where is Anabelle, anyway? Usually she comes for a cuddle as soon as she hears me.'

'She's with Miriam,' Charlotte mutters, processing Lily's words. She didn't breastfeed Anabelle . . . not surprising, given the medical interventions her daughter had needed. *God.*

'So? What happened to your head?'

Charlotte sits down on the sofa beside her friend. 'Car accident,' she says, running her eyes over Lily, trying to reconcile the friend she remembers with the woman in front of her now. Tall, slim Lily with the gorgeous, wheat-coloured hair that cost half her teaching salary to maintain actually has *roots*. Not only that, but her friend seems to have gone up at least three bra sizes. Lily's always envied Charlotte's bigger boobs, but . . .

'Oh my God. But when? I just saw you a few days ago! Thank goodness you're okay.' She gazes closely at Charlotte. 'You *are* okay, right? Sorry we didn't get to chat much when you came by. I was so tired I could barely utter a sentence and then you left so quickly, even before David! He just told us that you had to go and he needed to get back to work. Where was the fire?'

'Well, actually . . .' Charlotte pauses, wondering what Lily will say when she tells her she can't remember Anabelle. Dismay fills her at the thought of her friend's likely horrified response. Charlotte can't blame her – it *is* hard to believe a mother could forget their own child, even if it is only temporary. And for Lily, who struggled for so long to have a baby, it's probably even more horrific. Charlotte's world is shrouded in enough confusion and fear right now, and the last thing she needs is added confirmation from Lily.

Lily's baby starts flailing, and Lily switches the child expertly to her other breast, smiling gently as she watches it feed. Charlotte still has no idea if it's a boy or a child – damn gender-neutral clothing. 'Sorry, what were you saying?'

Charlotte shakes her head. 'Just, you know, it's wonderful seeing you so happy.' Tears prick her eyes as she takes in Lily's shining face, and she swallows back emotion. It really is good to see that her friend finally got what she longed for all these years.

Lily glances up from her baby and meets Charlotte's eyes. 'You know, everyone told us to give up and accept that it wasn't going to happen. Even Joseph wanted to stop trying. You know what kept me going?'

Charlotte shakes her head.

'You did,' Lily says. 'Watching you with Anabelle, seeing the bond you two had . . . I know you guys had a tough time in the beginning, but it was wonderful watching you become this brave mum who'd do anything for her baby.' She shakes her head. 'I'll be the first to admit I found it really difficult when you told me you were pregnant – I was a little sceptical about how you'd adjust to being a mother. But you surprised me with how strong you were – the way you gave up work, how everything you do is to help Anabelle . . . Char, you're just incredible.'

Charlotte forces a smile, her mind churning. She should be starting to get used to hearing what a wonderful mother she is. She's heard it from David and from Miriam, too. But it feels so odd that her oldest friend – the person who'd downed bottle after bottle of wine with her, who'd known how much she wanted to succeed at work, and who'd heard her say over and over that she didn't want kids – is not only praising her, but looking up to her as a mother.

Lily reaches out to touch Charlotte's arm. 'If I can be the same kind of mother to Liam as you are to Anabelle, I'll be happy.' She wipes her eyes. 'God, I've turned into a big ball of mush since becoming a mum! You warned me this would happen – how I'd be overwhelmed with emotion. It's just so amazing, isn't it? How you can feel so much love for someone, so quickly?'

Charlotte nods, struggling to find something to say. Was it like that for her, too – yet even more intense, since Anabelle was so ill? Charlotte always found the idea of loving something instantaneously strange, even if it was your child. Sure, there must be an instinctual connection, but to swoon with love the second you set eyes on something? Love grows – that's how it had been with David, anyway. She'd liked him straight away, of course, but you had to be sure of something before committing yourself. The first few months they'd dated had been so intense that David had often jokingly asked if he'd passed her probation period yet.

'Right, enough sap,' Lily says. 'I have five million questions written down to ask you. I've read every one of those parenting books at least twice, and I still don't have a clue what to do when he cries. Is he too hot? Too cold? Hungry? Needs winding? I know it's still early days, but I really need your help.'

Charlotte shakes her head, trying hard to hide her disbelief. Lily has questions to ask *her*? God, she's the last person on earth to dispense advice right now. She needs to tell Lily that, unfortunately, she's about as much help when it comes to babies as, well . . . as she used to be, but she still can't bear the thought of Lily's reaction. Besides, it's nice to see Lily being so chatty and open with her now, and the last thing she wants is to stop that in its tracks.

But before she can open her mouth, Liam starts screaming. As Lily juggles him from shoulder to shoulder, he deposits what looks like the whole of his feed down the front of Lily's shirt.

'Oh, *God*.' Lily hands the baby to Charlotte and runs to the loo. Liam starts shrieking, and Charlotte stares helplessly as he turns bright red, his little fists bunched into two balls as his cries escalate. What should she do with this thing? She starts to bleat out a nursery rhyme dredged up from the depths of her memory, but Liam's crying only intensifies; not that she can blame him. At David's last Christmas party she'd emptied the room during karaoke, although that could have been down to the fact that it was after 9 p.m., not her hideous singing.

'Thank God I brought a clean shirt,' Lily says. 'I'm definitely starting to learn!' She reaches out for the baby again, who immediately quietens in his mother's arms. Charlotte watches as he settles against her friend's chest, his eyes sinking closed. Had Anabelle nestled in her arms, warm and heavy like Liam is in Lily's? She tries her best to summon up the memory of a bond so strong that she put her life on hold to spend every second with her daughter, but she can't come anywhere close.

Lily's phone bleeps, and she digs it out of her pocket. 'That's Joseph – he's waiting outside. We'd better make a move,' Lily says, manoeuvring her baby back into the sling. 'Thank God you showed me how to do this thing. I hadn't a clue.'

'But you just got here!' Charlotte says, her heart sinking. 'Ask Joseph to come up. I can get you some coffee, and—'

'Coffee?' Lily looks at Charlotte like she's just offered cocaine. 'I can't breastfeed and have caffeine, remember? Liam started sleeping much better after I cut that out. Joseph said he'd only be ten minutes, and I'm about ready to drop. I would have got here sooner, but Liam did a huge poo, I had to try to change him in the car, and . . .'

Her voice drifts over Charlotte as she follows her friend down the stairs and out into the street, where the sun is now peeking through the clouds. She plods back up the stairs, the silence of the flat seeming even heavier after her friend's departure.

She picks up a grubby muslin that Lily has left behind, holding it out from her in case the smell should reach her nose. Her friend looks absolutely knackered, but then who can blame her? She's only a couple of weeks into motherhood with a baby that won't stop crying. But despite the exhaustion, Charlotte can't forget the look on Lily's face when she soothed Liam: the absolute tenderness and joy wiping away all traces of frustration and fatigue. Lily's achieved what she fought so hard for: to be a mother. And by the looks of things, she couldn't be more delighted.

Charlotte stares once again at the family photo where she's gazing at Anabelle with the same beatific expression Lily had worn. She must have felt that rush of love . . . a rush that washed away her former self, convincing even her oldest friend that she's changed – and that she's delighted with her new life, too. She *had* become another person. How much more proof does she need?

I'll try one more time to get David to talk about the past few years, Charlotte decides. And if talking to her husband doesn't help, she'll book an appointment with a consultant. She needs to get back to the mother she was and abandon this strange in-between state. Why bother hanging on to an outdated version of herself when that person could never exist in this new reality, anyway?

CHAPTER FIFTEEN

13 November

I can't believe how these nine months have flown by. This time tomorrow, I'll be wheeled into surgery to give birth. The midwife looked at me apologetically when she confirmed last week that my baby was breech and I'd need a C-section to deliver, but I wanted to punch the air in victory. I settled instead for a giant grin, which grew even bigger when the midwife raised her eyebrows at me. Did she expect me to mourn the loss of the natural birth our antenatal instructor had mooned on about? On what planet is a natural birth hyped up to be a wonderful experience – the best for both mother and baby – as if feeling shitloads of pain could catapult you into the stratosphere of World's Best Mother? 'I love you so much I'll put myself through pain for no reason' sounds more moronic than beatific, at least in my books. Brewing a baby in my body is enough.

A caesarean is way more convenient, more predictable and controlled. Not for me, the element of surprise . . . no living in fear my waters would burst during a work meeting. God, I can just imagine Vivek's horror if my bottom had started leaking. This way, I knew exactly when to start my leave and what to expect from the whole birthing process. No rush to the hospital and no pushing for hours. I'll be scrubbed and given a shot, my belly cut open, baby removed and placed on my chest. Sure, it might take longer to recover. But I'd trade an increased recovery time in a second for an element of control. I'm starting as I mean to go on.

Keeping David at the non-business end is an added bonus, too. For a while there, he was threatening to film the birth. *Shudder.* As if watching my body stretch to unnatural, surreal proportions as it attempted to squeeze a child from its cavities is something I'd want to see in glorious Technicolor, let alone remember.

And although I know it sounds a little ridiculous, I can't help but be proud of my girl, too. Because she sounds like me: stubborn and strong. She wants to be born her way, dammit, and she ain't shiftin' for no one.

Just like a good, strong woman *should* behave.

God knows I've had to be strong these past few months, and I'm proud of how I've kept it all together. Despite repeated trips to Vivek's office to reassure him I'll be back with bells on, as my pregnancy has progressed and my stomach has grown bigger, I've been shifted more and more to the back. When I've been out on pitches, I've sensed potential clients' eyes sliding over me and on to the next person in the room, like my baby bump has negated my presence. I've spoken up louder, showcasing my experience and knowledge that much more, then addressed the baby in the room by making it clear this child won't take me out for long – it doesn't subtract from my future value.

I managed to fit my remaining maternity appointments around work meetings, I never once left the office early, and over these last three months I've secured more clients than at any other time in my career. But when my maternity cover was hired – a man years younger than me and nowhere near as experienced – straight away, a big account I'd been itching to pitch was transferred over to him. I couldn't help feeling a little . . . threatened, even though this man has nowhere near my expertise or track record. My place in this company has always been more than secure; my route to the top practically guaranteed by Vivek.

Now it feels like I've been shoved on to a road to another place, and despite my attempts to get back on track, I keep getting knocked off.

Leaving the office for the last time today – heading towards the Tube and knowing I won't be back for at least a month – was such a strange feeling. Even though it was past seven on a Friday, my department was working just as hard as ever, showing no signs of slowing for the weekend. I shut down my computer, pushed back my chair and walked between the work stations. People were on the phone, busily typing up pitches and reports or rushing from one place to another. I could have announced my departure, but I didn't want to make it more evident – anyway, I'd be back before long. I slipped into the lift, telling myself over and over again that everything would be fine, despite the anxiety and worry rising inside.

This strange sense of vulnerability is making me even more determined to return to my job as quickly as possible and reclaim what is rightfully mine after so many years of working there; after so many years of proving myself. Having a baby *won't* subtract from my value. I've managed to juggle everything during pregnancy, and I'll do the same with motherhood, too. And on those rare occasions when Lily's words from our disastrous meeting all those months ago – how I won't be able to work; how I won't be able to travel – manage to find a way into my brain, I tell myself she's wrong. I *will*. Of course I will, with a partner like David set to take over.

I'm ready to take this exam and ace it; ready to take on motherhood and all it entails. I've used every spare second of these nine months to get myself to this point, even lying awake at night to previsualise life with a child: how David and I will juggle the night-time feeds, how I'll get ready for work on time, the baby sensory classes I've already enrolled us in on the weekends to help bring our baby on. We've even attended antenatal classes, revelling in our secure preparations, feeling miles above the rest of the bewildered parents-to-be.

Our bedroom is stuffed with everything our baby will need from the second we'll bring her home straight up to her first birthday: Moses basket by the bed, cot in the corner, change table beside it, with drawers packed full of the cutest little clothes you've ever seen and stacks and stacks of nappies. Our exhaustive research into the best pram – a project we embarked on with huge enthusiasm and dedication – culminated in a hulking black frame in the corner that will be hell to lift up and down the stairs, but will provide the best support for our daughter.

It was a rather rude awakening to realise how much baby gear one tiny child will need, but every time I look at the detritus of our formerly ordered flat, I remind myself this chaos is just for the first few months when the newborn's needs are so intense. Once things have settled, maybe we'll look into two-bedroom flats in the area. If I keep getting commissions the way I have been for the past three years or so, we should be able to afford something.

This is our last night, just me and David. Tomorrow, we will have our child – a perfect, tiny baby nestling in our arms. David is practically vibrating with excitement, riffling through the contents of our hospital bag with a huge grin on his face then striding over to the Moses basket and staring down, like he can't wait to place our baby inside it. And a couple of days from now, we'll be doing just that.

I'm eager to get started. Now that all the preparations are behind us, now that we're ready and the moment has come, I can't wait, either. Inside me, our daughter is ready, too. This pregnancy has been trouble-free, and my body has done what it should. We're not stepping off into the unknown: we're striding into our family's future, full of confidence and love. I'm not even scared of the surgery. Why should I be? It's been done a million times before, and our doctors know what they're doing.

We've got this.

Together, we've got this.

CHAPTER SIXTEEN

'She's finally out.' David rubs his eyes as he emerges from the bedroom and picks up the TV remote. It's been another long evening of trying to get his daughter to sleep, and Charlotte doesn't blame him for wanting to relax in front of some brainless telly.

Not tonight, though. Tonight, they're going to talk, even if she has to tie him down to the sofa and yank his mouth open. Her gut twists that it's actually come to this. Never in a million years would she have imagined the need to contemplate physical force just to exchange a few words with her husband.

She grabs the remote before the TV comes to life. 'Can we have a chat?'

David looks down at her with the stony expression she's come to recognise every time she tries to engage with him. He sits beside her, his long legs stretched out as if they're itching to run away. Maybe she *will* need to tie him down.

Charlotte sighs and turns towards him. Christ, he's not even facing her, he's staring straight ahead as if the telly actually is on. 'Look, I'm not any closer to remembering anything. And you did say we could talk, right? Maybe going through some things from the past will help jog my memory.' She pauses, waiting for a response, but the only change in David's face is a muscle jumping in his jaw. That's new – she's never seen that before. Has Anabelle's traumatic birth really affected him that much? It's not unexpected, she guesses, given how much it's changed her, but it was three years ago and Anabelle's fine now. David's always so positive, so upbeat. Why does he look so . . . beaten and *resigned*?

'Do we have any photos of me pregnant?' she presses on. 'With a bump or something?' If Anabelle's birth was so distressing, perhaps talking about her pregnancy would be all right. It seems surreal that her stomach stretched so much to accommodate a baby. Pictures might make it feel more real.

'No,' David replies almost curtly, still gazing at the blank TV. 'No photos. You were always trying to hide your bump in your work clothes, and you practically fell into bed as soon as you got back from the office.'

Charlotte nods slowly. Sounds about right. In a way, it's good to hear she hadn't dropped her proprieties just because she was pregnant, although of course she hadn't known about Anabelle's condition then. Maybe things would have been different if she had.

David's shuffling to his feet, but Charlotte tugs him back down. 'What about ultrasound photos of Anabelle? Do we have any of those? When did I first feel her kick . . . or hiccup, or whatever?' Way back in the recesses of her mind, she recalls hearing some women on the Tube talking about how weird it was when your foetus hiccupped. It'd sounded like something straight out of *Alien* to Charlotte.

'No.' David's face tightens. 'I wanted to get some, but you had a client meeting to rush off to.'

'Oh.' Charlotte bites her lip. God, that's a little . . . hardcore. Of course she'd had to meet her clients' demands, but this *was* her baby. How many chances would she get to have photos of something she was growing in her womb? Still, ultrasound photos were hardly a matter of life or death. If the baby needed her for something critical, she's sure she'd have been there.

'So everything was good up until the birth?' she asks tentatively, not wanting him to shut down.

'Everything was perfect, as far as we knew. It was after—' David cuts himself off, his eyes blinking as if trying to push away whatever images are swirling in his head.

Charlotte reaches out to grab his hand, a wave of sympathy and love washing over her. Her poor husband – he's been through so much and these memories seem to be bringing it all back again.

'David, let's do something. Let's go for a walk, go to the pub, I don't know – see if there's a film playing somewhere.' She speaks quickly before he can interrupt her and reject the idea. If he won't talk to her about the past, the least he can do is *talk* to her . . . and getting out of this flat might help. She's starting to go stir crazy.

'Come on, get your jacket.' She smiles and tries to pull him up, but he's looking up at her like she's lost her mind and is babbling in a foreign language. 'What?' she asks, his expression unnerving her.

'Charlotte,' David says, his tone incredulous. 'Have you forgotten about Anabelle?'

Oh, shit. Charlotte's heart drops. Well, yes – she had forgotten the little girl sleeping in the next room; she's forgotten she even has a daughter! Of course they can't just grab their coats and leave. Those days of spontaneity are well behind them. A sense of loss sweeps over her that she'll never be that carefree again.

'Okay, well. We can have some fun staying in, then.' She raises her eyebrow suggestively and climbs on top of him, desire rising as she straddles him. They haven't made love since the accident, and – from what she remembers – going that long without having sex must be a new record for them. There might be some emotional barriers, but they must still make love, right? That's always been sacred for them.

But David lifts her off him and turns away. 'I'll just go check on Anabelle,' he says, and before she can answer, the door to the bedroom has shut behind him.

Charlotte sits still, trying to absorb what's just happened. Her husband doesn't want to talk to her. Her husband doesn't want to go out with her. Her husband doesn't even want to make love to her! She understands reliving the past might be painful, but they're not in the past now. They're in the present.

Charlotte gets to her feet and crosses to the window, the empty pavements outside making her feel even more alone in this world. *I'll book that appointment with the consultant as soon as possible*, she decides. Maybe her husband can't – or won't – help her remember, but a doctor might. And if regaining her memories will make life now less painful, then she needs to do just that . . . and fast.

CHAPTER SEVENTEEN

14 November

She's here! Anabelle is here and she's perfect. The hard part (if you can call lying on my back, feeling nothing, as the doctor scrambles around in my womb 'hard') is over, and my daughter exists in the world now.

Everything went according to plan. The sun streamed from the brilliant blue November sky this morning when David and I headed to the hospital. I watched our flat recede from the back of the taxi and a mixture of emotions streaked through me, strangely similar to how I felt when I left work: determination that our life will remain the same despite this new addition, mixed with worry that, even though I'd done everything possible to ensure a smooth transition, I was being shunted on to a course from which there was no return.

But then David squeezed my hand and smiled, and the excitement I'd felt last night flooded through me, sweeping away any doubts. If ever a couple was ready, we were.

David held my arm as we entered the gleaming hulk of the hospital and made our way to the maternity ward. The soles of my shoes clicked smartly on the tiles beneath me, and in the metal of the lift doors, my newly coloured and sharply trimmed pixie cut gleamed. The cocoon coat I was wearing disguised my bulk, and if you cast a quick glance over me, you might not even know I was pregnant. I smiled as I realised that this time tomorrow, I wouldn't be – God, I couldn't wait for that. No more people's eyes raking my midsection. No more gooey glances from older women, and none of this 'when's it due?' nonsense. I'd be back to *me* – a mother, yes, but a person in my own right once again.

We checked in, I had an epidural, and several hours later I was lying on my back, my heart lurching when I heard my daughter's cry. The doctor placed her on my chest and she gazed up at me, her blue eyes blinking in instant recognition. And then they whisked her away to check her weight and make sure everything was all right. It was, thank goodness: she had ten fingers, ten toes and all the usual bits in all the right places. I held my breath until she was back by my side. I'll never forget how her eyes – so alert for a newborn – sank closed when she touched me.

As if she knew me; knew my body, the place she'd made home for the past nine months. Here she was, and now she was mine.

David bent down to kiss me, and I glanced up in surprise. I'd kind of forgotten he was there. Thank God he is, because I'm going to need him more than ever . . . now that we're a family.

Now that we have Anabelle.

Anabelle. I can't help smiling at the name, because it's certainly not one I'd ever have thought of choosing. It definitely wasn't on our list of top five names. But once we saw our baby, the traditional, solid names we'd settled on seemed so plain, so . . . unemotional, really, and ill suited to our beautiful girl. David and I stared at her for hours this afternoon, unable to look away. If I say so myself, she's gorgeous. Just enough hair not to look like a bald egg, but not too much that she resembles a gorilla. Her skin is unmarked and her head so nicely formed, she looks like she's come from a doll mould.

We dressed her in a pure white Babygro, taking it in turns to hold her snug little body up against us as she dozed for hours. David picked up Chinese and sparkling elderflower pressé and we toasted our new family – our new life – as parents. So far, so perfect.

Finally, just before David bunked down on the gym mat the nurse had left for us in the corner of the private room we were lucky enough to get, he turned to me and said, 'What about Anabelle?' He'd heard the name on the radio as we drove to hospital, and for some reason, it had stuck with him.

I would have dismissed it before as too cutesy, but gazing down at our daughter sleeping peacefully, her black lashes grazing her rosy cheeks, I couldn't imagine a better-fitting name. It was melodic and feminine, and our strong, healthy daughter didn't need a plain name to telegraph her strength: she would show it every day in the future.

And so, I'm Anabelle's mother. I'm a mother, and yet I don't *feel* any different. Despite my pre-birth assertions, a very small part of me still feared that by crossing the divide to motherhood, I'd instantly be changed . . . but I'm not. I still care about work; still plan to show everyone I'll be as committed as ever when I return. In fact, I'll confirm my return with HR once we're back home, now that I've had the baby and everything is all right.

It's only been a few hours, and already I can't believe how full of emotion I am for this tiny creature. But there's room in this life – in my heart – for me, too.

And I think we'll all get along just fine.

CHAPTER EIGHTEEN

16 November

I'm guessing at the date – our whole world has stopped. I can barely see to scribble on this page. God knows if what I'm writing is even legible. But it doesn't matter. I'm not writing this to be read. I'm writing this because I just . . . I need to get out this uncertainty, as if by penning the words, I can then cross them out.

Delete them.

Forget that this even happened.

Everything was going so well. Better than well, even: fantastic. I was in less pain, Anabelle was the best sleeper ever, and even though my boobs looked like twin missiles ready to eject from my chest since my milk had come in, I was confident we could take it from here – so confident I badgered the nurses and midwives to perform Anabelle's physical exam as soon as possible so we could be discharged. I longed to be back in my familiar surroundings, with all my carefully chosen baby gear at hand.

And then . . . Oh God, and then.

I can't believe it. Even though I'm sitting here, in this horrible room on this rickety rocking chair, I still can't absorb this has happened to us – no, that this *might* be happening to us, because nothing has happened yet. The nurse could be wrong. I'm hoping. I'm *praying*, even though I don't know to whom, that the doctors are just being overly vigilant. That the tests come back saying everything is wonderfully, beautifully normal. We'll take our daughter home and start our lives, even more grateful for our perfect child than we were before.

Not that I was grateful to begin with, actually. I'd taken Anabelle's health for granted, not even thinking something *could* go wrong. But oh, God, I will be grateful now . . . now that I know things can change in an instant.

Now that I know what fear really is.

I'd been so excited when the midwife came to collect me and Anabelle for her physical exam. She asked if I wanted to wait for my husband, but David had nipped out to get me a coffee (the hospital coffee is dreadful), and I was keen to get on with it. I hobbled down the corridor, wincing with every step, as the midwife cheerily wheeled along Anabelle in her glass-sided cot. She looked so peaceful, wrapped in a soft pink blanket that David's mum has given us. Even though I'd vowed not to force pink on my daughter, it was such a wonderful dusky hue and such soft fleece that I hadn't been able to stop myself shoving it in my hospital bag at the last minute. And now, it seemed to suit her, contrasting nicely with her almost translucent skin.

My daughter woke briefly as the midwife handed her to the nurse, her eyes fluttering open, then closing again. She didn't even stir as the nurse unpeeled her layers, examined her hips, then dug out the smallest stethoscope I've ever seen and placed it on my baby's skin. I tapped my foot impatiently.

She's fine, she's fine, I remember thinking. *Come on, just let me go home.*

But the nurse didn't hand my baby back. Instead, she took the stethoscope from her ears, and turned to face me.

'I'm just going to grab a doctor to have a quick listen to your baby's heart,' she said.

'Heart?' Immediately, my own heart fluttered inside me. 'Is everything all right?'

'I'm sure it's okay,' she said, her voice calm and soothing, as if she was used to dealing with neurotic first-time mothers. 'She does have a bit of a murmur, but it's quite common in newborns. Always good to let the doctor have a listen, just to be on the safe side.'

'Okay.' Back in her glass cot, Anabelle had fallen sound asleep again. *She's fine, she's fine.* My heart pounded out the rhythm.

'Hello. I'm Dr Graham.' A tall man with a kind voice appeared. 'I'm just going to have a listen to your baby's heart, all right?'

I nodded, watching as he repeated the same procedure as the nurse. But instead of telling me it was nothing, he listened again. And again. With every second that ticked by, my panic rose.

'There's definitely something there,' he said at last, settling the blanket back around my daughter.

'But it's quite common for newborns to have heart murmurs, right?' I parroted the nurse's words, holding on to them like a lifeline.

'It can be, yes. But the one in your baby is quite loud, and that can be a sign of something more serious. That, and she does look a bit cyanotic to me.'

'Cyanotic?' I echoed. 'You mean blue?' I peered at Anabelle. She did have a slightly blue tinge, but I'd figured it was just because her skin was so thin. *Something more serious?* The room began to close in around me as fear more intense than anything I'd ever known swept through me. It couldn't be that serious, surely, or one of the prenatal scans would have picked it up. That was the whole point of them, wasn't it?

Then I remembered, and I went cold. The anomaly scan – the one I'd ducked out of. The one I'd never rescheduled. *Shit.* I sucked in air, trying to fight my way through the terror gripping me. Our first scan was perfect. The ultrasound technician had almost completed the second scan. I was healthy. I had no problems in my pregnancy.

Everything would be okay.

'I'm going to refer you for some more tests,' the doctor said. 'Then we'll have a better idea of what we're looking at.'

'But I can still go home today?' My voice sounded plaintive even to my own ears, and I hated how Dr Graham and the nurse exchanged looks, as if they knew something I didn't – as if they felt sorry for me. I wanted to shake them, to tell them they had no reason. My daughter would be fine. She *was* fine.

'I'm afraid not.' Dr Graham shook his head. 'If there is something wrong with your baby's heart, we need to know just how serious it is before we can release you. Sometimes an infant will seem fine for the first few days or even weeks, but then the problem can make itself known.' He patted my arm. 'I know it can be worrying, but just try to relax. You're in the best place you can be right now, and your baby will get all the help she needs.'

I jerked away from his touch. I didn't mean to, but I couldn't help it. *Relax?* I glanced down at my child, and suddenly she seemed so fragile, so pale, so helpless in that dusky pink blanket.

Just be okay, please. I'd sent up a silent prayer. *Just be okay.*

And now, I'm back in the room with my daughter. She's still sleeping, and I'm writing this down before David returns, trying to grasp it all so I can force out the words when he comes back.

Trying to beat back the panic that rises each time I replay the doctor's words.

It's nothing, I'm sure. It has to be nothing. Because if it's not, and they do pick up something . . . Something that might have been spotted if only I'd gone back for that scan . . .

No. I won't think that. The doctors are just doing their job. I'm thankful to them, even if I wish I could be home right now.

Once we're back at the flat with our daughter in our arms, we'll laugh about this little hiccup. It'll become part of Anabelle's birth story, adding some drama to an otherwise straightforward tale. We'll clutch our daughter closer, thanking God our lives haven't been detoured in such a sudden, brutal manner.

Relieved that our family's future is still intact.

CHAPTER NINETEEN

20 November

Nothing exists except my daughter. My daughter, who's in a neonatal intensive care unit now, a needle in her arm and breathing with the help of a respirator until she has her open-heart surgery tomorrow – surgery she needs to survive.

My daughter, who's so weak that she can't even breastfeed.

My daughter, whose mother failed her – failed to help, failed to do everything she could to ensure her daughter's future . . . because of her job. Her fucking *job* was more important than her baby's health!

How could I have been like that? How could I have been so careless?

I want to scream and cry. I want to tear myself open and to rip out that part of me, but what good would that do? I can't turn back the clock. It's too late, and all I can do is wait. Wait, and try not to stagger under the guilt that presses down on me. A guilt that's so palpable, it's like another person in the room.

It's been four days since the nurse first heard Anabelle's heart murmur, yet it feels like we've been living this nightmare forever. When David returned from the coffee run that day, I couldn't bear to tell him straight away. I watched as he picked up our sleeping daughter, cradling her in his arms. Her rosebud mouth stretched in a yawn, and he smiled with such contentedness and absolute bliss that I felt my heart almost break in two.

'Did the nurse do the final checks?' he asked, his voice so quiet I could barely hear him. Anabelle stretched in his arms, and we were both silent until she was still again. It's funny how, even though it was barely two days at that point, already we'd adapted our behaviour to suit Anabelle's needs.

I looked up at him and swallowed, my heart lurching. Even though I refused to believe that anything could be seriously wrong, the very thought of planting a seed of doubt in my husband's mind made me want to be sick. And although I'd done everything possible to minimise the worry inside me, voicing the words aloud might make those fears real.

I took his hand and pulled him down on to the bed beside me. I leaned against him, weaving my finger into Anabelle's closed fist. I wanted us to be physically connected. I needed to feel solid and real.

'She did.' My voice was hoarse in the small, stale room. The sound of babies crying, phones ringing and a woman's laughter drifted through the air.

'We can go home, then?' David's voice lifted in excitement. 'Thank God.' He grimaced and rubbed his back. 'I can't say I'll miss that gym mat.'

'Actually . . .' I took in a breath. 'They want to do more tests.'

David's eyes swung towards me, and I felt his muscles stiffen. 'Why?'

'They think something might be wrong with her heart.' I forced the words out of me, and they hung in the air. I waited for David to bat them away but instead his features contorted with fear.

'Her heart?' His face had gone white, and panic clutched at me as I saw his response.

'Apparently she has a heart murmur, and she looks a bit blue.' I peered over at her. 'She doesn't look blue, does she?'

But the way David's lips tightened confirmed that, really, she did.

And before we knew it, a doctor had come to take our daughter away for an echocardiogram, to see inside her heart. David and I followed, me still hobbling like an old woman and David holding my arm . . . though, in reality, I don't know who was supporting whom. David was supposed to tell me I was being silly. He was supposed to boost me up, to say that this was just an extra check, to be sure. Instead, he seemed as lost as me.

And then the doctor blew our world apart – a world we hadn't even had a chance to properly construct. Our daughter has transposition of the great arteries, a condition in which things are flipped around inside the heart, so that blood without oxygen is pumped around the body instead of blood with oxygen. It's a condition 'not conducive to life', as the medic so bluntly put it, and Anabelle will need open-heart surgery to survive. Until then, they'll give her medicine to help her breathe and she'll use a respirator, if need be.

The doctor's words flowed over me, and I tried my best to keep them in. Operation in the next few days, moving us to family accommodation, family resource and support centre . . . we were caught in a current sweeping us down a river so quickly I couldn't get a grip on anything to save me, to haul me from this disastrous place I was drowning in. I looked at David and he was already under the surface, his eyes wide and unseeing, his mouth open in a silent gasp.

We followed a kind nurse to the neonatal intensive care unit, me holding Anabelle in my arms, despite the pain of her soft baby weight on my stitches. When the nurse stretched out her arms to take my baby and settle her into her new cot, I just . . . couldn't. My head told me I needed to, but my heart . . .

Finally David eased Anabelle from me and I stepped back as the nurse attached our daughter to tubes. I felt so empty, as if she had already been taken from us. She wasn't inside me any more, and she wasn't in my arms, either. She was existing in a hinterland between life and death, a place where I couldn't reach her. In the space of a few hours, our daughter had gone from a healthy newborn to one who might—

I stopped myself from travelling down that road. I couldn't travel down that road.

That first night in our family accommodation, I didn't sleep. I lay beside David, my eyes wide open. I didn't know if he was awake or not. Each of us was locked into our own separate world, unsure what to say or do to comfort the other. I longed for him to tell me everything would be okay; to revert to his blue-sky thinking as usual. But he seemed frozen, unable to utter even a word.

When David was asleep, I slid from beneath the starchy covers and opened up my laptop. I was desperate to absolve myself for my negligence; desperate to prove that even if Anabelle's condition had been spotted sooner, it couldn't have made any difference – to her, anyway. I might not have rescheduled that scan, but maybe it didn't really matter.

It *had* to not matter.

But instead of plugging the gaping hole of guilt inside me, what I discovered ripped it even wider. Because if the condition *is* picked up on scans before the baby is born, children usually have better short-term and long-term outcomes.

I doubled over as the hammer hit my heart. If I'd stayed that day until the machine was fixed . . . if I'd rescheduled . . . hell, if I'd just gone along to one of those naff prenatal clinics and got a video, then the doctors might have seen something amiss. They might have been ready to help Anabelle the second she was born. They might have even been able to help her before she was born – you always hear about these operations in the womb.

She might not be lying there, right now, with her life at risk. And even if she makes it through, her future might have been more secure.

I'm not sure what went wrong inside my body. What I've read says that, often, heart conditions occur for no reason – apart from genetic factors, which doesn't relate to us. Neither David nor I has relatives with heart problems; the nurses took our family histories.

I *am* sure what went wrong with me, though. All I'd cared about was work – work, and me. *My* life. And the consequences of my actions are brutal.

My daughter might die.

I haven't told David that I ducked out of the scan. I can't – I never will. I can't bear the weight of any added accusations. I'm already bent in half under my own.

And now, it's the night before the operation. David and I are hunkered down with our baby, huddled around her cot, our little family of three. Because as much as we don't want to think it, it could be the last time. Oh, the doctors have told us that only one per cent of babies don't make it through, but that's not good enough to allay our fears. One per cent is still a chance, a chance I know is real. After all, wasn't I in the one per cent who get pregnant on the pill? Ironic how that one per cent could now take our daughter away from us.

Our mothers have come and gone, with words so different it's like they're from different planets: my mum telling us Anabelle will make it through, that the doctors know what they're doing and things will be all right – the words I longed to hear, but now mean nothing in the face of all of this; and Miriam, who didn't say a word to me – she didn't tell me to relax. All she did was sit down beside me and take my hand. And in that simple gesture, I knew she got it. Knew that this child I'd carried inside me and still had yet to know was under threat, and that until someone could tell me my child was one hundred per cent well, nothing could help.

Nothing could ever help take away this guilt.

Not the countless messages from many friends, who David has kept informed through text (I couldn't even bear to read the words, let alone write them). Not the message from Lily, offering any help we may need. Not the well-meaning nurse who pats me on the arm each time I see her, telling stories of other babies who've pulled through. Not even the bottle of whisky David smuggled in one night, which we poured into plastic glasses in a desperate attempt to blunt our sharp-edged reality.

And definitely not my husband's embrace as he pulls me against him. I can't let myself fall into him; can't let myself lean on his warm body. I don't deserve his support and his strength, for what I've done to our child . . . or what I *haven't* done, rather.

There's a chance that, after tomorrow, I won't be a mother any longer, and David won't be a father. Remembering how I felt when I first got pregnant – the horror, the panic – I want to go back and kick myself. Perhaps this is my punishment for not appreciating what I had. Perhaps I'm about to get what I thought I wanted: a life where my sole responsibility is me.

But that's not what I want now. I can't imagine life without this little girl. I can't imagine *wanting* a life without this little girl.

If Anabelle makes it through this operation, I promise I'll cherish her like never before. I'll never take being a mother for granted again.

CHAPTER TWENTY

'And then the little slug slimed across the leaf, and . . .'

Charlotte smiles as she listens to David's voice on the monitor telling his daughter a very long, complex bedtime story, following her exacting specifications. Judging from the laughter coming from the bedroom, it seems they're both enjoying it, although Charlotte's not sure how conducive to sleep it actually is.

For the past few nights, David's made an effort to get home early and put Anabelle to bed, and the little girl has finally accepted that bedtime is Daddy's job. It's amazing how quickly kids adjust, although, according to Miriam's expert opinion, Anabelle's been extra clingy this week. Charlotte just nodded when she said this, thinking how strange it is that she wouldn't know if the child is extra anything. From the little she's seen, Anabelle's antics are standard three year old: demanding, stubborn and ear-gratingly whiny – with the odd dash of cuteness thrown in every once in a while, probably an evolutionary necessity to remind parents just why they had children in the first place.

God, she must have had the patience of a saint to deal with that every day . . . or perhaps she had a secret stash of booze locked away somewhere? She certainly wouldn't blame herself. The few minutes she'd spent with a tired and hungry Anabelle earlier today had tested her in a way that even the most annoying client hadn't. She'd resorted to deep breathing to keep from losing her cool after Anabelle pleaded over and over for her paintbrushes and watercolours, dissolving into tears and tantrum despite Charlotte offering every other option under the sun. Apparently it was one of their favourite things to do together, but the thought of trying to control a three year old with watery paints terrified Charlotte. If slathering tepid colour on soggy paper was their favourite thing, the two of them really needed to get out more. Now, mother-and-daughter manicures . . . that was something she could get behind. Perhaps she'll ask David if she and Anabelle have ever done anything like that.

Maybe after her appointment tomorrow with a top neurologist on Harley Street, she'll actually remember . . . and not a moment too soon. It's been a week since the accident, and she still feels like a favourite auntie biding her time until she can return to her usual fun, full life. It's a harsh slap when she remembers there *is* no escape. This is her life. This is her *daughter*, even if, between Miriam and David, she still barely spends any time with her. It's as if everyone's letting her tread water, waiting for the consultant to throw her a lifeline.

'But Daddy!' Anabelle's voice bursts through the monitor. 'Slugs don't have antennae!'

'Well, they sort of do,' David says. 'They're more like feelers, but still.'

The story continues, and Charlotte grins. *Do* slugs have antennae? How would Anabelle know that they don't? God, she sounds like a clever little thing. Charlotte listens as the story meanders onwards, her husband's warm tone softening more and more as Anabelle – she hopes – grows sleepier. For a split second Charlotte closes her eyes, wishing David was speaking that way to her . . . maybe not in relation to slugs, but just dissecting their days, like they used to. She'd tell him all about her latest workplace victories, he'd crack jokes about his deadbeat colleagues and even do one or two impressions of his boss that always made her laugh, and then they'd open a bottle of wine and settle down on the sofa in each other's arms. It was the perfect ending to the day in a place where she could relax and just be *her*. Tears fill her eyes now as she realises the *her* she's trying to become doesn't even seem to bother with her husband any longer – or maybe he doesn't bother with her. Either way, it gives her a constant pain in her heart.

But while David's guarded with her, he's been amazing with Anabelle. He might have been far removed from their daily routines, but he's quickly sorted out new ones. From serving Anabelle a crazy mixture of Rice Krispies and Bran Flakes with a flourish each morning ('Your cereal cocktail, madam!') to diving games in the bathtub to the endless bedtime stories, he's a natural. It's obvious he loves spending time with her and Anabelle is crazy about him . . . so it *must* have been Charlotte who was holding him back?

She bites her lip, an uneasy feeling tugging at her. She is a bit of a control freak – even Vivek would tell her sometimes that she needed to delegate better. When it comes to a child you're desperate to protect – something you love with every part of you – then it must be desperately difficult to let others in, even if that 'other' is your husband. But not only is David her husband, he's also Anabelle's father. Even if she did decide to stay at home, surely she didn't deny them a relationship. Is *that* why he's so frosty with her?

'She's asleep,' David whispers, closing the door softly behind him.

'I loved your story,' Charlotte says, grinning at him. 'Slugs?'

David shrugs. 'She's going through a bit of a slug obsession at the moment. She wants to know everything about them. I printed off some stuff at the office to show her, and she was so excited.'

God, he is such a good father. 'David, look.' Charlotte takes a breath, wishing he'd sit down instead of hovering over her like this. 'I'm sorry if I pushed you away from Anabelle. You know what I'm like sometimes, trying to take over everything myself.' She gives a little laugh, hoping it'll lighten the intense way David's staring at her. 'You two obviously love spending time with each other.'

David keeps staring at her and she clears her throat, an idea popping into her mind. Maybe the three of them just need time to gel as a proper family. They must have done *some* things together – the photos of them dotted around the place prove that – but they don't seem much like a threesome to Charlotte. Perhaps drawing David in more would help rebuild his connection to her, too.

'And you know, I was thinking. Why don't we take a holiday together, all three of us? You know, as a family? Have we ever done that?' She grabs the mobile. 'Let's book it tonight! I'm sure we can get a great last-minute deal to somewhere.' The more the idea grows in her mind, the more certain she is that this is exactly what they need. Even if her memories do start coming back in the coming days and her mothering sensibilities return, the holiday will already be booked, and she knows for a fact David would never cancel anything if it meant losing money. Growing up with a single mother has made him extra careful about any added expenses.

'Charlotte.' David's voice makes her head snap up; she's already googling last-minute holidays. 'There's something I need to tell you. Before you see the doctor tomorrow, and before you book anything. In case you remember.'

She takes his hand, stunned by the anguish in his eyes. 'It's okay, David. Whatever it is, I'm sure it'll be okay.' Anabelle is fine, the consultant will be able to help, and just the thought of lounging in the sun is making her feel better already. Why does he look so . . . tormented?

David laughs bitterly, a sound she's never heard coming from him. 'Isn't it usually me who says that to you?' He shakes his head. 'The thing is, I'm not sure it will be okay. You were so upset when I told you the first time, over at Lily's place.'

Charlotte raises an eyebrow. 'You told me at Lily's?' If this really is as big as he's making out, why wouldn't he tell her at home when they were alone?

'Not exactly the ideal scenario, I know.' David sighs. 'Lily wanted to show us her new baby, and I agreed to meet you at her place during my lunch hour. When I told you . . . well, you couldn't even speak to me. You just took Anabelle and left, and then you had the car crash. Sometimes I wonder if what I said caused the accident.'

'What is it?' Charlotte's heart is pounding now. 'What did you tell me?' Has he had an affair or something? She catches her breath at the horrible thought. The bond between him and her daughter she can fix, but she's not sure she could handle such a betrayal. It's hard to imagine her loyal husband sneaking around, but no harder to believe than what her life has become. It certainly would explain why he's so cold around her.

'Okay. Here goes . . . again.' David takes a breath. 'If we have more children, there's a slight risk they'll have a heart condition, too.' His face twists, and he runs a hand through his hair. 'Anabelle's heart defect has a genetic link, and it runs in my family. Remember when we were waiting for Anabelle's diagnosis, and the nurse took our family history?' He clocks Charlotte's blank expression, and he shakes his head. 'Of course you don't. Well, those questions made me wonder if there *were* any heart problems on my side – on my father's side, maybe – that I hadn't known about. Mum told me two of my dad's family had passed away as infants because of heart problems – one was his brother. I'd had no idea.'

He holds her gaze, facing her stiffly like he's in the firing line. But instead of the explosive reaction he's clearly expecting, all Charlotte can feel is relief. Is that all? Anabelle's condition is genetic? God, she'd wondered if he'd been cheating on her! To hear the cause of Anabelle's condition, well . . . it's helpful to know, but it doesn't really change anything.

But . . . she tilts her head, trying to puzzle it all out. 'Why didn't you tell me this sooner?' she asks, trying to keep her voice level. She needs to tread carefully; David looks like he might bolt at any moment. 'Anabelle's three, so why would you keep this to yourself for so long?' They used to tell each other everything, right down to what they'd had for lunch – mundane, but she always loved hearing every little detail about her husband's day; it made it seem as though they'd been together, even though they'd been apart.

And this wasn't some trivial detail involving tuna melts or chicken wraps. This was their daughter – the cause of her condition, a condition that could have been fatal. Why the hell would he keep it from her for *three years*? Fear shoots through her that perhaps there is more of a rift between them than she'd thought.

He sits down on the sofa, his legs bending so stiffly he looks more robot than human. 'I couldn't tell you. I could hardly bear to think about it myself. To know that I did this to her, that it's my fault, I—'

'David, *stop*.' Charlotte squeezes his hand. His fingers are like ice. 'You're being silly! It's not your fault. How can you control genetics? We had no way of knowing, no way of preventing this. No one's to blame.' She wills him to believe her, but judging from the set of his face, her words have barely made a dent.

He turns towards her, the muscle in his jaw jumping again. 'You can't understand. Of course you can't – not now that you can't remember, and not before either. To see your daughter barely able to open her eyes and attached to so many tubes, bandages swamping her . . . and to realise that you did this to her. That she's in that horrific situation because of you.' His eyes burn into her. 'You can't understand that. You never will. And the way you looked at me when I finally told you . . . it was like I'd destroyed you. Like you hated me. You grabbed Anabelle and left without saying another word, like you couldn't stand being near me. I tried to call you, but you didn't answer.' He shakes his head. 'And you know what? I can't really blame you. Not only did I put you through hell and back, I've taken something away from you. I've taken away a future you want.'

Charlotte shakes her head, trying to understand. 'A future? What do you mean? The only future I want is with you. And Anabelle,' she adds, remembering that she has a daughter.

'You want another baby,' David says bluntly, and Charlotte freezes.

'I want another baby?' *Fuck.* Her heart sinks as he nods, and she feels even more distant from the person she'd become. Imagine wanting another child after such a traumatic experience with her firstborn! Even if she hadn't known the risks at the time, she must have worried their next child could face some challenges, too. She must have really loved motherhood – loved her life – to give it another go after all that.

'Yes, you do. Or you did. You were so excited to talk to me about it . . . practically glowing. I hadn't seen you look so happy for ages.' He drops his head and she reaches for his fingers again, trying to signal again that it really is okay. Well, it is now, anyway. She can't even connect with the desire for one child right now, let alone two.

'I had to tell you then,' David continues, his voice shaking. 'I had to tell you that I was to blame for Anabelle – that because of me, Anabelle won't have a sibling and you won't have another child. I can't watch another baby suffer because of something I passed on.' He lets out a trembling breath. 'Anabelle's illness meant you gave up your job. It pushed you into becoming the wonderful mother you are today. I'm so in awe of how you gave yourself to her; how you put yourself aside and built a happy, safe world for her. You sacrificed everything to do that, and of course you want another child – you're a bloody brilliant mother. But I can't give you that. I can't give you more of what you had to become.'

He gets to his feet and looks at her with that resigned, defeated expression. 'One day you'll remember all of this. You'll look at me again like . . .' He rubs his eyes. 'I'm sorry, Charlotte. Just . . . just know that I'm sorry.' He walks away from her, moving so stiffly it's like his muscles have forgotten how to function.

'David, you have nothing to be sorry—'

The slam of the flat door stops the words in her throat and, once again, she's alone.

The ticking of the clock fills the room, punctuated every once in a while by Anabelle snuffling in her sleep. Charlotte shifts on the sofa, trying to absorb what just happened. She must have been furious that David only told her then about Anabelle's condition. He'd harboured this huge thing for years and while she can understand his guilt – even if, in her mind, he shouldn't feel the least bit at fault – the secret he was keeping didn't just affect him. It affected her, too. Why the hell hadn't he just told her?

And he's right: her whole world is about being a mother. To be told she can't expand, can't progress, is like taking up a job position and working like a demon to get promoted, only to be informed after years of hard graft that it's never going to happen. She can understand why she stormed out.

But that person who ran off isn't her – not now. With memories of Rome still bright in her head, the thought of feeling such anger towards David is shocking. She loves him, and despite the guilt and pain he's been through, she's sure he still loves her, too. She can understand his trepidation about what might happen when she remembers, but this is *them*. Life might be putting their marriage to the test, but they'll be strong enough to get through it.

It's impossible to imagine anything different.

CHAPTER TWENTY-ONE

21 November

The operation is over. It's over, and I'm still a mother . . . our daughter is still breathing. Granted, she's attached to a forest of tubes and it's only been a few hours, but she's still here, her heart victoriously beating.

The procedure was successful, although the doctors say she'll need check-ups as she grows to ensure there aren't any further complications. But right now, I can't think about the future. Right now, there *is* no future. There's just this beautiful baby in front of me, my child whom I love with every single bit of me. She is knitted into the very fabric of my soul, and I feel every tube, every pinch, every wound on her body almost as keenly as if it were my own.

Waiting for her operation to end was torture, unlike anything I've ever known. When they wheeled her away, it took every ounce of self-control not to run after them and snatch my baby from the looming darkness that could fall. From the possibility that, after today, I could be childless.

But I knew that if I didn't let her go, that looming darkness – a word I don't even want to say – would come anyway.

David and I stood there, our eyes trained on that squeaky-wheeled cot, unable to look away until the nurses turned the corner and our baby was out of sight. Then a nurse gently guided us to a lumpy sofa and pushed steaming coffee at us. I couldn't move. Couldn't talk to David, couldn't even turn my head. All I could do was focus on the wall in front of me and try to keep breathing.

I've never known time to move so slowly. Every second seemed to stretch, every minute spilling over with fear, hope, panic, love . . . and guilt. I did this. I put my daughter at risk through my negligence. I'm the reason she's lying there, her chest open, doctors prodding inside her delicate body. It was all I could do to stop myself from screaming, and in those seven hours we waited, I felt like I'd run a thousand marathons through freezing wastelands and burning deserts. I was scorched, then icy. I was sweating yet shivering at the same time.

And through it all, one thought echoed above all else, one pledge that circled inside. *If you live, I'll keep you safe. If you live, I'll keep you safe. If you live, I'll keep you safe.* Just *live.* Just keep breathing, keep your heart beating. Just get through this, and I'll do the rest. I'll protect you. I'll cradle you when you need it. I'll feed you when you cry. I'll make sure you have everything you need.

I promise. I promise. I promise.

And I think she heard me. I *know* she heard me, because we are connected. Linked together through the months she spent inside me, linked together through blood. Because she *lived.* She made it through the operation, and she's back in that glass cot. We'll be in hospital for a while yet and she still has a way to go, but she's out of immediate danger. There's always a risk of infection, fever . . . but for now, she's made it.

Not that I can relax. I'll never relax; never let down my guard again. I'll do everything in my power to protect my child.

A child I should have tried to protect sooner.

CHAPTER TWENTY-TWO

Charlotte opens her eyes, apprehension mixed with anticipation churning inside when she remembers that today she'll be seeing the consultant. After learning of the secret David kept and their argument before the accident, she knows now that the life she doesn't remember ended on anything but a happy note. They *will* resolve things, she's sure, but she's not exactly eager to regain those turbulent memories – to feel the fury David told her about. The state of her marriage at the moment isn't much better, though. The only way to move forward is to remember, and hopefully she'll be on her way today.

A few hours later, Charlotte's striding down Harley Street, grimacing as the waistband of her jeans rubs against her skin. She should have stuck with leggings rather than contort herself into clothes she hasn't worn in forever, but the automatic dress mode for 'outside world' kicked in. She even attempted to put on make-up until discovering the concealer she normally used is cracked, and her red lipstick is down to the end. Despite her hope of remembering today, her gut squeezes at the thought. She takes a deep breath and pushes it away.

Miriam had raised her eyebrows when Charlotte emerged from the bedroom.

'You look . . . nice,' she'd said, like she was surprised it could still happen. 'I haven't seen you that dressed up for a while. It's good to look your best for such an important visit.' Charlotte had nodded as

Miriam wished her luck, thinking that this used to be her *casual* outfit, something she might wear out to brunch on the weekend. Oh, how times had changed.

She pulls open the door of the doctor's office and announces herself to the receptionist, then takes a seat in a plush chair. She's only just flicked through a few pages of *Vogue* when her name is called, and she follows the receptionist down a silent corridor and into the consultant's lair.

A grey-haired man rises and shakes her hand, but Charlotte gets the sense that he barely even sees her. They both settle into their seats, and immediately the doctor focuses on the computer screen in front of him. 'Hello, I'm Dr Mitchell,' he says, typing on the keyboard. 'What seems to be the problem?'

Charlotte shifts in her chair, wishing he'd actually look at her. For God's sake, they're paying him a crazy amount for this. *It'll be worth it, though*, she tells herself. She'd pay almost any amount to stop feeling displaced in her own life.

'I had a car accident just over a week ago,' she says, lifting a hand to her head. She's taken off the bandage and the bruise has faded, leaving only a tiny black line of dried blood where the wound is healing. For the first time, she's grateful for the otherwise annoying fringe she decided for some reason to grow. 'And now . . .' She swallows. 'And now I can't remember the past four years of my life.' It sounds like a plotline from a soap opera when she says it aloud; if someone told her that, she wouldn't believe them. 'I can't even remember having my daughter.'

She waits for a reaction of shock and horror, but Dr Mitchell just nods. 'Right, then. Let's do the necessary tests and we can see if there is any reason to worry.'

Besides the fact that I can't recall my own flesh and blood? 'Okay.' She nods.

'But I should tell you that, more often than not, we aren't able to find anything wrong.' The doctor pushes up his specs on his very thin nose, and Charlotte watches them slide back down again. 'People come here all the time looking for answers, but the brain isn't something that functions in black and white. There's a lot we still don't know, and we can't always get to the bottom of things.'

Way to big up your services, Charlotte thinks as she follows him through to the diagnostic room. 'Can't you just give me a knock on the head and make everything come back again?' she jokes.

But Dr Mitchell doesn't seem to get the humour. 'Unfortunately not,' he says. 'Regardless of what you may see on television.'

Charlotte can't help rolling her eyes.

'All right, so I'll leave you in the capable hands of our technician, Dorota,' he says. 'She'll do all your diagnostic tests, and I'll see you later in the afternoon to review the results with you.'

'Okay.' Charlotte watches him leave the room, thinking that he probably doesn't even know her name. And by the looks of things, he has even less interest.

Several hours later, Charlotte is back in the waiting room, leafing through the same magazine. Her brain has never been so well photographed: a star in its very own film. If something is wrong inside her head, she's sure they must have found it. Dr Mitchell has to err on the side of caution, so as not to raise people's expectations, but he is an expert, after all. He'll be able to help, even if it's just to tell her how long this memory loss will last. Any other alternative isn't worth thinking about.

When her name is called, she jumps up and forces herself not to run to the office.

'Have a seat,' he says, as monotone as ever. 'I've had a chance to look at your images, and as far as I can see – and let me tell you, if there were something to see, I would have seen it – your brain appears to be functioning normally.'

Charlotte stares, unable to believe what he's saying. 'But . . . but it's not functioning normally. Not when I can't remember the past four years. Not when I can't remember giving *birth*, for God's sake. Having a *daughter*.' Her voice rises, sounding even louder in the hushed room. 'That's not normal!'

Dr Mitchell blinks. 'Memory is a funny thing, and the part of the brain where memories are stored isn't something we fully understand yet. While it's possible the accident damaged that area, it's not showing up on the scan.'

'So . . .' Charlotte leans back in the chair. There has to be something he can do; something he can tell her. 'I should be able to remember, then? If everything is okay?'

'I didn't say everything was okay. It might be; it might not. I said that, as far as we can tell at the moment, your brain is fine. You may regain some of your memories, and you may not.'

Frustration bubbles inside her. 'What can I do? What can I do to remember?' She *has* to remember. She can't carry on this way!

'The best thing you can do is just live your daily life, and try not to force it. Memories may trickle back in, or they may return in a rush. They may not return at all. It's really impossible to say.' He smiles distractedly and glances at the door, indicating the session is over.

Charlotte stays in the chair, unwilling to move. That's not an answer. That's not even close to an answer. If anything, this so-called expert has only muddied the waters even more. There's nothing wrong, but there is. She may remember everything, or nothing at all. Life may return to normal, or it may never be the same again.

Fear and panic twist her insides, and she clenches her hands. How can she ever be a mother again if she can't remember her child – if she doesn't *love* her own child, or not like she should? How can she live this life, trapped in a place light years from who she is now . . . from what she wants? And how can she begin to heal the rift with David if she's not even the same person he argued with?

Charlotte longs to scream and beat her feet on the floor, but instead she says thank you (not that it matters – Dr Mitchell is fixated on his computer screen again) and forces herself to stand.

Out on the street, cars rush by and a taxi honks when she almost steps in front of it. She lifts a hand in apology and tries to breathe. She knew regaining her memories wouldn't be a straightforward process, but she hadn't let herself think that she'd simply never remember – that she'd be stuck here forever. Plodding down Harley Street, past door after door of top-notch consultants promising everything from the latest cosmetic surgery to videos of babies in the womb, she remembers her earlier apprehension about regaining her former self. Now, she'd give anything to dive into the cauldron of memories and let them fill her up again, no matter what challenges she might face.

Live your daily life, the doctor had said, and Charlotte feels determination flood through her. That's exactly what she'll do. She'll immerse herself in her daughter, following the path she'd laid out years earlier. Her memories will have to return. Because if they don't . . .

She shakes her head. They will, and that's all there is to it.

CHAPTER TWENTY-THREE

19 December

Anabelle is home! She's been home for just over two weeks now, actually. It's hard to believe it's only been that long, because it feels like forever. In fact, I can barely remember life without her, although I dimly recall a place where dishes didn't clog the sink and laundry wasn't piled in corners of the bedroom.

The flat is a disaster, with muslins draped on every surface. Half-drunk cups of coffee – those I start but never get further than a few gulps before Anabelle starts crying – dot the flat. I used to wonder what mums did all day at home, and now I marvel if I'm able to get in the shower. My stomach is spongy and soft, my hair is greasy, and I'm lucky if I can even form a coherent thought right now – that's how tired I am. And as for preparing for Christmas . . . Scoffing down a box of mince pies is the closest I've got.

But I don't care about any of it, because at last, I can be a mother – a *real* mother. Not just one standing stiffly by a cot, hoping for the best, but one who's filled with such a fierce, protective love that nothing could diminish it. One who can pick up her daughter and jiggle her around, let her kick on the play mat, who can breathe in her scent . . .

A scent I'm still not all that familiar with, swaddled as she was for the past couple of weeks in bandages and scratchy, stiff hospital blankets. I camped out with her in the NICU for those long, endless days after surgery, sleeping upright in a chair in the corner of the room. David tried to give me a break, and even Miriam offered to take a shift. But I couldn't leave my girl. It felt like the second I stepped away, her body would fail. She would feel my absence in her heart, and it would stop working. And although I know it can't possibly be true, a small part of me fears that my lack of emotion during pregnancy – excitement, anticipation, love – directly affected my daughter's heart, as if she didn't feel my devotion.

Like she somehow knew my first priority wasn't her.

I'll never banish the image of her after surgery: so tiny, so frail, so defenceless. I'll never forget the terror while doctors performed the procedure. I'll never recover from waiting to hear if I was still a mother – waiting to hear that my child had survived.

And then . . . the absolute relief, like all the heavy, sludgy blood had drained out of me, to be replaced by a frothy light liquid. Like I'd been lifted right off my feet and floated up into the sky. My daughter was *alive*.

I'd be lying if I said I wasn't scared now. For as much as I wanted to have my baby home, once the moment arrived, I was petrified. I made a vow to keep my daughter safe. But what if I can't? What if she falls ill, or her heart stops working, or . . . Although the doctors are quite sure she'll make a full recovery, there is still a risk of complications in the years ahead. What if I fail to protect her once again?

Her future is in my hands, and only mine. I can't even think of burdening David with my fears when I'm the one who set us on this path. If only he knew . . . I can't bear to ponder his reaction. Better to leave him be; better to keep the silence between us than open up a channel of communication right now. I don't deserve his comfort, his reassurance. I can barely see him through the guilt fogging my vision, anyway.

He's making noises about getting up to speed on everything so he's ready to take over when I return to the office. *Return to the office.* The words sound so foreign that I can't begin to process them. Right now, the only thing I can focus on is Anabelle. Anything else . . . My brain will not allow it. My heart will not allow it. I'm marooned here with my daughter, and I don't want to be rescued. I need to stay here.

I *will* stay here.

Because I've quit my job at Cellbril. I'm never going back, and the sense of relief when I said those words almost bowled me over.

It all started this morning when the human resources woman (Tina? I can never remember her name) left a message on my voicemail, asking if she could confirm my start date at work in two weeks' time. *Two weeks!* I held the phone away from my ear, my heart squeezing as I remembered thinking, right after Anabelle was born, that I'd confirm the date as soon as I was home. And then . . .

Then everything changed.

I couldn't return to work in two weeks' time – no way. For God's sake, my daughter was barely off the operating table, and I'd only just started getting to know her. I rejected the notion of leaving her without even thinking about it.

I rang Vivek up straight away, unsure what I'd say other than that I needed more time – my daughter and I needed more time. Hearing my boss's familiar deep voice was jarring, like looking through a cracked window into a dusty, far-off place. I'd cared so much about it, but now I barely recognised it.

I told him I wouldn't be returning in two weeks, trying to explain as unemotionally and succinctly as I could about Anabelle's heart condition. As the words fell from my lips, nausea swirled in my stomach and a bitter taste filled my mouth. I wasn't even back at work, and already I was glossing over what had happened to my daughter, making my decision palatable and justifiable to my boss. Already my daughter was taking a back seat in my conversation, with work first and foremost.

Vivek responded with incredulous sympathy, quickly moving on to develop a strategy so none of our accounts would suffer until I returned. I sank down on to the bed as his words poured over me, anger rattling inside. How could I do that? This job and my determination not to let anything affect it had put my child at risk; yet here I was, shoving my daughter to the background once again. My newborn daughter, who'd almost died.

God.

I couldn't go back there. I couldn't let myself fall into that trap again, be sucked into caring more about a job than my child . . . to want to be a VP more than a *mother*. I cringed, remembering writing just that in this diary. That job is like an addiction to me, and if I couldn't shake it after what had just happened, I'd clearly never be able to.

I needed to go cold turkey.

So, I told Vivek I didn't just need more time. I told him I wouldn't be back, full stop. I kept my tone firm and unyielding, like he'd taught me. He tried to persuade me to wait a bit longer before making such a drastic decision, talking quickly in his sales-patter voice about how I was so talented, how hard I'd worked, how I was on the way to becoming VP, and how he was certain I would want to come back after a little time to 'adjust to everything'. I'm sure he expected me to be flattered, but instead of boosting me up, every word rubbed raw, the guilt pouring into open wounds. I had to cut him off with a final 'no'.

His disappointment echoed down the line as he said goodbye, his formality a million miles from his usual jovial tone. I knew I'd let him down, but that was the least of my worries. I'd let myself down by risking my child. And even worse, I'd let Anabelle down.

As soon as I hung up, I yanked all my work clothes from the wardrobe, shoving them into an empty suitcase we keep under the bed. Out of sight, out of mind – I couldn't bear staring at them, as if they were responsible for betraying my daughter. I could hardly even touch them, and I heaved a huge sigh of relief when they were safely zipped into the case.

I don't know what the future holds for me now, or if I'll ever go back to wearing those clothes. But one thing is clear: I'll never put my daughter at risk again.

CHAPTER TWENTY-FOUR

Charlotte closes the flat door quietly behind her and leans against the solid wood. This is home – this is the world she existed in with her daughter, and the space she must now inhabit while frantically praying she'll remember everything. If the consultant said to live her daily life, she'll do just that . . . with bells on. Anabelle's laughter floats from the lounge, and Charlotte pushes off the door.

'I'm back!' she calls out, forcing a bright and energetic note into her voice, though her heart drops when she spots Miriam and Anabelle at the table with the watercolours – the very last thing on earth Charlotte wants to contend with.

No, she tells herself firmly through gritted teeth. *I love watercolours! I absolutely adore them! It's my favourite thing to do with Anabelle.* Shame repeating the words doesn't make them feel any truer. Still, she needs to try.

'Hi, guys. Can I join in?' She leans over to examine Anabelle's painting . . . Surprise, surprise, a giant slug, with definitely no antennae.

Anabelle glances up at her with a face like pure sunshine. If Charlotte hadn't been cursing the coming paintjob, Anabelle's joy at seeing her might have made her feel a little bit better. 'Mummy! Yes! Come sit.'

Miriam pushes back her chair and Charlotte can't resist looking at what her mother-in-law is creating. To her surprise, it's actually an accomplished painting of the view from their window . . . quite a feat, given the shoddy brushes and paints.

'Wow! That's great!' Charlotte says, unable to keep the disbelief from her voice.

Miriam shrugs. 'I've been doing some watercolour classes for the past few years, you know, just to pass the time and meet a few people. The days can seem very long when you're on your own.' Her face softens from its usual brisk expression, and Charlotte catches a rare glimpse of vulnerability. For once, she can relate to how long the hours can be – time has never dragged more than this past week, when she was alone in the flat. Is that what Miriam's life is like all the time? She lives for her sons, and even though they adore her, they have their own worlds now that she's not part of, despite her best efforts. She has nothing of her own . . . except watercolours. God, how depressing.

A stab of fear goes through Charlotte. Is that what she has in store, too?

'I can't wait to have you lot all with me, all the time,' Miriam continues. 'It'll be so nice to have noise in the house again.'

Charlotte nods, her mind whirling. Does diving back into the life she was living mean having to embrace all her previous decisions, good or bad? She can see that Miriam is lonely, but living with her . . . ? Maybe they could take Anabelle over to visit a bit more; perhaps a sleepover every once in a while. Had Charlotte ever done that, or had she been too fearful to let Anabelle be with her grandmother, too? She may have thought she knew best, but it seemed she was denying her daughter relationships with other people in her life.

'Anyway.' Miriam clears her throat, staring hard at her daughter-in-law. 'How was the appointment?' An alarm on her phone goes off, and she glances down in horror. 'Oh, goodness. My parking time's up. I'd better run – they're like vultures here. Give David a hug for me and call me later to let me know how it all went. Bye!' She rushes out and the door slams shut before either Anabelle or Charlotte can even say goodbye.

'Well.' Charlotte forces a smile at the little girl – at her *daughter*, she needs to drill that into her head – and sits down in Miriam's spot. 'What shall I paint?' She darts a glance at the clock. One more hour before she can start making supper, then a half-hour until bath, then bedtime . . . she might be able to clock off around eight? *This is not a job*, she reminds herself. *This is your life. A life you chose, and that you will remember eventually.*

'Can you paint a giant leaf? A giant purple one? Slugs like purple.'

'Well, I'm not sure leaves are purple,' Charlotte says, unable to resist reality. 'I could do a green one?' She points out the window. 'See? The leaves are green.'

Anabelle's bottom lip comes out and her brow furrows. 'No. *Purple.* Slugs like purple.'

'But Anabelle, slugs don't see colour.' Do they? Goodness, her slug knowledge is truly lacking. 'They don't care. They just want to eat.' Why is she even bothering to explain this? Why can't she just paint the bloody leaf purple and get on with it? She sighs. 'Okay, purple.'

Thirty minutes later, she's painted about fifty hideous purple leaves while Anabelle has created an army of slugs. Charlotte's hands are covered with purple paint, Anabelle has brown streaks across her face, and the table resembles a Jackson Pollock canvas. Charlotte can't help laughing as she surveys the paintings in front of them. It's like a psychedelic Planet of the Slugs, and against all odds, she actually had fun helping her daughter create it.

'What are you two up to?' David's head pokes around the corner of the lounge, his eyebrows rising in surprise as he spots Charlotte and Anabelle at the table. 'Charlotte?' he asks tentatively. 'Did the consultant help you?'

Charlotte shakes her head, the same fear and dismay running through her. 'No, unfortunately not.' She pushes back her chair and wipes her hands, then crosses to where David's taking off his tie. She smiles, thinking that some things never change. It's still the first thing he does when he gets home. 'The MRI couldn't pick up anything wrong with my brain. The consultant said the memories may return or they may not – I just have to live my life and see.' She watches him for any sign of reaction, but his face is like a mask.

'They'll come back,' he says, turning away and heading into the bedroom to change. 'If there's nothing wrong, then I'm sure they will. It might take a bit more time, that's all.' He sounds like he's awaiting an execution rather than getting the last version of his wife back. Given how they ended things before the accident, she can understand he might be anxious, but . . .

Charlotte follows him and sits down on the bed, desperate for something – anything – to help her get through this. Even if she does understand David's coolness now, it's so hard to reconcile this distant man with the affectionate husband she remembers.

'Look, the last thing I want is to push you and Miriam away again,' Charlotte says. 'It's been great to see you and Anabelle connect, and I know Miriam's really enjoyed spending time with her, too.'

David meets her eyes and, for the first time since he came home today, she can see some warmth and happiness on his face.

'But . . .' She swallows. 'If I am going to remember, then I should do things now exactly as I did before the accident.'

'Right.' David's face closes up again and he turns to hang up his suit. 'Sure. I'll tell Mum that we won't need her to look after Anabelle.'

'Okay.' Charlotte plays with a thread on the duvet, hating the tension between them. 'So I guess I'll do the bath and bedtime routine, and . . . everything else?'

'Fine.' David pulls on a pair of trackies and Charlotte can't help noticing that his butt is as cute as ever. They still haven't made love, and a shag would definitely do David some good. He's coiled so tightly he's going to implode if he clenches any harder.

'David . . .' She shifts on the bed. 'I might have been really angry when you told me about Anabelle's condition, but you know . . . I wasn't myself. I mean, I wasn't who I am now – the person I am today. I can't remember that person.' She sighs in frustration at the confusion on his face. She's getting confused herself.

'It's not what I feel right now,' Charlotte says, desperate to get her meaning across. God, when did it get so hard to communicate? It sounds a cliché, but they used to know how the other was feeling just by looking at each other. 'I'm not angry, not at all. I love you. And we'll be fine. Right?' Her voice cracks and every muscle in her body tenses as she waits for his response.

David looks down at her and her heart lurches at the sadness in his eyes. 'I love you, too, Charlotte.'

She waits for him to add that they'll be fine; to reassure her that of course they'll make it. Instead he jerks a T-shirt over his head, obscuring his face, then turns to the wardrobe once again.

Does he think we won't *be fine?* she wonders, staring at his back. That she'll be so angry she can't have more babies that she might actually leave him? Or that she really will blame him for faulty genes?

No. No way. If he thinks that, then he doesn't really know her at all. She freezes as it hits her that *she* doesn't know the person she'd become.

Well, at least he still loves me, she tells herself. That's something, anyway. She'll hang on to that.

'Mama!'

Anabelle's shout interrupts her thoughts. Charlotte gets to her feet and heads back into the lounge, her mouth dropping open at the sight in front of her. Anabelle is sitting in the middle of the floor, happily slathering purple paint across the wooden floorboards.

'Anabelle!' Charlotte's voice rises to a shriek. 'What on earth are you doing?'

Anabelle's head swings around. 'Painting more leaves, Mama,' she says in a tone that makes it clear there must be something wrong with Charlotte's eyesight if she can't figure that out.

Charlotte takes a deep breath to try to quash the frustration and anger, then picks her way across the floor, dodging paint. 'Right.' She lifts her daughter – for a small thing, she's certainly heavy – from the floor and, ignoring the kicks and protests, carries her to the bathroom and dumps her in the tub. 'Let's get you cleaned up.'

And as Charlotte runs a bath, she realises she may have just learned the most important lesson to help her get through the next few weeks: never *ever* leave a three year old alone.

CHAPTER TWENTY-FIVE

Just over a week has passed in Charlotte's new life . . . a life in which her world revolves around one thing: her daughter. From morning (very early morning) until bedtime, Charlotte takes care of Anabelle full-time. No more Miriam, and no more David coming back from work early to put their daughter to bed. It's a crash course in parenting, squeezing three years of knowledge into seven days, and it's very often by trial and error, but she's getting there. She knows now, for instance, that letting Anabelle eat a chocolate lolly is like injecting sugar straight into her daughter's veins. That taking a toddler out for a 'relaxing coffee' is the farthest thing from relaxing you can get, and that pulling wellies on to a child's foot burns more calories than a 10k run. Charlotte's amazed how much she's learned, but then, when you're working 24/7, of course you pick things up quickly.

Right now, despite going through all the motions, taking care of Anabelle still seems just that: a job – something she needs to do to reach the end goal of actually feeling like a mother. This child belongs to her and she knows that, after all they've been through, she should feel incredibly lucky. But she still doesn't . . . doesn't feel the depth of emotion that would make this new life meaningful. She misses a job she remembers choosing . . . misses having adult conversation between the hours of eight and seven.

And she misses David most of all. Despite her attempts to prod him out of his shell – kissing him when he's home from work; babbling on about her day with Anabelle – he seems as distant as ever. He skirts around her, eating the meals she's cobbled together (she may have been a cook extraordinaire in the past, but one step at a time – at least she knows how the oven works now) while staring at the telly. And even though she knows their argument is hanging over his head, every time he turns away it is still a slap in the face. He *did* say he loves her, right? Surely he'd want to try to bring them together again, even if he is afraid of what might happen when her memories return . . . if they ever do, that is.

It's only been a week, she tells herself, when despair and frustration threaten to overwhelm her. When you're stuck in a life you don't want, though, that week seems like forever. That same restless urge to do more burns inside her, increasing her determination to emulate the mother she once was. To that end, she's going to make a big meal tonight if it kills her – and it might do just that. David's going to be home at a reasonable hour for once, and they can all eat together before Anabelle's bedtime. Charlotte has decided to cook a roast chicken and potatoes, one of David's favourite meals when they go to visit Miriam. How hard can it be to stick a chicken in the oven and boil some potatoes?

'Come on, Anabelle. Let's hit the supermarket!' The huge Sainsbury's on Cromwell Road is nearby, and while Charlotte's managed to get by this past week using what's already in the cupboard, right now the kitchen resembles an empty wasteland. In the past she used to rely on the off-licence to plug any gaps between the takeaways, but she doubts it sells the horrible pig-shaped biscuits her daughter keeps whining about, not to mention a whole chicken. God knows the last time she actually visited a supermarket.

Anabelle looks about as enthusiastic as if Charlotte had suggested beheading her Barbies. Her lower lip juts out and her forehead lowers, and Charlotte's heart sinks. Uh-oh.

'No. Not going.'

'Come on! It'll be fun!' Charlotte's tone sounds false, even to her. Who is she trying to kid? She used to avoid the megastores like a plague: the flickering fluorescent lights, the screaming kids who run trolleys into the back of her heels, the people who block every aisle, staring at spaghetti as if it contains the secrets of the universe . . . She shudders. Actually, she can remember being Anabelle's age and *dreading* trips to the shops with her father. He used to bribe her with an ice cream every time. *Not a bad idea*, she thinks, raising an eyebrow.

She crouches down to meet her daughter's eyes, trying not to smile at her stubborn expression. As annoying as it is right now, Anabelle's determination will serve her well in life. 'How about we both have an ice cream once we're finished at the shop?' she asks.

Anabelle's eyes light up instantly. 'Two scoops?'

Charlotte shrugs. 'Sure, why not!'

'But Mummy, you never let me have two scoops! You always say one is enough.' Anabelle hurls herself into Charlotte's arms. 'Thank you, Mummy. Thank you!'

Charlotte hugs her daughter back, thinking how wonderful it is that such small things can provide so much happiness – and how nice it is to be hugged . . . to be loved with such abandon. Things might be tricky with David, but at least she'd never doubt Anabelle's affection – even if she doesn't share her strength of emotion just yet.

After wrestling with the car-seat buckle for well over ten minutes while fielding fifty million and one questions from Anabelle about every subject under the sun, they're finally on their way. Charlotte jams the gearstick into first, sighing as the unfamiliar car judders in protest, then reluctantly shifts. The mechanic deemed it 'good as new' after the accident, and it feels bloody new to her for all she remembers driving it. She can barely recall driving, actually: it's been years since her dad coaxed her into the family car, despite her protests that taking the Tube was faster than being stuck in endless London traffic. He'd paid no heed, telling her that one day she might need to know how to drive.

She never could have imagined that she'd do so with her three year old, on the way to the supermarket for the weekly shop in the middle of a workday. She couldn't have imagined doing a weekly shop, full stop – let alone trying to make a roast dinner. Like driving, making a meal feels about as familiar as swan-diving off a cliff. In fact, she'd definitely find that more enjoyable.

She parks the car, unclips Anabelle from her car seat, finds a pound coin and secures the trolley, all the while trying to insert appropriate responses to Anabelle's steady stream of conversation. Does that child ever keep quiet? Steering the trolley with one hand (harder than it sounds – it keeps veering right) and clutching Anabelle's wriggly fingers with the other, Charlotte crosses the car park and into the huge, brightly lit supermarket. Right, where to begin? She stops, ignoring Anabelle pulling her forward. Ugh, she should have made a list. That's what people do, right?

She lunges for a nearby packet of romaine lettuce and chucks it in the trolley, then grabs some organic peppers despite having no idea what to do with them. Well, she has to start somewhere and Anabelle's definitely not one to linger, tugging her along at the speed of light. Ah, potatoes – she swipes some as they pass, her eyes widening as she spots the different varieties. Who knew there were so many kinds of potato?

Half an hour later, Charlotte pushes her heavy trolley towards the till. Anabelle trails behind, her face smeared with the remains of the chocolate bar Charlotte said she could eat if she stopped grabbing everything from the shelves. God knows what Charlotte will do with half this stuff (smoked sardines, anyone?) but at least they have food – and wine, although ten bottles might be a few too many. Her Mother Goddess self probably doesn't drink, but that's one area where Charlotte is willing to deviate. She might have gone overboard with the food for just one weekly shop, but perhaps she can avoid coming back here next week.

'Anabelle! Put that back!' Too late, she notices that her daughter has grabbed a particularly trashy tabloid from the rack by the till and has somehow managed to turn to a page featuring women with hardly any clothes on.

'Mummy! Look! That lady has really big—'

Charlotte yanks the paper from her hands and Anabelle yowls in protest. Desperate to prevent a full-on meltdown, Charlotte gives her the debit card to keep her quiet while she unloads the groceries on to the conveyor belt. Silence at last.

'Sorry, Mummy.' Anabelle's small voice makes her head jerk around, and her heart plummets. Her daughter has bent the debit card so far, there's a huge white crease down the middle. It looks more like a teepee than a card, and scanning it will be impossible.

'Anabelle!' Charlotte grabs the card. God, what had she been thinking, giving it to a toddler, anyway? *Stupid, stupid, stupid.* No matter, she has another card for her own account. She hasn't used it since the accident and, thankfully, it's still there in her wallet. She hands it to the woman behind the till, breathing deeply to try to stay calm. If anyone had told her a shopping trip with a toddler would raise her blood pressure more than pitching to big companies, she'd have said they were mad.

'I'm sorry, but your card has been declined,' the checkout lady says, handing back her card.

'Declined?' Charlotte squints at the card. Has it expired, maybe? No, the date on the front says it's valid for another year. 'Can you try it again, please?'

'Sure.' The woman takes her card and runs it through another time, then shrugs. 'Sorry, it's still not working. This machine can be a bit funny.'

A queue is building up behind them, and Charlotte feels her cheeks grow warm. Her mind scrambles for a solution, not an easy feat with

Anabelle now trying to balance on her feet. 'Can you hang on to our groceries? I'll just go the cashpoint and see if I can get it to work there.'

The woman nods. 'Of course. There's one inside the entrance.'

Charlotte hurries Anabelle along with her to the cashpoint. She taps in her code, then hits 'Cash', hastily selecting one hundred pounds. There should be more than enough in her account – although she was never one for saving; her comfortable salary meant she never had to scrimp at the end of the month.

'Anabelle, just wait . . .' Her voice trails off as two words on the screen pop up: 'insufficient funds'. *What?* She quickly taps the button to check her balance, her heart dropping when the machine relays its current status: –£16.24.

She blinks. She's overdrawn She's never been overdrawn in her life – not even when she was a poor student. Okay, it's not by much, but still.

Then it hits her. She doesn't have a salary any more. She doesn't have a job. There's only one way her bank account can go, and that's *down.*

Everything inside her goes cold.

Charlotte takes Anabelle's hand and plods out to the car park, feeling heavy and weighted, despite leaving with no groceries. She'd known she wasn't working, but it hadn't sunk in that she's totally dependent on David. She can't envision going to her husband and *asking* for money, even if she did need something. How could she stand there, meek and grateful, as he dishes out cash?

Even if being a stay-at-home mum is a valuable, important role in society, not earning an income makes her feel . . . insignificant. She's always had her own money, right from the age of sixteen when she worked in a fast-food restaurant on weekends, flipping burgers and burning her arms on the grease from the deep-fat fryers. Christ, she still has the scars.

But it's not just about the job or the money. It's the ability to stand on her own two feet, like she did when paying her way through university and putting down a sizable deposit on the flat. It's being able to buy what she wants, when she wants – even insanely expensive turquoise curtains that cost as much as a small car.

It's about her *independence* . . . yet another important part of her that she can't believe is gone.

Charlotte fastens Anabelle into her car seat then sits for a moment behind the driver's wheel, desperately trying to conjure up her earlier resolve to find a way back to her pre-accident life. She still wants to, of course. She still needs to, for herself and for her family. But with every day that passes, the more she discovers how much she's changed. So many things she holds dear are gone, as if someone has flicked a switch on those parts of her.

The things I used to hold dear, she reminds herself. She couldn't have thought them important any longer, or she wouldn't have been able to function.

Charlotte takes a deep breath and starts the engine, leaving another piece of herself behind.

CHAPTER TWENTY-SIX

2 January

Today is the day I was supposed to return to the office. The second of January: the start of a new working year, and the date I'd thought this mothering gig would feel old hat. My baby would be settled into a routine, sleeping through the night, her feeds regulated. I'd fit back into my old wardrobe, and my brain would be firing on all cylinders instead of just one (if I'm lucky). I'd put on my high heels and slide back into my life.

I couldn't be further from that life if I tried.

I wouldn't have even remembered this date, actually, but I'd set the alarm on my phone before going off on maternity leave – God, I really was chomping at the bit to return. The persistent buzz jolted me awake at 6 a.m., and I wanted to murder my former self when I figured out what the noise was. I hadn't heard it in a while – there's no need for an alarm with a newborn in the house, let me tell you. Anabelle is our personal siren, alerting us that it's time to snap to it. I'm not complaining, though. I *can't* complain, not after everything we've been through. If she wants to feed 24/7, bring it on.

And so, instead of rising to dash out the door, I turned over in bed and listened to my baby breathing. In, out, in, out . . . I'd never heard a sweeter sound, and I'd never been more grateful for anything in my life. I need to savour this, to remember how lucky I am, and to be thankful every day that things turned out as they did. What more could I ask for than a healthy child?

Anabelle and I are like one now. It's hard to know where she stops and I begin. She's next to me at all times, and the rhythm of her day and night has become mine, too. Christmas came and went in a mist of fatigue, barely recognisable as a different day. In the past, I couldn't have imagined not marking the holiday with my usual over-the-top gifts and decorations, but now I'm happy to have every day the same . . . wonderfully, boringly, the *same*.

David feels a bit like an extra, an unnecessary appendage in my world, where only one thing matters. He tries to change nappies, to do a feed and to put our daughter to sleep, but the truth is, I can't accept his help. I need to do everything to prove I'm worthy of this. He stares at me sometimes like I'm a stranger, like he's trying to figure out how I got here. In many ways, I suspect I *am* a stranger to him now: a person who threatened the dearest thing to him. Not that he'd ever say that – he doesn't even *know* that – but I know. My secret's like a jagged thorn wedged in my heart, twisting deeper with each breath, amputating everything but love for my child. And even if I wanted to get close to him, I couldn't. I'm too scared his kindness will ease out that thorn, tempting me to tell him what happened. And I can't. I can never tell anyone. I can barely even think of it now myself.

When I told David that I wasn't returning to Cellbril, he blinked in surprise and disappointment. My heart gave a pang – I knew how much he'd been looking forward to being with Anabelle, but I just couldn't let go.

'But why?' he asked. His fingers tightened around mine like he was trying to anchor us – to what, I didn't know. 'I mean, I can understand asking for more time to be with Anabelle, especially after what happened. But *quitting*? What about your career? What about becoming VP, and everything you've been working for?' His words echoed Vivek's, and I flinched. I didn't need reminding of how driven I'd been; how much I'd risked. 'I know the past few weeks have been tough . . . really tough, but we're over that now, right? Anabelle is fine. There's no need to give up a job you love because of a birth defect.'

'*A birth defect?*'

David made it sound so minor – not something that would have killed our daughter without a major operation. I should have been grateful that he downplayed its severity; but I'd never, not in a million years, see it the same way.

'Look, why don't you take a few more months,' he carried on. 'Call Vivek and tell him you've changed your mind. I can put off my leave from work for a bit.'

I shook my head. I wouldn't change my mind. I couldn't. 'I know money might be tight on just your salary, and that we won't be able to look for a bigger place,' I said. 'We can forget any holidays, and we won't have money for the cleaner or any of that, but we should be able to get by if we're careful.' I bit my lip. I hadn't even thought about the financial implications of not going back – of not having my own income any longer. It was just something I had to do.

I stared down at my husband's hand, surprised at how big and heavy it was after Anabelle's tiny one. 'I can't go back there,' I said, meeting his eyes again and praying that he wouldn't make me try to explain. 'I need to be home. I need to be with Anabelle.'

'All right.' David slid his hand from mine, his expression unreadable. I'd thought he'd be happy, but instead he seemed . . . weighed down. 'I suppose you can always find a job, if you do want to go back at some point.'

I nodded, but I couldn't even contemplate that. All I could think about was the life I was so lucky to be building. I hadn't realised the value of what I had, but I'll never forget now.

I'll never forget what my daughter means, and how fortunate we are to have her.

That much is certain.

CHAPTER TWENTY-SEVEN

'Okay, what do we do next?' Charlotte squints at the recipe on the tablet. A dusting of flour covers its surface. 'We need to add two eggs.' She glances down at Anabelle, only just able to reach over the countertop even with her step. 'Do you want to crack them?'

'Yes, please!' Anabelle reaches out for an egg and smacks it hard against the bowl. It collapses completely, shell and all, into the mixture. 'Oops.'

Charlotte can't help but laugh at the disaster in front of them. It seems her daughter has inherited her defective cooking genes. Even with lots of practice over the past two weeks, Charlotte is as bad as ever. The roast chicken dinner she finally managed to make was diabolical – the potatoes boiled over, the chicken didn't cook all the way through, and despite saying he'd be home early, David had turned up well after Anabelle had gone to bed. He hadn't even touched the roast, opting for a simple sandwich instead . . . not that Charlotte could blame him.

But despite Charlotte's horrific kitchen skills, Anabelle's begged over and over to bake some treats together. Apparently it was something they used to do, and so – in the interest of remembering, to which she seems no closer – Charlotte had agreed, although she'd rather face death by firing squad than make cookie dough.

But actually, she's been enjoying it. So far this week, they've made a sponge cake (burnt), a lemon loaf (raw), and today they've moved on to chocolate chip cookies (hopefully, edible). To Charlotte's surprise, Anabelle's a great helper, although her assistance has had no bearing on the outcome of their efforts. Their disasters have become something of a joke, both of them breaking out in giggles at the monstrosities they've made.

'Okay. Let's start again.' Charlotte sets aside the eggy bowl and reaches for the flour. Too late, she discovers she didn't close it properly last time, and flour flies through the air, landing on Anabelle's head.

'Anabelle! Your hair is white!' Charlotte grins, holding up a shiny tin so Anabelle can see her reflection.

'More!' Anabelle reaches up to touch her hair. 'More, please!'

And before Charlotte knows what she's doing, she's sprinkling more flour on her daughter's hair. The sprinkle becomes a handful, and the kitchen is engulfed in a cloud of white, coating everything. Anabelle's delighted laugh floats around her, and for a brief instant, Charlotte feels pure joy – something like the way she felt as a child, when the whole world could seem magical. She leans down to swoop her daughter up in her arms, spinning them in circles.

'What on earth . . .' David's voice trails away, and Charlotte glances up to catch his incredulous expression. God, is he actually home early for once? She holds out a hand. 'Come on, join us! It's the Wonderful World of Flour.' She throws another handful of flour in the air for added effect, trying to ignore the thought that soon she'll need to clean all this up.

For a split second, it looks like David might actually take a step forward and join in, but then he shakes his head. 'You two enjoy that. I'll just go and get changed.'

Charlotte sighs as she watches him walk away. What will it take to make him relax just a bit? If the Wonderful World of Flour won't crack his façade, then what will? She knows he's afraid, but avoiding her at every turn is hardly the answer. Ever since that day at the supermarket, she's been dying to talk to him about their finances – *his* finances, rather, since she has none of her own – keen to understand if they're doing okay, what their monthly income is and how much she can spend. But he's hardly even around any more, disappearing into the office even at the weekend, claiming he needs to catch up on some files. Since when has he ever felt the urge to 'catch up'? He's never even cared about his job, let alone staying on top of it. Things must be bad if he's taking refuge there.

Fear darts through her. Does David really believe that things are over between them – that his revelation and their argument was the final impasse? Does he really think she won't be able to forgive him for keeping his secret; that their love isn't strong enough after all? He must, if his absence is anything to go by. He's pretty much checked out already.

But what if she never remembers? How much longer can they go on like this, living in limbo, waiting for the axe to fall? Her stomach churns at the thought of them splitting up. She'd be alone with a three year old she doesn't remember, broke, with no prospects – Jeremy Kyle's wet dream.

Something has to give. Either her memory, or . . .

'Come on, let's tidy up,' Charlotte says to Anabelle now, abandoning all hope of chocolate chip cookies. Sighing, she gazes down at the little girl, who's trying futilely to catch the flour still swirling in the air. She *is* cute, and over the past couple of weeks, Charlotte has actually enjoyed spending some time with her . . . *some*. She's had fun, but it's not nearly enough to compensate for the life she's leading; not enough to plug the holes in her heart when she thinks of David and a life without him.

Charlotte wipes a cloth across the counter, sending more flour flying. She'll keep trying to be the mother she was, keep going on the path that's been set out. Eventually, she'll get there. She just hopes that when she does, her husband will still be by her side.

CHAPTER TWENTY-EIGHT

14 February

It's Valentine's Day, and I didn't even remember. I *did* have it marked on the calendar, but not as a romantic holiday; as 'Anabelle Three Months Old!' And while I should probably feel bad admitting that – while all the baby books make a point of saying 'Make sure you remember you're a couple, too' – the baby books haven't been through what we have . . . what *I* have. Caring for a child who had such a traumatic start combined with all the usual newborn needs is enough to knock anyone flat, and by the end of the day, I can barely form a sentence, let alone be romantic.

Truth be told, when I think of David . . . well, I want to run away. I want to run from his tender glances, his praise, his constant encouragement to go back to work and his continuous offers of help. Because I don't deserve it, and if he knew everything, he wouldn't be so loving. I turn away from him, that thorn jabbing my heart, and redouble my efforts with Anabelle to prove – to him, to me, I don't know – that I'm sorry. I can see the hurt flickering on his face, but I can't fall into him. Not now.

So when David came home early from work tonight bearing roses and chocolate in a garishly red heart, I didn't swoon with romance. Instead, I felt like fleeing. Most parents would jump at a night out after three months straight with a newborn, but not me. How could I smile and accept tokens of love, knowing I might have risked the dearest thing to us – knowing I could have eased her journey into this world and helped secure her future, but didn't? Knowing that if he had even an inkling of what I'd done, he might flee from me, too?

I took a deep breath and tried to smile, dodging his hug to set the flowers and chocolate on the side table.

'Mum has agreed to look after Anabelle tonight,' he said, and I could see he was trying to hide his disappointment at my lacklustre reaction. 'And I've booked us a show at the Royal Court and dinner at the Botanist afterwards.'

I jerked towards him, my mouth dropping open. 'You *what*?' It was already six o'clock, I'd been wearing the same clothes for two days and God knows the last time I'd washed my hair, which was scraggly and threaded with grey now.

But that wasn't really it. I couldn't sit next to my husband all night, pretending we were fine – smiling and acting like the past three months were nothing; like my negligence was absolved. Guilt weighs on me with every breath I take, and some silly romantic evening out won't shift that. Not to mention that leaving Anabelle for a whole night is out of the question. What if something happened? I'd never forgive myself – again.

'I thought it would be a treat,' David said, biting his lip. 'You've been superwoman these past few months.' He shakes his head. 'Super*mother*, I should say. I think it's time to let your hair down a bit. Come on, you deserve it.'

Supermother. Right. I turned away and gulped in air, trying to clamp down on the emotions swirling inside.

'It's a nice thought. Thank you.' I forced myself to face him, lifting my lips in what must have been the fakest smile ever. 'It's just, well, I'm a little tired, and—'

'I think we'll always be a little tired from here on in.' David caught my fingers. 'Come on, Charlotte. Please? I feel like we haven't properly talked for ages. Let's ditch the show. We can just go for a drink or something. The Prince Albert?'

Something shifted inside me at the mention of the pub across the street, the place we used to go for a Friday night drink together at the end of the long week. We'd stay for more pints than expected, then stumble across the road and into bed to make love. Longing flashed through me, but as soon as I recognised it, I pushed it away.

'I can't,' I said, shaking my head.

'Not even for a quick pint? We don't need to stay long. Come on, it will do you good to get away.' He swallowed. 'I miss you.'

I looked into his eyes, his words echoing in my ears. Who exactly did he miss? Madam Vice-President, like he used to call me? The woman who'd cared more about her job than making sure her child was okay?

'I'm sorry,' I mumbled. 'But I need to stay here.' My heart ached, but I steeled myself against it.

Then I spun away from my husband and into the room where Anabelle was sleeping.

CHAPTER TWENTY-NINE

'Come on, it will only take a minute. Snip, snip, and you're done!' Charlotte tries to drag an unwilling Anabelle into Moby's, a hair salon just off the King's Road. Her daughter's fringe is now covering her eyes, and a haircut is well overdue. But Anabelle's having none of it, gripping on to the doorframe.

Charlotte grits her teeth, bearing down on the impatience and frustration boiling inside. After a fractious night in which Anabelle couldn't settle for some reason, they'd both woken up on the wrong side of the bed. The morning had been punctuated by tantrums and crying, and Charlotte had looked forward to this appointment as the temporary light at the end of a very noisy, sticky tunnel. She loves hair salons: the sense of peace when you walk in the door, the feeling that you can switch off and indulge your love of trashy magazines with no one to judge you, and leave refreshed and revived, a better version of the person who'd walked in the door.

Even though this is for Anabelle and not for her, she couldn't wait. She'd pictured her daughter sitting placidly in the chair while Charlotte chatted to the hairdresser, having a little human interaction for once. She'd never realised how isolating staying at home with your child can be, and although she's in no hurry to chat up other smug mums, it would be nice to feel she's not alone in this world.

Finally Charlotte manages to prise Anabelle's clinging fingers off the door frame and coax her over to the stylist with a smile firmly nailed on to her face.

'Are you Anabelle?' the stylist asks, checking her clipboard. 'Hello.' She gestures to the chair, and Charlotte lifts her daughter into it, feeling sweat trickle down her spine. 'And hello, Mum.' She turns her grin on Charlotte. 'How are we today?'

Hello, *Mum*? Is that her new name? Apparently so, because that's how the stylist addresses her throughout the whole torturous session, every instance setting Charlotte's teeth on edge more and more.

'I'm Charlotte,' she snaps when she can't bear it any longer.

The stylist turns to her in surprise. 'Oh, sorry.' She raises her eyebrows at her colleague and they exchange a look, clearly not caring that Charlotte can see them.

As Charlotte does everything in her power to keep her daughter still – she's seconds from being jabbed in the eyeball with the scissors at one point – her mind spins. To these women and everyone else she meets, she is a generic 'mum', just another woman who stays at home while her husband goes out to work. That is her job, her role, her identity, now and for the foreseeable future. She looks up at her reflection in the mirror, taking in the mumsy brown bob and grey roots. This is *her*.

'How quickly do you think you can cut my hair?' The question bursts out of her before she can stop it. She hadn't come for a new style, but now that she's thought of it, desire flares inside.

The stylist glances over at her. 'What do you want done?'

'Short pixie cut,' Charlotte says, without having to think twice. That's how she remembers herself. That's who she is.

'Thirty minutes, give or take,' the stylist says. 'If you don't mind not having a blow dry afterwards. I can do you straight after your daughter.'

Oh, *Anabelle*. Charlotte glances down at her daughter, remembering that she's there. Shit. 'Anabelle, I'm going to get my hair cut after you, okay? It won't take long.' *And hopefully it won't cost too much*, she thinks, realising she still needs to talk to David about finances. Two haircuts in some Chelsea salons would buy a small car in other parts of the world.

'Nooooo!' Anabelle lets out a wail. 'Home after this. I want to go home!'

Charlotte draws in a breath, having learned that showing her frustration will only make Anabelle dig in harder. She wants this haircut. She needs this haircut – regardless of the cost. Time to bring out the big guns. 'Right, how about an ice cream afterwards at that place you love around the corner? *Three* scoops!'

Anabelle's mouth drops open. 'Three? Promise?'

Charlotte nods. 'Absolutely.'

Half an hour later, long locks of Charlotte's mousy brown hair lie in clumps on the floor. She shakes her head and smiles, loving how light she feels – both inside and out. It's not just a haircut: it's embracing who she is now. 'God, that's better. Thank you.'

'No problem. You'll need a colour again soon if you want to cover those roots.'

Charlotte nods. She'll pick up a box of black hair dye on the way home after ice cream. David will be stunned when he sees her – he always loved her with short hair, nuzzling her bare neck. She bites her lip. Or will he even notice? He barely looks at her any more, even when she swoops over to kiss him when he's home from work – on the rare occasions she's not already snoozing on the sofa. They're more like roommates these days than husband and wife.

Anabelle glances up from the magazine she's been ripping apart, her mouth dropping open when she spots her mother. 'Mama! Where's your hair gone? What happened?' Her little face crumples. 'I don't like it! Put your hair back on! Mama, please!'

She dissolves into tears and Charlotte stares at her, unsure what to do. She'd never have imagined Anabelle would react this way to a haircut, of all things. Then a memory flashes into her mind of when her father shaved his beard – she must have been about three? She'd taken one look at him and started sobbing. It had been him and yet it wasn't, and the change had been overwhelming. According to her father, she'd cried for a week.

She feels the stylist's eyes on her, and she bends down to engulf her daughter in a hug. 'It's okay, Anabelle. It's just hair. I'm the same person you always knew.' She swallows, knowing that's not true. 'I'm still your mother.' The word sticks in her throat, and she realises it's the first time she's said those words aloud.

She's not the same person Anabelle knows, but whoever she is now, she *is* still a mother . . . and maybe, just maybe, she's getting a little bit better at being one. She lets out her breath as Anabelle's tears subside now that she's in Charlotte's arms.

'Come on.' Charlotte wipes Anabelle's tears and gives her another quick cuddle, relieved that, unlike her younger self, Anabelle's not going to cry for a week. 'Let's go and get that ice cream.'

Anabelle slides from the chair and grabs Charlotte's hand, chattering away once again. As they head back out to the front, Charlotte glimpses herself in the mirror. Even with the soon-to-be-gone grey streaks and the few extra wrinkles, she looks like herself again – the professional, switched-on woman who wore business suits and was a shoo-in to be the next VP. Then she takes in the rest of the image: Anabelle clinging to her hand, her jeggings and her faded T-shirt. Charlotte blinks, trying to assimilate her newly coiffed head with the rest of the reflection, but the juxtaposition is so jarring.

Will she ever be able to completely let go of the person she was before Anabelle came along? Does she even *want* to now? She'd followed the doctor's advice and tried to walk the path of motherhood, but that doesn't seem to be working. It's been well over a month since the accident, and although she does feel more connected to Anabelle, she keeps waiting for the rush of maternal love that Lily spoke about – and that she herself must have experienced to sweep her life off-track. She's starting to think it's never going to happen.

And with every day that passes, her desire to return to that path is only diminishing.

CHAPTER THIRTY

'Park! Park!' Anabelle shouts through a mouthful of Cheerios, early one blustery morning.

'Hmm . . .' Charlotte chews her cereal, heart sinking at the thought of going back to the park. Despite living here for years, she'd never even *been* to the park around the corner until recently, but she's definitely making up for lost time. Over the past few weeks, she and Anabelle must have gone there at least once a day. And while there's something so invigorating about breathing in fresh air, she's not in the mood to hoist her daughter up the sand-encrusted ladder or dig with a stick in the woodchips. Not to mention that the weather today isn't exactly inviting.

'Let's do something besides the park,' she says, grabbing her phone to scan her weekly calendar. She cringes, noticing the only indoor activity available is a music class at a nearby church hall. According to her calendar, she used to take Anabelle there quite a bit. Lots of kids shoved into a small room with jangling tambourines doesn't exactly sound like the ideal way to pass an hour. But actually, she can kind of understand now why she'd go there: at least there's adult company. Some of the women she must have met at these places have messaged her over the past few weeks asking where she's been, but she hasn't responded. In fact, she hasn't talked to anyone over the age of three since the outing to the hair salon – her husband excluded, of course. But then, you could barely call what they did 'talking'.

She sighs, remembering his reaction to her new hair. By the time he'd got home that night, she'd transformed her locks from their hideous brown-grey to a glossy black. She'd even put on make-up, making her eyes a sultry grey and her lips bright red. A full face of make-up had looked ridiculous with jeggings and a T-shirt, so she'd thrown on a leopard-print jumper she'd found shoved to the back of the wardrobe and a pair of black skinny jeans that she could just about fit into. Then she'd perched on the sofa and waited for David to come home – not quite sure what she wanted him to do, but hoping that, maybe, her transformation would trigger something between them; remind them of how they used to be.

David had taken one look at her, raised his eyebrows, then gone straight to the bathroom to have a shower. Unable to damp down her frustration any longer, she'd followed him and yanked the door open.

'Do you like it?' she'd asked. 'What do you think?'

She knew he liked it – he'd told her the haircut suited her so many times in the past – but she wanted to hear him say it. If she couldn't get him to say he loved her, at least he could say he loved her hair.

'It's nice,' David responded with a sigh, as if even those words were too much to utter. 'But didn't you always complain it was a lot of upkeep? And really expensive to go to the stylist every six weeks, too?'

He'd turned on the shower before she could even answer. Charlotte had backed out of the bathroom, disappointment and hurt stinging inside. For the first time, it felt like he wasn't just rejecting the woman he'd argued with, the mother who'd wanted more kids. He was rejecting *her*, the woman she'd been before Anabelle. The woman who'd relied on him to calm the whirlwind inside her, and the woman who loved him now without the complications and burdens the past three years had heaped upon them.

But he's not the man she remembers, she realises with a jolt – the man who'd always been there. He'd kept a vital secret from her for years, and had allowed himself to be held at a distance from their daughter.

The David she knew would never have stepped away; would never have let guilt drag him down.

He'd changed, like she had, too. And she doesn't know him now, any more than she knows the woman she'd become after having Anabelle. The thought digs uncomfortably into her brain as her doubts balloon. Is it possible to reconnect, if they've both changed so much? Who *are* they as a couple now?

What she really needs right now is a friend. Maybe Lily could come over – or they could hit the music class together? Lily might treat her as mother extraordinaire, but at least she knows the old Charlotte. Charlotte's tried calling several times, but despite her hope of rekindling their friendship, she hasn't managed to connect with Lily since her visit weeks ago. Given how much work a three year old is, a newborn must be excruciating, and Charlotte can understand why most of her friends faded away once they had kids. Even so, Lily must still be chomping at the bit to get out of the house. Liam's too young to hit a drum, but he might enjoy the music, and she and Lily can chat without worrying about their kids crying and disturbing others, at the very least.

Charlotte clicks on Lily's contact information and hits 'Call', turning on the TV to keep Anabelle occupied for hopefully longer than a minute. She'll never take making a phone call in silence for granted again.

'Hello?' Lily's voice is a whisper.

'Lils? It's Charlotte.'

'Oh, hi. Sorry, I've just put Liam down for a nap.'

Lucky thing, Charlotte thinks. She'd give anything to put Anabelle down for a nap, but the one day her daughter did drift off in the afternoon, she didn't go to sleep again until ten at night. David had shaken his head, asking what on earth Charlotte had been thinking, before realising she didn't know any of that stuff. She'd quickly brushed up on it, learning never to give Anabelle a lie-down if you wanted an evening of silence. The hour of peace wasn't worth the evening of pain.

'Listen, Anabelle and I might head to a music class in St Matthew's Church in about an hour. I know Liam's a little young, but I thought you guys might like to join us? It's a good way to kill an hour or two!' Charlotte winces at her words, remembering too late that she apparently cherishes every minute with her daughter.

But Lily doesn't seem to notice. 'Does the outside world still exist?' she asks. 'God, I can barely remember the last time I left the flat. It's all been such a blur, and to be honest, this breastfeeding thing is bloody hard. I mean, I love it,' she adds quickly, 'and I thought we were getting on fine. Turns out Liam's not gaining enough weight.' Charlotte can hear the stress crackling in her friend's voice. 'I don't get it. I mean, he feeds for *hours*. How can he not be gaining weight?'

Charlotte stays silent, wanting to comfort her friend but unsure what to say. If she ate for hours, she'd be the size of a baby elephant. Clearly it's not the same for newborns.

'Anyway.' Lily swallows. 'I think we'd better stay in. I don't know how he'd feed in a noisy place, and I don't want to risk him losing more weight. I just want to crack this, you know? Then I'll be able to relax a bit. I really want to enjoy this time, after trying so hard to have a baby.'

Charlotte nods, thinking how funny it is that she's in the same place as Lily: they've both faced challenges when it comes to children, leading them to narrow their focus. The only difference is that, for Lily, it's still very early days in her journey as a mother. It makes sense that she'd want to pour everything into her newborn; he'd need that from her. But in Charlotte's case . . . well, it's three years on, and she's still giving everything to her child. That's fine if it makes her happy, but right now, she's anything but.

'Well, maybe you two can come over here later this afternoon? I'll make sure it's nice and quiet.' Charlotte's voice is tainted with desperation now, and she swallows it down again. She's not desperate. Well . . . maybe a little. She just needs someone familiar in her world, someone who cares for her and loves her. She blinks back the tears that have come from somewhere, telling herself to get a grip.

'I'd love to, but we should probably stick around here,' Lily says, and Charlotte's heart sinks. 'I'm not sure how much company I'd be, anyway – I'd probably fall asleep on your sofa. The other night I drifted off when I was trying to eat a piece of leftover pizza while holding Liam at the same time. When I woke up his little head was covered with pepperoni!'

Charlotte bursts out laughing at the image, and despite the dismay in Lily's voice, she starts laughing, too. For a second, it feels just like old times.

'Okay,' Charlotte says slowly. 'Well, we're free all week.' God, were they ever. 'What are you guys up to tomorrow?'

'The health visitor is coming over to check Liam's weight,' Lily says. 'And the day after, he has an appointment with the cranial osteopath. I'm hoping that helps his feeding.'

'Right.' Charlotte's more disappointed than she wants to admit. 'Lils . . . We should book a night out, just the two of us.' The thought flashes into her mind, and she grins. What a great idea! What she wouldn't give for an evening out to escape from all this for a few hours. 'In a few months' time, I mean,' she adds hastily, remembering Liam's weight issues. 'And you know what? We could even do a girls' weekend away! Just the two of us, somewhere with a posh spa. Loads of champagne and relaxing massages . . . that would be bliss.'

Excitement filters into her at the thought. She and Lily haven't been away together in ages! Even before they had children, Lily stuck to her fertility schedule, while Charlotte was often too busy working then relaxing with David. But they don't have those obstacles now, do they? They can leave the babies with their husbands and *escape*.

It would be good to get away, too, and do something outside of London. Charlotte used to love leaving the city every once in a while, even just for the day. Driving back along the motorway, with the high-rises glowing orange as the sun set behind them . . . something always stirred inside her, reminding her that for all the countryside's virtues, *this* was her place.

Well, until they move to the suburbs, that is. Her heart sinks just thinking about it.

'Oh my God, remember that time you booked us a weekend away on one of those last-minute discount sites? Where our "secret top-grade hotel" turned out to be a caravan in the middle of a field?' Lily laughs.

'And where the "spa" was actually an outdoor mud bath . . . well, more like mud puddle,' Charlotte recalls with a snort. That weekend should have been a disaster, but she and Lily had a blast rolling around in the mud as rain poured from the leaden sky. Their caravan had no heat, no TV and a toilet that barely flushed, but somehow the time had flown by as they made their way through the stack of board games and trashy paperbacks while sipping the paint-stripper cocktails Lily had concocted.

'I promise it'll actually be posh this time,' Charlotte says. 'With heating.'

'Maybe.' Lily's voice is hesitant. 'Right now, Liam starts crying if I put him down for even a second. It's hard to picture being away from him for that long. But maybe in a year or two, when I'm finished breastfeeding. Some mums in my group are planning on breastfeeding as long as their kids want to. I'm not sure I'll go that far, but I am aiming for two years.'

Charlotte tries to stop a yelp from escaping. *Two years?* What about work? Lily loves her teaching job, and despite her constant complaints about her students, they love her, too. Charlotte's seen the little notes and cards they give her at the end of each school year, surprisingly touching for secondary school hooligans. 'You're not planning to go back to teaching?' The question pops out before she remembers that perhaps she should already know the answer.

'We'll see,' Lily responds. 'I want to savour these early years – they'll only come around once. I love my students, but I don't want to be pulled between them and Liam. I don't want to be a crap teacher *and* a crap mother, and to be honest, I'm not sure I can do both well.' She pauses. 'Most of the mums in my group think the same way. Only one is going back to work after three months, and we all feel so sorry for her. I can't imagine being away from Liam all day, every day.'

Only *one* is going back to work? *Shit.* Charlotte had thought her all-in attitude towards motherhood was an exception, propelled forward by her daughter's tough start. But maybe there are more women out there like her than she'd thought – women who haven't been through what she has and who still want to give their all; women who'd had good jobs and a full life before kids.

Women who prefer to put 'mother' as their primary occupation.

Surely it hasn't always been like that? Charlotte thinks back to her own mother, who went on a work trip to Kenya for three weeks when Charlotte was only a few months old – she still has the doll her mother brought back somewhere. And her mother wasn't alone. Her mum's friends were similar, heading off for nights out and leaving their children in the care of teens who were barely out of childhood themselves.

Her mother. As Liam's cries filter down the phone and Lily hurriedly says goodbye, Charlotte wonders when she last spoke to her mum. She's been travelling on and off since the accident, and despite an elaborate game of phone tag (typical for the two of them), Charlotte has yet to tell her of the memory loss. It's always been like that: whenever Charlotte had a problem, she'd go to her father for help and support. After his death, she would turn to Lily . . . and then David. Her mum was the one to provide practical advice and workplace strategies, not emotional support, and Charlotte was fine with that. They may not have had a typical lovey-dovey mother–daughter relationship, but her mother was a great role model. She was the first to encourage Charlotte to work harder, to never take no for an answer, and to never let anyone derail her from her chosen career path. Charlotte had tried her best to emulate her – with success.

What did her mother think of her daughter now that she was a stay-at-home mum? Would Charlotte have talked to her about how happy she was being a mother, or would she have shied away from disappointing the woman whose drive and ambition she'd always admired?

Suddenly Charlotte feels the urge to talk to her . . . to someone who knows what it's like to want more from life than procreation. She pulls up her mother's contact and hits 'Call', praying she picks up this time.

'Charlotte!' Her mum's smooth voice comes on the line. 'Long time no talk, my dear. I'm sorry, it's been absolute craziness over here, as per usual. How are you? How's my granddaughter?'

'We're all fine,' Charlotte says, pleased that, despite the passage of time, some things have remained the same. For as long as she can remember, it's been 'absolute craziness' at her mother's office. 'Well, some of us more than others.'

'Oh?' Charlotte can hear her mother clacking away on her laptop; she's always been the queen of multitasking. Charlotte would be offended, but she knows her mum can do half a dozen things at once much better than someone focusing on one thing at a time.

'I was in an accident a few weeks ago,' Charlotte says. 'And, well . . . I can't remember anything from the past four years or so. I mean, not getting pregnant, not having Anabelle, none of it.'

'Crikey,' her mum says without missing a beat, and Charlotte smiles. Typical Mum, taking everything in her stride. 'Have you been to the doctor, just to make sure everything's okay?'

'I have,' Charlotte answers. 'A top neurologist in Harley Street, who told me the memories may or may not come back. All I can do is wait.'

'Well, that's helpful,' her mother says with derision.

Charlotte laughs. Exactly what she'd thought. God, it's good to talk to her. 'I know. And I've been trying to carry on as I did before the accident, but . . . it feels so weird. I mean, I feel like I'm living someone else's life.' Her voice tightens as frustration churns inside, and tears fill her eyes. 'It sounds like I was incredibly happy, staying home with Anabelle. But right now, I can't help feeling I've thrown away everything I used to want. And I miss it, you know. I miss going to the office, the meetings, everything. I miss being *me*.' The words leave her mouth in an anguished cry, and a tear streaks down her cheek as she realises just how much she means them.

'Oh, my dear,' her mum says in a soft voice, and for an instant, Charlotte would give anything to have her mother's arms around her, even though she can't remember the last time they hugged. 'It must be an incredible adjustment for you right now. I can't begin to imagine. How are you holding up?'

Charlotte sighs. 'I'm trying. I'm doing everything I can to remember being a mother, why I wanted to stay home. But . . .'

'But?' her mum prompts.

'Well, there are some good bits,' Charlotte says in a rush, as if to justify what she's about to say. 'I mean, Anabelle's a great kid. And it *is* nice to see the outside world in daylight. It's fun doing silly stuff with her.' Charlotte smiles as she thinks of the slug painting and the fun they'd had with flour. Anabelle's bright face flashes into her mind, and a warm feeling goes through her. 'But just staying home . . . it's not enough. I wish it was, but it's not.'

Her mum laughs. 'It wasn't for me, either.'

'What do you mean?' Charlotte's mouth drops open. 'You never stayed home with me – not for a long time, anyway. You were back to work after weeks.'

'Yes, that's true,' her mum says. 'But within a few months, the company made me redundant. I was the easiest candidate, since I'd come back from maternity leave, even if I wasn't off for long. I was home with you for a few months while I looked for other work, and I have to say that those few months – even with your father around – were the most challenging of my life. I was chomping at the bit to get back to work, although your father said he could find a job and let me stay at home.' She pauses. 'That doesn't mean I loved you any less, that I didn't care about your future, or that I was any less of a mum. It just means that that set-up wasn't for me.'

'Oh, I know,' Charlotte says quickly. 'But I was happy before the accident, you know? Happy with this life. It *was* for me.'

'Perhaps you were content,' her mum said. 'But things change, and there's no right or wrong way to be a mum. You need to do what you think is best for your family . . . and for *you*. You may have a child – a child who had a difficult start – but you are still a person in your own right. I sometimes wondered if you'd forgotten that, although you rabidly denied any suggestion of it. Maybe this is your chance to remember.' She laughs. 'Bad choice of words, but you know what I mean.'

Charlotte nods. 'I do know what you mean.'

There's a voice in the background, and her mother sighs. 'Right, I'd better go,' she says. 'Call me later, if you want. We can chat more then.'

Charlotte clicks off, gazing over at Anabelle as her mother's words run through her head. *There's no right or wrong way to be a mum.* Is she right? Does every woman need to make their own way forward through the tangle of clashing identities, needs and wants to strike a balance that works for them? Charlotte knows with absolute certainty now that she can't stay at home with her daughter any longer, but *is* it possible to embrace her career with the same pre-kid fervour and be a mother at the same time, or – as Lily worries – will she fail at both? She's only really starting to learn how to be a mother again.

She pictures herself living the life her mum did: rarely seeing her daughter on weekdays, working late into the night and flying off for weeks on end, and something twists inside her. How would Anabelle cope? Would she miss her mother and cry for her at night? After all, the little girl has been with her non-stop since she was born, barring those few days after the accident. Charlotte watches as she happily shoves a dolly's hand into her mouth. She'll adjust – that's what people always say about kids, isn't it? That they're so adaptable? As her own mother did for her, she'd be providing Anabelle with a brilliant role model.

And as for David, well . . . he might be distant, but hopefully he'd jump at the chance to bond with his daughter again by taking over some of her care, as he did after the accident. Maybe Charlotte going back to work will ease some of his guilt about Anabelle's condition, too. Or maybe not? She sighs, wondering again if they will be able to reconnect.

She'll miss the time she's spent with Anabelle, Charlotte realises suddenly. But it's time to take her life off pause. Maybe her memories will come back in a gush or a trickle. Maybe she'll never remember those few missing years. But there's one thing she knows for sure: this life of absolute motherhood isn't for her, any more than it was for her mother.

CHAPTER THIRTY-ONE

14 May

Already it's been six months since Anabelle was born . . . six months of fear, of worry, of guilt, of *love*. Six months, and my world has changed beyond all recognition.

Life goes on outside the flat. The buses heave past the window, their brakes squealing as if in pain. Green leaves have sprouted on trees, and pollen dances in the golden sun. Heavy grey skies give way to blue, and bare shoulders and legs appear in place of winter woollies as people hurry to work.

But instead of blossoming like the world around me, I'm still in winter mode: wrapped up snugly, keeping what's dear close by. My life consists of these four walls. I know every squeak of the floorboard that threatens to wake Anabelle, and my eyes have traced each crack in the ceiling as I wait for her to sleep. I know the number of steps from our bedroom to the lounge and back again, as I jiggle her back and forth, back and forth. I know how the patch of sun moves from the front window to the back, telling me what time it is without me even looking at the clock.

This is my domain now, mine and my daughter's, with David like a guest in our household. He hasn't spent the hours here each day like I have – the hours I hadn't, either, before Anabelle was born. He doesn't know the dog that barks each day at eleven o'clock, or the *thunk* of the post at two. These daily markers anchor my day, and they're all foreign to him.

He doesn't know Anabelle like I do, either: the shuddery sigh that means she's succumbed to sleep, or the high-pitched squeal when something delights her. She is a subject I've studied exhaustively, almost as if I'm going to be tested. Her latest check-up shows I've passed: her weight and development are right on track, she's wonderfully chubby, and the stronger she gets, the more the sharp pain of what I've done eases. So far, I've managed to sidestep the consequences of my carelessness, and I've never been more thankful.

David seems happy to hand her care over to me; he's finally moved aside. Where before he'd attempt to give her a bottle, now he looks at me when she cries. He doesn't try to take her out to the park without me, and he doesn't dress her without consultation on temperature, weather and general atmospheric pressure. He doesn't give me that look any more when I worry if she's ill, or not eating, or that she feels a little warm – a look I still can't decipher.

He's stopped trying to get me to go out, too. I have to give him credit: he persisted for a while after the disastrous Valentine's Day, only backing off when I told him he could book us dinner at the Ritz and I still wouldn't go; that nothing he could offer would tempt me away from my daughter. The words were harsh and I regretted them the instant they were out, but his kindness was killing me. He wouldn't be kind if he knew what I'd done . . . or, rather, what I should have done.

We haven't made love since Anabelle was born. And now that I'm over those exhausting newborn days, I *do* miss him – miss the closeness and intimacy – but I still can't open myself up. The heavy weight of guilt pressing down on me is only just starting to shift, and the thorn inside my heart is twisting less . . . or maybe I'm getting used to it. I can breathe now and look around; I can fill my lungs instead of gasping with my eyes shut tight. But I can't move towards anything other than my daughter, and it's easier to push him away and tell him I'm tired. Half the time, he falls asleep on the sofa. Not wanting to disturb me and Anabelle, he ends up staying there all night.

Miriam keeps going on about baby groups, play dates and music classes. She even printed out a schedule of all the activities in the area, highlighting ones she thinks I'll enjoy and talking about the benefits of meeting other stay-at-home mothers. The phrase made me jerk: is that what I am? Although I've quit my job, I've never really thought of myself like that, and something about the words made my gut shift uncomfortably.

Even if I am a stay-at-home mum, I can't picture myself striking up friendships with the mothers I see when I *do* take Anabelle out, on those rare occasions when the sun actually shines: all bouncy hair, immaculate make-up and back in their skinny jeans already. I'm lucky if I can fit a leg into mine, but then losing weight hasn't exactly been high on my list of priorities. I couldn't care less how I look right now. I've even started growing out my hair so I don't need to hit the hair salon every six weeks like I used to. Anyway, I don't need more company. Anabelle and I are happy together, just the two of us.

The only person I've seen more than a handful of times is Lily . . . Lily, who's still trying to have her baby. I'd feared our friendship was over, but she's surprised me by dropping in every few weeks, bearing gifts: soft toys for Anabelle, bubble bath and chocolate for me (chocolate devoured; bubble bath still unopened). She stares at Anabelle with a mixture of such envy and longing that I have to look away. I understand, in a way I never did before, how lucky I am to have my daughter. Seeing Lily is a harsh reminder of how flippant I was about having children, and how woefully negligent I was with my daughter in the womb.

In her eyes, I am different now. I'm not the person she met over dinner just a few months ago . . . the woman who was heading back to work after just six weeks. *Six weeks!* I'm a mother – a mother who almost lost her child, and she treats me with gravitas, asking question after question about Anabelle's health and how she's getting on, telling me how much she admires my total dedication to my child. It almost feels like she's put me on a pedestal, as if my desire to protect my child, that fierce maternal instinct she thought I lacked, will somehow inspire her body to procreate. I hope it can. If anyone deserves it, it's her.

After each visit from my oldest friend, I'm left feeling off-balance, like there's a mismatch between what she's seeing and what I actually am. Because my decision to quit my job wasn't just down to a desire to be with Anabelle. That was a huge part of it, of course, but it was also down to guilt – guilt, and a fear that I might let that job hurt my daughter again. Stepping away from Cellbril was a kind of atonement, a way to prove to myself that I am worthy of my daughter, despite my earlier actions.

Six months later – six wonderful months cocooned with my daughter – and I'm only too happy to have left that world. I had to, for me and for Anabelle. I'll never regret it. But lately, in the dark of night when everything is silent and it's just me awake, I get out of bed and pad to the kitchen – past David on the sofa – and stand there, gazing out the window. I stare at the life on the street below, and I remember striding down the pavement in my high heels, the potential of the day pulling me forward. I remember feeling my brain buzzing, my phone bleeping.

I remember being more than a mother.

Maybe I will be again. Maybe, with time, I'll be ready to emerge from this protective place; this enclosed world with my daughter. My shell will have hardened, and I'll face the outside world without being sucked in. I'll hug my husband and let his love lift me up, instead of feeling like it might crack me open.

Not now, though. Not yet.

CHAPTER THIRTY-TWO

'Hello! I'm here!'

Charlotte grins at the sound of Miriam's voice, nerves rushing through her at the thought of the evening ahead with David. After talking to her mother yesterday and deciding to go back to work, she's felt so energetic and lit up, buzzing in a way she hasn't since the accident. Now she just needs to talk to David about it, and getting him out of the flat into neutral territory seems the ideal way to do it. Miriam jumped at the chance to babysit, and even though Charlotte's still fuzzy on their financial big picture, their joint bank account balance looked healthy enough to cope with a splurge on last-minute tickets to see one of David's favourite cellists at Wigmore Hall. They were a bit pricey, but she'll be working soon, so . . .

Okay, so it's a little last minute – and a bit of a risk, given the state of their relationship. She used to plan surprises for him all the time, though. Checking the *Time Out* listings and booking something each weekend was a regular occurrence before they had Anabelle. David would jokingly dare her to book the most outlandish show possible, and in the years they'd been together, they must have been to every fringe theatre in London, no matter how hidden away or small.

Charlotte grimaces, remembering the 'immersive' performance in a grotty pub in Peckham where the actors threw jelly at the audience.

She and David had emerged slimy and sticky, but they'd laughed about it for years.

'Thanks for coming,' Charlotte says, ushering Miriam in. 'David's on his way home now, and Anabelle's—' She stops as her daughter rushes into Miriam's arms. *That's them sorted*, she thinks, watching Anabelle drag her grandmother into the lounge. She feels a slight pang that she won't get to finish that book she and Anabelle started reading for her bedtime story last night. Unusually, Anabelle had fallen asleep halfway through. Charlotte had stayed snuggled up with her, cosy and warm in the darkness, almost falling asleep herself.

She heads to the bedroom to get ready, wondering what to wear – feeling almost like it's a first date again. She pulls the curtains, then slides off her clothes and selects the only suitable outfit she can find: dark jeans and a plain black top that she jazzes up with a pendant necklace, completing the look with sparkly dangling earrings. The clothes are a bit tighter than she remembers, and here in the chaos of the bedroom, the earrings feel a little . . . over the top. She makes a face, remembering how silly she felt when she'd slathered on the make-up and dressed up after her haircut, only to be pushed aside.

Is she being naïve to hope that a night out, a great outfit and a new outlook will be enough to bring them back together? Because it's not just a new outlook for her: it's a chance for them to work as a team, caring for Anabelle together for the first time since she was born. The past three years may have changed her husband in ways she couldn't have imagined, but perhaps they can all find a new way forward. Hope flares inside that they can make it through this.

'Mummy, where are you?'

Charlotte jerks at Anabelle's voice. 'Coming!'

She throws open the door with dramatic flair and strikes a pose, then prances into the lounge. Miriam and Anabelle clap and cheer, and Miriam even lets out a wolf-whistle. Charlotte cocks her head towards her mother-in-law in surprise. She hadn't known Miriam had it in her.

Then again, she hadn't known much about her at all – besides her desire for grandkids and her devotion to her sons. And while Charlotte still doesn't know her well, she understands her more – and respects her. Being with Anabelle these past few weeks has shown how difficult being a mother is, and to do it all on your own with three children . . . no wonder Miriam is still so invested in her sons. Raising them alone had claimed all of her, and Charlotte can now grasp just how consuming that must have been.

Charlotte does another shimmy and a wiggle before tripping over a toy and falling, shrieking, on to the sofa. Miriam and Anabelle collapse in giggles.

'What's going on in here?' David's voice cuts through the noise, and they all look up to see him staring askance at them. He gives Anabelle a kiss and a cuddle then hugs Miriam.

'Kiss Mummy!' Anabelle cries out. 'Daddy, kiss Mummy!'

Charlotte can't help smiling at Anabelle's insistence, even though David's expression is carefully blank. He lowers his head towards her, and she grabs his shoulders and plants a huge kiss on his lips, tightening her grasp so he can't move away. For a second – for just a split second – she swears she can feel him relax into her embrace.

'Right, I'm taking you out tonight!' she says, striking while the iron is hot – or, at least, not frigid. 'Miriam's going to babysit.'

'What?' David's mouth drops open. 'No, no. That's fine. I'm knackered. Mum, thanks for coming, but it really wasn't necessary. Stay for dinner, please. I'm sure Charlotte can knock up something delicious.'

Charlotte's heart drops. She'd known she would face resistance, but she hadn't expected David to reject the idea outright – not with her already dressed and Miriam here.

'No, no, *no.*' Miriam wags a finger in David's face, like he's her little boy again. 'You two deserve an evening out. It's been ages since either of you let loose a bit. I just hope you last a little longer than last time, Charlotte!'

Charlotte's brow furrows. Had there been another time? She'd thought she'd been glued to Anabelle's side. 'What do you mean?'

David sits down and kicks off his shoes. 'You went out with some other mums a while back, and, well . . . I don't know what happened, exactly. All I know is that you rushed home and straight into Anabelle's room.' He pauses and Charlotte strains to remember, but nothing comes to mind. A night out with other mums sounds like fun – if there's alcohol involved. She's surprised she actually went along. 'Okay, then. Since Mum came all this way, I guess we'd better not waste her time.'

It wasn't exactly the enthusiastic response Charlotte had craved, but at least he'd agreed. 'Great!' she says, forcing herself to sound upbeat and positive. 'Go and get changed, and let's get out of here!'

Half an hour later, she and David head down the stairs of their building and into the street. Charlotte takes a deep breath, relishing the evening air while at the same time hoping Miriam remembers where Anabelle's toothbrush is. She had pointed it out before leaving, but Miriam had been more focused on *Teletubbies* than on her instructions. She laughs under her breath, shaking her head. Here she is on her first night out in weeks and she's thinking about *toothbrushes*.

'What are we doing tonight, anyway?' David asks, looking straight ahead as they walk down the pavement towards the King's Road, where they can grab a taxi.

'I'm taking you to see Park Min at Wigmore Hall!' She grins at him triumphantly, anticipating his reaction.

'Park Min?' David's mouth drops open and he turns to face her. 'Really?' His eyes are bright and, for the first time in days, his face is alive.

Charlotte nods, thinking how handsome he looks tonight. He's ditched his usual out-of-office uniform of baggy jeans and a T-shirt for dark, slim-cut jeans and a crisp black shirt. If you didn't look too closely at the pair of them, they could almost pass for their pre-baby selves.

'I knew you'd like it.' She squeezes his hand. 'I thought we could see the concert, then have dinner in the area afterwards.'

'But Charlotte, those tickets must have cost a fortune.' David pulls his hand away, his long legs picking up pace as they stride down the pavement. 'It's just that we have to be careful, you know. With you not working, and—'

'David.' Charlotte grabs his arm, forcing him to a stop. 'Look, I wasn't going to tell you this until after the concert, but I don't want you to sit there worrying about money.' She takes a breath, excitement stirring inside. 'I want to go back to work,' she says. Anticipation flows into her just saying the words.

David's face stays neutral, in that blank expression she's come to know so well.

'I know I was happy to stay at home before, and I've tried to be again. I really have.' God, has she ever. 'Anabelle's a great kid,' she continues. 'Funny, bright . . .' A flash of pride goes through her that this clever girl is her child, and she can see from David's face that he's proud, too. 'But right now, I need more. I can't sit around hoping that one day I might remember . . . not any longer. We need to face the possibility that I might never regain my memories.' She pauses as a police car flashes by them, the siren drowning out everything in her head.

'I may never be that person who wanted more babies,' she says gently, and David's face twists. 'I may never be the mother who was content to make her child her life. I miss my career . . . so much. And I just need to get out there again.' Her voice breaks and she watches him carefully, hoping he'll understand. He must, right? He knew her before they had children. He knows what she's like.

David stares at her and silence falls between them. She holds his gaze, wondering for the millionth time what's running through his head.

'Before we had Anabelle, I was going to be the one to stay at home while you carried on with work,' he says finally. 'And you know, I was so excited. If you remember – you remember that bit, right? – I hated my job. To think I could trade it in to do something wonderful like raising our daughter was like a dream come true, a way for me to be what my father never was for me. A way to build something special, something I never had.'

Charlotte nods, cringing inside. She can't imagine how difficult it must have been for him to be pushed aside, stuck in a dead-end job while she lived out his desires. He'd clearly lived on the periphery of their lives, with hardly a look-in. Why had she done that to him?

She reaches out to take his hand again, drawing back when she discovers he's clenched his fingers in a fist. 'I'm sorry, David.'

'You don't need to apologise!' His voice rises, and Charlotte steps back in surprise. She can't remember the last time she heard him shout. He clears his throat and looks down at the ground. 'You might have pushed me away, but I let you. That was the price I had to pay for Anabelle suffering the way she did. For making you so scared, so fearful, that you felt you had to give up everything to protect our daughter.'

'David.' The word floats out of Charlotte's mouth in an incredulous tone. 'You don't need to pay a price! Anabelle needs you. I need you. And we'll need you even more when I go back to work. I might have work meetings, or travel, or—'

'If you want to go back to work, then you should,' he interrupts her. 'I'm hardly going to stop you, am I? Not after what happened with Anabelle.'

Charlotte lets out a puff of air. 'David, for the millionth time, what happened to Anabelle wasn't your fault. And you couldn't control my response to it, either. You need to stop beating yourself up about it.' What will it take for him to stop blaming himself?

'The only thing is . . . I probably won't be around to help out much,' he says slowly.

Charlotte freezes, fear shooting through her. 'What do you mean?'

'Before the accident, I was offered the opportunity to head up a new branch in Exeter.'

'You? Exeter?' She can barely get out the words.

David nods. 'It's a great chance for me to break into management. Not to mention build a team and a business from the ground up.'

Charlotte blinks. Does he actually look *excited*? 'But . . . but you hate your job.' Hadn't he just said that? She draws in a breath as it hits her that, for someone who hates his job, he seems to spend an awful lot of time there. She'd put it down to their difficult situation, but maybe there's more to it than that.

David laughs, but his face doesn't change. 'I did hate it, yes. But when you decided to stay at home, I was . . . well, I was stuck, in a way. If I couldn't help you at home, at least I could make a good life for the two of you. And so I threw myself into work, and somewhere along the way I started to like it. Maybe not the work itself, but feeling needed, valued. I may not make the big bucks, not like you did, but these past three years I've worked like a dog. I've been promoted twice, and this job in Exeter is a huge step forward.' There's a note of pride in his voice and Charlotte shakes her head. It's so odd to hear David speak about working his way up the ladder, not her.

'So . . . so we'd move there? To *Exeter*?' It might as well be to Mars, as far as she's concerned. How will she ever get a job there?

David lowers his head. 'Well, I figured I'd stay up there during the week and come home at weekends. Most weekends, anyway. Once or twice a month I'll need to be there on Saturdays.'

'*What?* You'd be gone all week?'

David runs a hand through his hair. 'Well, to be honest, I rarely see Anabelle during the week, anyway. I'm out the door before she gets up and she's in bed by the time I get home. I'll miss her, of course, but she probably won't even know I'm gone.'

But what about me? Charlotte wants to scream. What about *us*? Her mind's eye envisages night after night alone on the sofa, shovelling a takeaway into her mouth then heading to that big bed alone. She stares at him, realising with dread and disappointment that he *is* a stranger. Not only has he changed, he's changed almost beyond recognition. The David she knew – the *husband* she knew – would never have considered being away from her for so long. He would have found his way through anything – guilt, blame, pain – to be by her side. And what about Anabelle? David had always felt his father's lack of presence in his life, and now he was going to do the same thing to his daughter.

It was almost unimaginable.

'So you said yes?' Charlotte's voice emerges thready and weak.

'I haven't given them a firm answer yet. They haven't officially posted the job, but apparently I'm the top choice. They wanted to float it by me and give me a chance to think about it. The opportunity only came up the day before your accident, and of course I wanted to talk to you first.'

'But you want to go.' Heaviness presses down on her as the pieces fall into place: his reluctance to engage, how he'd continued to pull away even as she tried to draw him out. He *had* already checked out. 'Even if I don't want any more children? Even if we can work past what you told me at Lily's?'

'Charlotte . . .' David shakes his head. 'It's not just about having children. Things between us, well . . . they haven't been right for ages. And I don't know how to fix it. I don't even know where to start.'

Charlotte holds his gaze, her mind spinning. What can she say? What can she say to this stranger before her – a man who says he still loves her, but one she doesn't even know any more? What can she say when she doesn't even *remember* what went wrong in the first place?

'I think . . .' He draws in a breath. 'I think this will be a good chance to give us both some space, maybe a chance to reset,' David says. 'And obviously I'm not going anywhere until you and Anabelle are one hundred per cent okay. It'll be a few months before I need to go – they're constructing a whole new building for us. You were keen for us to move in with Mum so Anabelle could attend the great state school there. Maybe we could make the move sooner rather than later. Having Mum around might balance out me being away.'

Charlotte winces at the thought of the move she'd been planning . . . and all because of *schools*? There must be a million and one schools in London that Anabelle could attend. What had she been thinking? And moving in with Miriam would hardly be consolation for losing her husband! At least Anabelle would be raised be a beloved grandparent, not a nanny. Still . . . how will their daughter react when both her parents disappear from her life, popping up only at weekends? If Anabelle freaks out when her mother changes her hairstyle, how will she cope when that whole face is replaced by someone else's, even if it is her grandmother's? Because, like David, Charlotte won't be able to be home most nights before half seven or eight.

'It'll be super-convenient to have Mum right on hand, even if you don't find work straight away,' David continues, warming to his theme. 'And if you do eventually regain your memory and decide you don't want to work any more, you'll still have Mum there to keep you company. I don't like to think of you alone in central London.'

Then don't go! Charlotte wants to scream it aloud, but she knows there's no point.

Her head starts throbbing, and she puts a hand to her temple. What an idiot she's been, thinking this could be a new beginning for them, when her husband has already made plans to leave. Tears fill her eyes and she wills them not to spill over, not wanting David to witness any hint of vulnerability in her now. The last thing she wants from him is pity.

'Do you still want to see Park Min?' David asks, looking at her hesitantly. 'It'd be a shame to waste the tickets, but I understand if you don't . . .'

'Sure.' Charlotte lifts her chin and forces a smile, although it's the last thing she feels like doing. 'Let's go.' She's not going to let him see how her insides feel torn to bits, pain and grief oozing from them. He's not the person she'll turn to any longer. He's a person who's hurt her now.

Her, and Anabelle. A fiercely protective emotion swarms over her for an instant, surprising her with its power.

'Okay, then.' David looks hard at her again, then glances at his watch. 'We'd better hurry if we don't want to be late.'

And even as they walk down the pavement together, they've never seemed further apart.

CHAPTER THIRTY-THREE

20 October

Anabelle is crying, but I had to write. My mind is buzzing – with ideas, with thoughts, with *excitement*. Because something happened today. Something that yanked me out of the protected place I was in . . . something signalling that maybe, after almost a year with my baby, I'm ready to open up again. Anabelle will stay my top priority, of course. I'll never stray from that; I won't let myself. But perhaps it's time to start thinking about letting the world back in.

I was hauling the buggy frame in one hand and Anabelle in the other up the stairs when my mobile rang. Assuming it was David calling to say he'd be late yet again, I grabbed it from my back pocket and barked, 'Yes?' without even looking to see who was ringing.

'Charlotte, hello. It's Vivek.' The voice in my ears was a blast from the not-so-distant past, and I froze, trying to get a grip on my past crashing into my reality.

'Vivek! Hi.' My voice was breathless. Wrestling with the buggy frame, my daughter squirming in my grip, I cradled the phone between my shoulder and my ear and managed to open the door. In the process, the phone slipped from my grasp and skidded across the floorboards.

Shit! I dropped the buggy and ushered Anabelle inside, plopped her down in her cot to keep her contained and scooped up the phone.

'Sorry about that,' I said, trying to sound like I had everything under control.

Vivek laughed. 'Don't worry. Are you all right to talk now? It won't be for long, I promise.'

'Um, sure,' I answered, my mind spinning as I sank on to the sofa. What on earth could he be calling about? The last time we'd spoken was when I quit . . . when my world had been swirling in a storm of guilt, fear and exhaustion. I peered into the bedroom, where Anabelle was bouncing on the cot mattress, inches from hitting her chin on the bars. I cringed, praying she'd stay quiet and injury-free for the next ten minutes.

'I'm sorry to bother you,' Vivek said. 'If you're anything like my wife, you probably don't have a second to spare. I know what it's like with kids.'

'It is pretty crazy,' I said, that strange discomfort sliding over me at my new role as stay-at-home mum. It felt even more disconcerting talking to my boss, who'd only known me in a professional capacity.

'Right, well, Ed's assigning someone to pitch to Avema to renew their contract, and we couldn't find the last presentation you'd done for them. I told him you wouldn't mind a quick phone call to ask. It's not like you're with a competitor or anyone.' Vivek's voice was jolly, and my gut clenched. No, it wasn't like I was working for a competitor. It wasn't like I was working at all. A spark of jealousy crackled through me, and I shoved it away. I couldn't be jealous of Ed, the half-wit who'd taken over from me when I went on maternity leave.

'Oh, sure.' I cast my mind back, surprised at how quickly the information filtered into my brain. 'It'll be saved on the desktop, under the "pitch presentations". They should all be arranged alphabetically.'

'Hmm, well, Ed got a laptop upgrade when he was made VP,' Vivek said. 'I'm not sure if the folders are still in the same place.'

'VP?' I almost dropped the phone again. I couldn't have heard that correctly. He'd only just started a few months ago! 'Ed is VP of business development?'

'Yes, he's really exceeded our expectations,' Vivek said, and I could barely move for the jealousy churning inside me. 'The team love him, and he gave a solid, inspiring presentation to the board to bid for the position. He was the best candidate by far.'

After me, of course, I longed to add, but obviously I'd crossed myself off the list.

'But what about you?' My voice came out shaky, and I cleared my throat. 'You're not actually leaving, are you?'

'I guess the grapevine doesn't travel all the way to Chelsea,' Vivek joked. 'Well, I've decided it's finally time to retire. I'm taking off next week – just sticking around now to make sure Ed has everything in order.'

I sagged back on the sofa, anger rushing through me. I could have been VP. I *should* have been VP. I'd put in the years of hard work and training under Vivek. I'd excelled, I'd led the team and I'd been primed to take over.

The only thing I'd done wrong was have a baby.

My anger deflated suddenly, like a balloon had burst . . . because that wasn't the only thing I'd done wrong, not by a long shot. I'd made the right choice to leave, beyond a doubt. I'd never regret that. And of course I could never be VP, not now, not with Anabelle. I couldn't even risk returning to Cellbril, let alone taking on a position with more responsibility.

'You don't have the presentation on a memory stick or saved anywhere else, by any chance, do you?' Vivek's voice cut into my thoughts.

'No, I don't think so.' I pulled myself out of the cloud of emotion and tried to focus on his words. 'But listen, tell Ed that whoever's pitching to Avema needs to remember . . .' And I was off, information rolling from my tongue so easily it was like it had been waiting to be resurrected. 'Tell him to call me if he has any questions,' I continued. 'And—'

'I will,' Vivek interrupted. 'Thanks for all this; it's been really helpful. But listen, I can hear your baby crying, so I'd better let you go. Thanks again, Charlotte.'

And with that, he was gone. I jerked towards Anabelle, for the first time hearing her screams. I hurried over to the cot and picked her up, rocking her back and forth as I struggled to get a grip on the feelings rocketing through me. It had felt so good to talk about something I knew so much about – besides sleep schedules and weaning, that is. It had felt good to have someone *ask* me to contribute, even if it was just the location of a presentation.

I wanted more of that. I *needed* more of that, I realised suddenly. A blind had been yanked open inside, letting light stream in. I didn't want to close it again. I'd never go back to Cellbril, to the dark place where I risked my child. But maybe I could find a new way forward: a part-time job, a less intensive position, somewhere I could use my brain again.

I took a deep breath and set Anabelle on the floor, grinning as she lurched towards the sofa with her arms raised in victory. Walking before she's even a year old! I couldn't be prouder. She's ready to widen her world, and maybe it's time to take a page from my baby daughter's book.

It's been a year of uncertainty, of guilt and of fear, but that year is almost over. We made it through, and while I'll never forgive myself – never forget what I did; never dream of putting anything above my child again – perhaps it's time to start a new chapter.

I am ready now, and I can't wait.

CHAPTER THIRTY-FOUR

Even though the pouring rain traps Charlotte and Anabelle indoors, the day still passes quickly . . . well, relatively quickly. It's amazing how having something else to focus on – something besides her daughter – helps the hours tick by. Bedtime comes and goes, and Charlotte hardly knows where the time went. Okay, so only part of her brain was engaged with Anabelle, but you hardly need full brainpower to build up and knock down a set of bricks over and over. She nods and smiles, her mind running through what she needs to do to start her quest for gainful employment.

Having something to keep her mind off David's bombshell has been useful, too. Sitting beside him in the quiet concert hall last night had been pure torture. A million words had swirled through her head – words laced with fury, with pleas, with love. But when the lights had come on and they could talk again, she'd been paralysed, unable to release even one sentence. She still can't believe he's moving away, and she has absolutely no idea where they'll go from here. Bump along in separate lives until they finally call it quits and get divorced? She shudders just thinking of the 'd' word in relation to them . . . or, at least, the 'them' they used to be.

Once Anabelle is asleep, Charlotte realises with a start that she's barely genuinely interacted with her daughter all day . . . and she actually *misses* her. Anabelle was such a good girl, in high spirits and full of giggles. Charlotte really should have taken advantage of that and done something other than activities involving the least possible amount of input. Anabelle had begged constantly for watercolours, but Charlotte had put her off.

I'll make more of an effort tomorrow, she tells herself, pushing aside the rogue guilt that pricks her. Right now, she needs to work on finding a job.

First things first: she'll talk to Vivek. Fingers crossed he hasn't retired . . . Despite his rumblings, she'd give him a good ten years yet. Like her mother, work is his life. When he finds out that Charlotte wants to return, hopefully he'll be able to ease her way back in. After all, she is – was – his prodigy, and she did bring in one of the biggest contracts the company had ever seen. She sighs when it hits her that, actually, that was over four years ago. Still, her skills are invaluable, and it would definitely be easier to jump-start her career at a place she knows so well.

Charlotte glances at the clock. It's just after seven in the evening – Anabelle went down early for once – and Vivek will probably be in the office for another good few hours yet. Heart racing, she picks up her mobile and flicks through her contacts, clicking on his office number. It might be a call from the blue, but as Vivek always says, why bother emailing if you can ring? She'll show him she hasn't forgotten his advice.

She hits 'Call' and waits for a response, praying that Anabelle stays asleep.

'Ed Salter here.'

Charlotte yanks the phone from her ear. *Ed Salter?* Who the hell is that, and why is he answering Vivek's line?

'Hi, Ed. It's Charlotte McKay.' She pretends to know who he is, trying hard to keep her breathing even. Vivek's first rule of thumb is never to let anyone know you can't remember them.

'Charlotte McKay . . .' He pauses, and she rolls her eyes. Clearly this Ed bloke needs more training.

'I used to work there a few years ago, before I went off on maternity leave?' she says, trying not to reveal her exasperation when it becomes clear he won't be moving on until she identifies herself. Maybe they've never met, but this man really should learn how to bluff.

'Oh yes! *Charlotte!* God, it's been a while, hasn't it? I took over from you when you went off on mat leave, didn't I? How's the little one?'

'Brilliant.' This clown took over from her when she left? She feels sorry for her accounts . . . and almost relieved, for once, that she doesn't remember. It must have been torturous passing over her hard-won clients to someone else, even if she had thought it'd be just for a short time. 'Listen, is Vivek around?'

'Vivek?' There's a pause, and Ed lets out a low laugh. 'You really have been out of the loop, haven't you?'

More than out the loop, she thinks. More like out of her mind – not that she'd ever let Ed know that. *Is her former boss all right?* she wonders. He always did work too hard. Despite all his talk of retirement, he used to joke that when his time was up, he'd be happy to pass on to the next world from the comfort of his office. In fact, one of the last things she remembers is him telling her to simply roll his chair out when he's gone and take over.

'Didn't you know he retired?' Ed asks, when it's obvious she's not going to say anything.

Retired? So he actually went through with it. Charlotte's heart sinks as she realises her biggest champion is gone – and the position she'd been driving towards for years has been filled by someone else. 'Oh yes, I did know that,' she fibs. 'It's just, I heard he was still around the office from time to time, and I thought I might drop him a line. To, er, get a reference.'

'Well, I don't know who you heard that from, but he hasn't been in since he left, about . . . two and a half years ago now? Moved to Spain, apparently. Life in the sun and all that. But listen, I'd be happy to give you a reference. As the VP and everything.'

Charlotte freezes. '*You're* the new VP?' Her maternity cover – who's been at the company for a fraction of the time she had – has bagged the VP position she's been eyeing for ages? Anger sweeps over her and she tries her best to keep her tone steady.

'Well, not so new any more,' Ed says. 'But listen, I could really use someone like you on the team, if you're thinking of coming back. You'd need to do a refresher course on all the new pitching techniques I've developed, but at least we wouldn't have to train you from scratch. We only have a junior position available right now, but it's a good place to get warmed up. I'm sure it'd all come back to you, just like riding a bike.' He lets out a jovial laugh that Charlotte's clearly expected to join in with, but all she can do is grit her teeth.

Refresher course? *Junior position?*

'And it goes without saying that we need someone insanely dedicated,' Ed continues. 'Like, two hundred per cent dedicated. No leaving early for the school run or working from home if your kiddie is sick. I've implemented a strict office-only working policy, and you wouldn't believe how much more efficient we are.'

'I can imagine,' Charlotte manages to spit out, thinking how messed up it is that she, who's worked at the company *years* longer than Ed, would need to prove her commitment. 'I appreciate the kind offer, but I've had other offers more commensurate with my experience.' She'd never return to her old office as a junior, going right back to where she started over ten years ago. Obviously Ed wants to lord his new position over her and show her who's boss. Even if he *had* offered her an account director position, she wouldn't want to work with him, anyway.

'Good luck,' Ed says. 'But the offer still stands. Do let me know if you'd like to take me up on it at any point.'

When hell freezes over, Charlotte thinks, but she manages a polite goodbye.

Right. Well, so much for that. She takes a deep breath, reminding herself that it has been over three years since she left. Of course things would have changed at her old company, although Vivek retiring was the last thing she'd expected . . . about as likely as a new hire becoming VP. Had she known back then that Vivek was planning to leave so soon? Would it have made the slightest bit of difference? Or was she too worried about her daughter, too much in love with her new life as a mother, that it would have just rolled off her . . . even if she could have been VP? Resentment tugs at her insides.

There's no point dwelling on the past – what's done is done. Determination rushes into her, and she grabs her laptop. She may not be VP at her old company, but she'll find something better, if it's the last thing she does. Junior position – as if.

As she opens her laptop lid, her brain is already skipping ahead to next steps. If returning to her old company isn't a possibility – and it definitely isn't; she'd rather eat her own arm than work under Ed – then she'll need to get that reference from Vivek and update her CV. Perhaps she already has a reference on file somewhere?

She taps in her password and navigates to the folder where she keeps all her work files. No, no letter. *God.* What had she been thinking, leaving her job without even requesting a reference? She may not have been keen to go back to work at the time, but had she planned never to work again? *That's all right*, she tells herself. She must have Vivek's personal mobile number somewhere – if he hasn't changed it, that is. She'll hunt for it later.

Okay, time to work on her CV. She smiles, thinking of the last time she remembers updating it. Vivek had marched over to her workstation, telling her that after winning the company's most lucrative contract, it was high time she got promoted to senior account director . . . and team lead. All he needed was an updated résumé of her 'many and varied accomplishments' to give to HR, and he'd get on it. She'd spent the rest of the day in a glow, typing up the document. When she'd scanned the finished product, she'd felt incredibly proud. She'd worked hard and she deserved this step up.

She squints as documents filter on to the screen, her brow furrowing as she notices that the most recent CV isn't from before she was promoted, but from only two years ago – when Anabelle would have been just a year old. *Hmm.* Why would she have been going through old CVs if she'd never planned on going back to work? Perhaps she'd needed it for something else – volunteering, maybe? Running one of those playgroups she seems to have been so involved in? It's still so hard to believe she did nothing for three years. Well, nothing except toddler-wrangling.

Three years. Okay, so it wasn't *too* long, but in her industry – where keeping up with ever-changing regulations, maintaining your network of contacts and staying on top of the constantly evolving landscape of companies were essential – it was a little . . . challenging. She herself had interviewed women who'd taken significant time out to have families, and she'd never once recommended hiring them for those very reasons. Given the choice between hiring someone who'd been living in another world and a candidate who'd been working in the industry, she'd always selected the one with current experience. It just made better business sense, but the memory makes her wince now. Maybe she should have given those women a chance. If they could deal with demanding toddlers day and night, they'd be more than capable of handling clients.

Hopefully she'll come across an employer who thinks the same way. They must exist, right? She'll study up on current regulations, and with this CV – ending with securing that huge global trial for a new psoriasis drug – her list of accomplishments should be enough to overcome the barrenness of the past few years. At least she finished on a high note.

But wait – that wasn't how her time at the company had ended, was it? She bites her lip, thinking that she doesn't actually know how it ended, apart from the fact that she took maternity leave and then, at some point, said she wouldn't be back. Vivek wouldn't have been thrilled with that move, that's for sure. Is that why she doesn't have a reference?

No, she tells herself, to placate the growing panic. It's probably down to everything that happened after Anabelle's birth. She was probably in such a state that she wasn't thinking clearly.

Right, back to the CV. Her fingers hover over the keyboard for a minute as she contemplates adding something to cover these past three years. But what can she put? 'Wonderful stay-at-home mother'? 'Skilled at tidying up, constructing Lego towers and overseeing strategic park ventures'? She tilts her head, thinking of the fact that she'd pulled up her CV a couple of years ago. Perhaps she *had* run a playgroup or volunteered. If so, at least it's something to add.

'Hey.' David creeps into the flat and throws his briefcase on the sofa.

'Hey.' Despite her anger and hurt, she longs to lean her head on his chest and cuddle him close like she used to; to do *something* to break through to him. Instead she steels herself against him, staring at the screen, and he disappears into the bedroom.

'David . . . did I do anything in the past three years?' she asks in a businesslike tone when he emerges in trackies and T-shirt. 'Any volunteering, starting new groups, anything like that? I'm just working on my CV.'

David frowns. 'No, not that I know of. I mean, you were pretty involved with the playgroups and you met up with the mums a few times, but nothing that you yourself organised, no.'

'Okay.' God knows why she'd been poking around in her old CV folder, then, but it hardly matters.

'I wouldn't worry too much about taking a few years off,' David says, and Charlotte's heart lifts that he's actually reassuring her about something. 'You were the most dedicated and passionate employee, and I'm sure anyone you talk to will pick that up straight away. They'd be a fool not to take you on.' For just a split second he sounds like his old self, and Charlotte can't help smiling. Then she remembers about Exeter and her stomach squeezes painfully.

Focus on the things you can control, she tells herself. Things with David might be far from ideal, but at least she'll have her career back on track.

Somehow, though, even that doesn't feel like much of a consolation right now.

CHAPTER THIRTY-FIVE

2 November

It's amazing how quickly the blanket of false security can be yanked from you. How one minute you're carrying on with your day, merrily believing everything is fine. And then you're jerked to another place, a place of fear and dread. A place I know so well, but whose memory had dimmed – dimmed enough to let me start to think beyond it, anyway, and to crave more than what I have . . . more than my daughter. It's been revived now in shades so intense they scald my eyes, my brain, my heart.

The beeping of the monitor. The hiss of the oxygen. The harsh fluorescent lighting that burns through your eyelids, even when they're closed . . . even when you're so tired, so desperate to grab just one minute of slumber.

The terror. The *guilt*.

Anabelle has pneumonia. I was so relieved to hear it's 'only' pneumonia; with her heart issues, it could have been something much worse. Even so, for a child that young who had such a tough start, pneumonia's no joke. Thankfully her breathing is stable and her temperature started dropping as soon as the antibiotics took hold. But seeing her so helpless, lying there with tubes coming out of her nose and arms, was a terrible throwback to the time when we really *weren't* sure if she'd live or die.

When the doctor said they'd admit her to the ward because they didn't want to take chances, my gut twisted and I thought I might be sick. Because although I'd been vigilant – she'd had a runny nose for days, a bit of a cough and a very slight fever – I had taken chances. I hadn't been as present, as all-in mentally, as usual. My brain was off cycling through recent job adverts I'd seen, being bombarded with images and thoughts of how to return to work.

David couldn't have been happier when I'd told him I wanted to go back, even sending me links to websites he thought would be helpful. Instead of pretending to be asleep when he came home from the office, I found myself waiting up for him, eager to show him the latest adverts I'd found, wanting to discuss the latest opportunities. It felt like a bridge had been built between our two separate worlds, drawing us closer together again.

The more job adverts I read, the more I couldn't wait to get back to work. I could almost envision myself striding down the street towards the bus stop, clad in a suit and high heels. I could feel my fingers clicking over the keyboard, and hear the ping of my email as someone summoned my opinion.

I even got as far as pulling up my CV – my most recent one, the one I'd put together just after I'd won the biggest contract of my career. I stared at the sentences in front of me, reading them over and over as desire bubbled up inside.

I was with my daughter 24/7, but my heart wasn't.

If it was, maybe I'd have noticed sooner. Maybe I'd have picked up on the fact that Anabelle only pecked at her breakfast, or just wanted to watch her favourite cartoon rather than head to the park. Instead, I flopped down beside her, only too glad of a second to surf websites and drool over yet another job. I put her down for her nap, pleased that for once she fell asleep without much fuss, and went back to my browsing.

But when I went to wake her up . . . her little face was red and her breath rasped in and out. Heart pounding, I put a hand to her cheek.

Panic swept through me at the heat radiating from her skin. My hands shook as I took her temperature, the familiar fear washing over me when it was over forty. I scooped her up and she lay her head on my shoulder, not even having the energy to do her usual happy wiggle. I could feel her chest heaving against me, and I grabbed our coats, my keys and mobile and went down to the street to hail a cab. I was going straight to A&E.

It was only once we were in the waiting room that I thought to call David. I'd been locked in this life with my daughter for so long, it almost felt like there were just the two of us – like everything that happened to her was down to me. Well, it *was*.

And so, we're back. Back to where all this began. Back to the hospital where I became a mother, where I pledged to keep my daughter safe . . . to never take her for granted.

I haven't followed through, have I? One phone call from the outside world and suddenly I'm jetting off on a different track . . . a track towards the place where I damaged my child, where the part of me that claimed I'd never be satisfied 'just' being a mum has been reignited. Looking over at my sleeping daughter now, I want to kick myself for thinking of wanting more. For God's sake, Anabelle isn't even a year old yet. We could have lost her, if the pneumonia had progressed. We *would* have lost her a year ago, if it wasn't for open-heart surgery. How many more reminders must I be given to treasure my child?

Anabelle needs me. She'll always need me, to watch over her and to be fully present. This illness is a kick to the desire that was starting to spiral out of control. It has jolted me back to the place where everything fades away – everything but the child in front of me . . . the child etched firmly into my heart, so deeply that every flutter of the eyelids, every twitch of her lips makes me ache with love.

I need to protect my daughter, not just from outside forces, but – once again – from me, too. I'd thought that by quitting Cellbril, I was safe, but that's clearly not enough. It's not the office, or the job. It's me.

I need to change *myself* – to purge any trace of the person whose ambition and drive threatens my daughter. I'm an all-or-nothing woman. I can't do things by halves. Not when it comes to jobs, and not when it comes to life. And now, it's time to commit to the most important position I'll ever have.

Not just commit, actually. To become a new person, consisting of only one thing: mother.

CHAPTER THIRTY-SIX

With David at work and Anabelle engrossed in watching some random woman open Kinder Surprise Eggs on YouTube, Charlotte decides to hit the job sites . . . just for a half-hour or so. She'd pledged to engage more with her daughter today, but the urge to get her search started is overwhelming, and no child ever died from thirty minutes on the tablet, right? Charlotte used to spend hours watching TV, and she turned out fine.

She's still not thrilled with the state of her CV, but it seems there isn't much more to add, so . . . well, she'll just have to blow them away in the interview. She's yet to track down Vivek for a reference – his mobile number isn't working – but she has managed to get through to one of her old line managers, who promised to send one through. It's been ages since they worked together, but something is better than nothing.

Anyway, all of that is just fluff. Experience and a proven track record are the most important things, and Charlotte has both of those in spades.

She logs on to the website where most of the pharmaceutical jobs are advertised, hope and optimism flooding into her as a multitude of posts fill the screen. It's a booming industry, thriving despite the uncertain economy. 'Everyone needs drugs,' Vivek used to say, and judging from the demand for employees, that certainly seems to be true. If there's such a high demand, maybe she could even start work next week!

She scans the screen, noticing that most of the adverts are placed by recruitment agencies and headhunters. Back in the day, she'd been a desirable candidate for them, fielding phone call after phone call as they tried to lure her from her job on behalf of competitors. In fact, there was one recruiter she'd become friends with – well, telephone friends, anyway – through their almost-daily conversations. Whenever something juicy popped up, she'd call Charlotte first. And while Charlotte was content to stay at Cellbril, it was nice to know she was such a good catch.

What was that recruiter's name? Charlotte taps her fingers as her brain works. Ah yes, Kirsty, that was it. From Top Executive Search. Charlotte googles the company name and finds the phone number. A huge smile grows on her face as she calls and the phone rings. She asks for Kirsty then scoots into the bedroom, crossing her fingers that Anabelle stays quiet.

'Hello, Kirsty Jensen speaking.' The voice is exactly as Charlotte remembers: chirpy and enthusiastic.

'Hi Kirsty, it's Charlotte McKay. I used to be in business development at Cellbril?' She clears her throat, cursing the note of uncertainty in her tone.

'Charlotte!' Kirsty screams. 'Oh my God, it's been a while! What have you been up to? We tried to reach you at your old job, but they said you'd moved on.' She laughs. 'So cheeky, looking for a new position without even letting me know! I could have got you something stellar. Never mind, though. Bygones and all that. I'm very confident we can find you something now.' She pauses for breath, thank goodness. Charlotte can hardly keep up.

'What is it that you're looking for at the moment? Did you move up into an executive position at your last place of employment? We've just had a VP of business development post come through at a pharma company that I think you'd be *perfect* for. Oh, I'm so pleased you got in touch! What wonderful timing!'

'That sounds fantastic, and just what I've been looking for.' Charlotte wants to punch the air.

'Brill. Absolutely brill.' She can hear Kirsty typing. 'I'll just email their internal HR right now to set up the interview, but I know they'll love you. When can you come in?'

'Any time.' The words pop out before Charlotte can stop them, and she bites her lip. She doesn't want to sound desperate, even though that's exactly what she is. But a VP position! She'd die for that.

'Great, great . . . and we'll need you to send us through an updated CV . . .' *Clack, clack, clack.* 'While I'm speaking to you, why don't you tell me a bit about your current position? It'll help me sell you to the company even better, not that you need any bigging up!'

She laughs, and Charlotte grips the mobile. *Shit.* Well, she'd known this was coming. 'My daughter was born with a heart condition, and I took some time off to be with her.' No one can fault that, can they? Even though she can't even remember making the decision, suddenly she feels incredibly defensive about it.

'Oh, I'm so sorry.' Kirsty stops typing. 'I had no idea you were even pregnant!'

Charlotte stays silent, thinking that she probably hadn't wanted to make a big fuss about it.

'Is your daughter all right now?' Kirsty manages to make it sound like she's personally interested, but Charlotte knows what she's really thinking: anyone with a poorly child is not the right candidate for a busy, demanding position.

'Oh, she's perfectly fine. Completely healthy.' Charlotte peeks around the side of the door, where Anabelle is now watching an animated music video featuring dancing sharks bopping along to some anodyne tune.

'Right.' Kirsty pauses. 'And so . . . your daughter is how old?'

Charlotte knows she's more interested in figuring out how long she's been out of work. 'She's three now,' she responds. 'And while I may not have been in the office, I'm up to date on all the industry regulations, mergers and developments. As you know, I secured Cellbril's biggest contract ever. I'd be a real asset to any company.'

'Oh, I know, I know. That's one of the reasons we were chomping at the bit to have you. But listen, my love. I'm just not sure the VP position is—'

'If you don't think the VP position is a good fit, then I'm open to something else at the director level,' Charlotte says, her heart beating fast. 'I can guarantee I'll grow the client list within weeks if I'm just given a chance.'

'I've no doubt you could,' Kirsty says. 'I've no doubt you could. But . . .' She falls silent, and Charlotte can almost hear the recruiter's mind ticking. 'If I'm being one hundred per cent honest, it may be a little difficult to place you in the positions we have available. They're mostly at a senior level, and I can't parachute you in there with such a big gap in your résumé. Surely you must know that?' Her tone softens.

'But . . . but . . .' Charlotte's mouth is dry. 'I have solid experience. I can get results. I'll work as long as they need me to; hell, I'll sleep under the desk if I have to. Please, just—'

'I'll let you know if we do come across anything suitable,' Kirsty interrupts in an apologetic voice. 'Lovely speaking to you again, Charlotte. Take care.'

And with that, she's gone.

Charlotte collapses on the bed, anger flaring as she replays what happened. She knew the gap in her CV would be a problem, but she'd thought . . . well, that her experience and results would count for *something*. How is she supposed to wow them in interviews if she can't even get a foot in the door? God, this is so unfair. If she could, she'd go back in time and not only hire all those women she'd turned away but give them medals of courage for running the gamut of biased employers.

'Mummy!' Anabelle calls from the lounge. 'The tablet stopped working!'

Charlotte draws in a deep breath and gets to her feet. Okay, so maybe she's been a little naïve to think she could start right where she left off. She's willing to go down a level – not as far as a junior position, but maybe to account manager level. Once you get to that stage, it's all semantics anyway, isn't it? Maybe Kirsty won't help her, but there must be other recruiters who can. Taking a bit of time off doesn't mean she's lost her edge. If anything, she's readier than ever to prove herself.

Charlotte fixes the tablet and gives it back to her daughter, the hours ticking by as she sends out more CVs, leaves more messages with recruiters and scans job sites. At last her eyes blur over and she sits back on the sofa. She's done everything she can for now – the calls and emails will start streaming in any day, she's certain. Now that she's started down this road, the longing to get back to work is like a physical ache.

'Mummy?' Anabelle's voice interrupts her thoughts and Charlotte jerks towards her daughter. God, she'd almost forgotten Anabelle was there! 'Mummy, I'm hungry.'

Charlotte glances at the clock, stunned to see it's hours past lunchtime. No wonder her daughter is hungry! Guilt filters through her as she realises she was so engaged in her job search that she completely neglected her daughter . . . not just emotionally, but physically, too. If she's like this now, what will she be like when she starts working again?

It'll be fine, she tells herself as she hurries to the kitchen to knock up some pancakes for lunch. She quirks an eyebrow and smiles. 'Knock up some pancakes for lunch'? This mothering gig has definitely taught her some new skills.

But it's not just new skills, she thinks, deftly mixing flour and egg. Life since the accident has opened up a new view into herself, too. She's learned how much fun it is to be silly, and how she treasures the time spent outside every day. She's discovered how much she enjoys creating things and using her imagination, from painting watercolours to telling stories at bedtime. And while she may never want to dedicate her life solely to her child, she's realised that being a mother isn't the horror show she'd imagined it to be. It's gruelling, often boring and definitely not always instinctive, but to have a child love you with all their heart . . . well, that's pretty special, even if it is a huge responsibility. She may never feel that overwhelming tidal wave of love and emotion, but she knows now that she *can* be a mother and an okay one, too – when she's not forgetting to feed her child lunch, that is.

She and Anabelle wolf down their food, and Anabelle helps her clear away the plates. Charlotte glances out the window, where the white stucco terraces gleam in the streetlight like frosting on cakes. After sitting inside all day, every inch of her longs to get out of this stuffy flat, to stretch her muscles and work off the restless energy coursing inside her.

'Come on, Anabelle. Let's get some exercise.'

'Exercise?' Anabelle slides in her sock feet across the floor, turns and slides back again. Charlotte grins. Looks like they both have excess energy to work off.

'You know, like running and stuff. Making your muscles work. It's good for the brain.' She catches her daughter on her next slide and corrals her into her trainers, then goes into the bedroom to look for her own. They must be here somewhere. She may not have been very sporty over the past few years, but she must own some form of sporty footwear? Not that she and Anabelle are going to do anything hardcore, but it'd be nice to wear proper footgear for once.

She roots around in her wardrobe, uncovering some Spandex leggings and her Brighton Colour Run T-shirt, smiling at the memory. She loves running alone – she always gets way too competitive if she's alongside someone else – but this time, she'd cajoled David into doing the run with her. It was an untimed race and the whole point of it was to have fun, jogging and skipping through a cacophony of colour. They'd gripped each other's hands as paint rained down on them, staining their faces, arms and legs until they looked almost like alien creatures. The sky was bright blue, the sea sparkled in the sunshine and gulls wheeled above them. It was like a dream, and they barely noticed when they crossed the finish line. They would have kept going forever, if they could, in that perfect state.

Tears fill her eyes now, and she takes a deep breath. Things *had* been perfect. So why had they decided to have children? They must have thought they could integrate a child seamlessly into their lives; and maybe if Anabelle had been born healthy, they could have. But she wasn't, and they didn't. Instead, they've ended up miles apart – soon, quite literally. Before she can wipe them away, the tears spill down her cheeks.

'Mummy, what's wrong?' Anabelle crawls on to her lap and winds her arms around Charlotte. 'Does something hurt?'

Charlotte leans into her daughter, breathing in her warm soapy scent as the emotions inside her quieten. She rocks Anabelle back and forth, feeling the little girl's limbs relax into her as the tight knot inside her relaxes, too. She'd known she could calm Anabelle, but she hadn't realised her daughter could calm her, too. The warm heavy weight of her body is beyond comforting, unlike anything she's ever experienced.

'I'll be okay,' she says, hoping that's true. It *has* to be true, because she needs to hold it together – not just for herself now, but for Anabelle, too.

'Right.' Charlotte forces a smile. 'Let's get going.' She laces up her Converse trainers, having been unable to uncover her proper running shoes, then takes her daughter's hand and they head outside. As she races Anabelle down the pavement, she thinks that while it might not be the 10k run she used to do every day, at least she's running again . . . this time with her daughter by her side.

CHAPTER THIRTY-SEVEN

25 December

It's Christmas, and this one couldn't be more different to last year. Back then, I was so shrouded in the trauma of Anabelle's birth and the exhaustion of the newborn phase that I barely knew what day it was and clung to our routine like a lifeboat. Today, I have submerged us in a sea of Christmas, eager to celebrate what we have; eager to highlight the difference between then and now.

Eager to show that at last, I'm ready. I am all in . . . all mother.

This feels like our first real Christmas as a family, even if our daughter is over a year old now. I can barely believe it, but then I watch her stagger across the floor to grab a shiny ornament, and it's obvious she isn't the tiny, translucent infant who nestled in my arms. And although many mums say they wish they could turn back the clock, I wouldn't go there for anything. I can't, anyway. I'm nothing like that fearful person, terrified I couldn't keep my daughter safe. I was right to be scared, as it turned out. But now, well . . . that woman is gone. She has to be. There's no other way.

Anabelle's first birthday, just days after her release from hospital, felt like a birth day for me, too: a new beginning, a fresh start. I've made horrific mistakes, but that's all behind me. It's still early days, but I'm slowly starting to close the gap between how others see me (the 'wonderful mother') and how I see myself; how I feel about myself. I *will* become that wonderful mother if it kills me.

It was a small birthday party – I didn't want to excite Anabelle too much – with just David, Miriam and me. Mum had a meeting at work and Lily was still teaching, but Miriam turned up with bells on . . . literally. I couldn't believe it when she jingled in dressed as a clown, but Anabelle loved it.

Watching Miriam with my daughter has made me appreciate her in a whole new way – well, appreciate her, full stop. I love how she drops everything to help her granddaughter; how she's always been there to lend a hand, even when she's not actually needed. How she sat in the hospital room recently with me, when David had to go to work and the days stretched, long and lonely, at Anabelle's side. How she never forgets to bring Anabelle's favourite rice cakes when she visits, and how my daughter's face lights up when she sees her grandmother. Her children and her family are her world, and it's something I need to learn. Something I *am* learning.

I never thought I'd look up to Miriam as my role model. I'd always considered Mum the ultimate one to emulate. But . . . my heart gives a pang when I think of how little she knows about her granddaughter, and how she doesn't seem bothered. The birthday gift she sent was the same thing she gave us when Anabelle was born (a super-soft bunny with *The Velveteen Rabbit* book), and Anabelle was as perplexed by her Christmas gift of brush-and-comb set as I was, given there's still hardly a hair on her head.

I don't expect Mum to make Anabelle a top priority. I know what she's like, because I was like that, too – or I would have been, if things had been different. But I've chosen another route now, a path that follows Miriam's rather than hers. A path where my child is my world, now and in the future.

So this Christmas is all about Anabelle. I went a bit overboard – David kept cringing with every new purchase, but couldn't he see it was worth it? – buying a huge fake Christmas tree we could barely fit inside the lounge, a handmade stocking for Anabelle, the most gorgeous red smocked dress with tights, and present after present. What with all her birthday gifts, too, she has so many toys that we can barely move without tripping over something, but her squeals of delight as she tore off the paper were priceless. Granted, she was more interested in the box half the time than the toy inside, but that'll come. I snapped photo after photo until my phone ran out of storage, glancing through them with nostalgia before the day had even finished.

I was so caught up in making this her first proper Christmas at home that I let the side down a bit when it came to buying David's gifts. In the past, I'd always showered him with armloads of presents, from expensive boxers to bottles of cologne to watches. Despite his pleas to tone it down – that he didn't need anything – I'd wave them away and go wild. I loved him, and I wanted to show it. Besides, Christmas wasn't about giving people what they *needed*, right?

But this year, well . . . I thought I'd take my husband at his word. He wasn't one for excesses, and besides, we both had this new little person on whom to shower our love. I got him a few bits and bobs, but even I have to admit my main gift to him of a silk tie from M&S was a little underwhelming. It was just that . . . unlike previous years, when I knew exactly what he was eyeing up and lusting after, this year I had no idea.

I had no *space* in my mind for any idea – I had to throw myself into fully embodying my new role. Ever since Anabelle's recent discharge from hospital, everything has been about her . . . not that, outwardly, it's any different to how things were before. Inside, though, I feel different. I don't miss anything about my old world now, not even my husband. It feels like my love for David is part of my former life; part of the person I had to bury. In order to access it, I'd need to resurrect that woman, and there's no way I'm risking that – there's no way I'm risking my daughter.

Not again.

I could tell by the flicker of hurt on David's face when he opened my gift that he expected something more, though. That he *had* hoped I'd made room for him in my mind . . . in my heart.

'It's perfect,' he said, meeting my eyes with what looked like a forced grin. 'It'll go wonderfully with my grey suit.' He cleared his throat and put it aside, and I bit my lip. I hadn't meant to hurt him. I just needed to focus on Anabelle.

'Here, give this to Mummy,' David said, reaching behind him to grab a rectangular-shaped box. He sat back and smiled as Anabelle kicked her way through the shiny foil littering the floor and practically threw the box at me.

'Thank you, honey,' I said to her, even though I was really thanking David. The box was heavy in my hands and I glanced over at him, wondering what he'd bought me. In past years, I'd always given him a list, preferring to receive gifts I wanted rather than the element of surprise. But this time, I realised, I'd given him no clues at all.

I tore off the wrapping paper and removed the top of the box, revealing the most high-tech pair of trainers I think I'd ever owned (and I'd owned many over the years). They were so white they practically hurt my eyes, and the fluorescent orange and pink trimming, which could have been so garish, contrasted perfectly. I lifted one from the box, revelling in how it felt so light yet solid at the same time. Before I could stop myself, I'd slipped both of them on, flexing my feet and envisioning how I'd fly through the park. I could almost feel the steady beating of my heart, the way the fresh air cleansed my lungs, how—

'I knew you'd love them.' David's voice interrupted my reverie; I'd almost forgotten where I was. 'It's been so long since you went for a run. It's well past time for you to do something for yourself again.'

I met his steady gaze, the glorious images in my mind blanching to white then turning black. The trainers felt like concrete on my feet, dragging me down towards a well of guilt and fear – towards the person who'd planned to run until her waters broke; someone who'd never even *thought* running might damage her child. Yes, they were just shoes, but they were also a signpost to a past littered with carelessness and mistakes, and I could no more hit the streets with them now than I could turn back time.

But I wanted to run. Oh, how I wanted to. Desire surged inside of me, almost taking away my breath with its intensity.

I jerked the shoes off my feet like they'd scalded my soles, ignoring David's surprised expression. I couldn't let myself slip backwards. I couldn't let one crack appear in this still-fragile mould of a mother I wanted so desperately to harden, in case it should fall completely apart. I *am* all in, and I'll find another way to fly.

This time with my daughter firmly in tow.

CHAPTER THIRTY-EIGHT

A week passes, and then another, and Charlotte is no closer to finding a job – a job that she wants, anyway, with pay levels and responsibility that reflect her expertise. She's registered with countless recruitment agencies, sent out a multitude of CVs and even had an interview, but . . . nothing. And while she knows these things can take time, she can't help feeling frustrated that it's going so slowly – and that it's not just one recruiter who has issues with her résumé gap. It's pretty much all of them.

Charlotte shakes her head, anger rushing into her, just thinking of the last recruitment consultant she'd spoken to. He'd advised that instead of telling employers she'd spent three years at home with her daughter, she should simply say she took a career break to write a book or climb mountains for charity . . . anything but raise a child. Never mind the fact that she hasn't the foggiest how to pen a novel or that she's terrified of heights. Apparently anything is better than eschewing the world of work to care for your daughter.

Although she can't even remember making the decision, she's starting to feel incredibly defensive about it. Staying at home is hardly a holiday – in a way, it's even harder than working. It's non-stop from morning to night, and women hardly take time off to indulge themselves. They're raising proper human beings, for goodness' sake.

David's pitching in to help, despite his own busy schedule, making it home most nights in time to put Anabelle to bed and taking her out for a few hours at the weekends so Charlotte can focus on her search. He even helped her pick out a suit for the one interview she'd had, where it transpired she'd be more of a PA than the account executive the advert had led her to believe. It's good he's helping, but she can't help wondering about his motivation. Does he actually *want* to help, or is he just trying to cram in as much support as he can before taking off? Is he keen to get her and Anabelle settled so he can leave sooner rather than later? Part of her wants to scream at him to just leave now – that they'll be fine – but he *is* still Anabelle's father.

Rain streams down the windows, and she sighs at the thought of another day inside. They've used up all the watercolours, the Play-Doh has dried up, the tablet needs recharging . . . and she and Anabelle need to get out of the house. In desperation, she checks the WhatsApp mums' group she muted weeks ago, eyebrows rising when she spots there's a playgroup in a nearby church today. She's so bored that it actually sounds like a good idea, even if she does need to face all those smug mums alone. Maybe she'll try Lily again, just in case . . . She picks up her mobile and dials her friend's number, but there's no answer.

Right, well, Lily may not be free this week or any time in the foreseeable future, but Charlotte needs to get *out*. It might be hell, but at least it'll be a different kind of hell.

Hopefully with coffee.

One hour later, Charlotte can confirm that it is indeed hell. With rain slicing through the air, the whole of Chelsea (anyone with offspring, anyway) seems to have had the same idea, making their way to the church to let their kids loose. Stuffed full of children ranging from infants to preschoolers, the noise is deafening, with screams, bangs and laughter echoing off the high ramparts. Charlotte loses sight of her daughter within seconds as Anabelle streaks towards the crowd of kids racing madly from toy to toy, clambering through nylon tunnels and shoving their chubby bodies into too-small plastic cars.

At least Anabelle's safe here, Charlotte thinks, folding herself into a small wooden chair clearly meant for someone a quarter of her size. Not even a madman would come within fifty feet of this place.

'Charlotte! Oh my goodness, is that you?' A woman with the kind of tousled, dirty-blonde hair that looks natural but actually costs a fortune to maintain swoops into the chair beside her. Charlotte notes with envy how her bottom fits neatly into the small seat, while her own is hanging off the side. 'We haven't seen you for ages! I texted you but you never responded, naughty girl. Everything okay?' She lifts her head. 'Jo! Come here! Look who I've found!'

A fine-boned, dark-haired woman turns from the counter by the kitchen, where she's clutching two mugs of steaming liquid as if they're more precious than diamonds. 'Charlotte! Where the hell have you been?' Jo laughs and crosses to them as the first woman shoots her an evil look – Charlotte's not sure if it's mock or not. 'Whoops. Sorry, Jemma. Guess I shouldn't swear in a church. Wouldn't want you to lose the back-up church-school place you've been gunning for by hanging around with us heathens.'

Jemma rolls her eyes, and Charlotte laughs, already liking Jo . . . a far cry from the type of smug mum she thought she'd find here. Maybe she should have replied to those messages, after all.

'So? Where *have* you been?' Jemma turns to lift a drooling baby from a car seat. 'Can you hold her for a second while I sort out this one?' Charlotte glances down at the toddler hanging on to his mother's legs. God, she hadn't even noticed that one.

Charlotte nods and takes the baby, trying to avoid the drool dripping from her mouth. She looks up to meet Jo's curious gaze and forces a smile, jiggling the baby on her lap with what she hopes resembles a practised air. Ugh, that drop of drool is getting closer and closer to falling on her leg . . .

'Great. Thanks.' Jemma lifts the baby from her arms just in the nick of time, seemingly oblivious to the smear of drool that's now transferred to her arm. Charlotte wonders at what point you stop noticing your child's bodily fluids.

'Poor thing,' Jemma says, stroking the baby's head. 'She's been stuck in his car seat pretty much all morning. By the time you get to number three, they're lucky if you can remember their names.'

Charlotte gulps back a gasp. *Three* kids? God, this woman must adore being a mum. Either that or she's certifiably insane.

'Thank God I stopped at one,' Jo says, sitting down. She carefully sets Jemma's mug beside her on the floor. 'I can't imagine dealing with Henry's tantrums and coping with a baby at the same time. You are a very brave woman.'

'I wouldn't even attempt to do it without a nanny.' Jemma gestures towards a woman who's trying to stop a little girl with two golden plaits from hitting a boy over the head with a spade. She turns to look at Charlotte. 'Have you given any more thought to what I told you? About schools for Anabelle? Such a shame you didn't put her name down for Penworth at birth. She and Felicity could have started together. It'll be impossible to get her in now.'

Charlotte shakes her head, trying to process the flow of words. At least they're not talking about where she disappeared to any more. 'Er, yes, I know. Such a shame. I—'

'Layla!' Jemma's voice cuts through the noise around them. '*Layla!* Get Felicity *down* from there.' She points to the front of the altar, where the blonde-haired girl is now climbing up a stone column, but Layla is busy chasing after the toddler. Jemma sighs and gets to her feet, lunging towards the column. Jo and Charlotte watch her in silence, Charlotte admiring her trim figure after three babies – and one barely out of the womb.

'How are you?' Jo flashes her a smile, then sips her drink. 'I'm sorry I haven't been in touch for so long.' She grimaces. 'You know how it is.

After a full day with Henry, I barely have enough energy to crawl into bed. And then I see people like Jemma who have three and who still make them organic meals every day. Sure, she has a nanny, but still. Three! I'd gouge my eyes out.'

She makes a grotesque face, and Charlotte can't help but laugh. God, it's good to talk to someone else who feels the same as her – that motherhood is bloody *hard*.

'We need to organise another girls' night out,' Jo says. 'Can you believe it's been almost a year since our last one? And no running off early this time!' She wags a finger at Charlotte.

Charlotte meets her eyes, wondering if she's talking about the night that David and Miriam have told her about. What the hell happened? 'Sounds good,' she manages to say through the questions circling her brain.

Jo peers closely at her. 'Are you okay? You don't seem your normal cheery, chipper self.'

Charlotte manages a smile despite the shock of hearing herself described as 'cheery' and 'chipper'. She's been described as many things, but never that. 'I'm all right. Just tired, you know.'

'Do I ever. I'd give anything for a good night's sleep. I swear to God, if someone had told me that at age three, he'd still be waking up, I'm not sure I would have ever got pregnant.'

'As good as Layla is, sometimes she really needs to pay better attention.' Jemma plonks back into the chair beside them, still holding the drooling baby in her arms. 'If I hadn't spotted her, Felicity would be halfway up that column by now!' She shakes her head. 'She'd better get her head screwed on right before I go back to work next week.'

Charlotte's mouth drops open. Jemma works? With three kids in tow – one of them only a few months old? Shame creeps into her that she's judged these women before getting to know them. Hell, she's even judged herself before understanding, railing against the choices she made.

'I'm thinking about going back to work, too,' she says, desperate to talk to someone about it.

Jo and Jemma both swivel towards her, their eyebrows flying up, and Charlotte cringes. She could have said she was stripping in Soho and they wouldn't have looked more shocked.

'Well, that's a turn-up for the books,' Jemma says wryly, deftly wiping the baby's chin while drinking her coffee at the same time. 'You kept telling us how happy you were, and how being home with your daughter was a privilege. I never once heard you utter a negative word . . . unlike the rest of us. You were even starting to make me rethink my decision to return to work so soon!' She sighs. 'I should be used to leaving the kids – I've gone back after two maternity leaves – but it really is hard at first. Even after all this time, Felicity still cries when I go to work in the morning. Layla has to pry her off me.'

Charlotte winces at the vision: a child crying desperately for her mother as someone tears her away. God, that sounds brutal. How does Jemma deal with that every day? Would it be like that with Anabelle, too?

'What made you change your mind?' Jo asks, leaning back in her chair. 'I mean, you know how I feel about it. If I hadn't been *made* redundant last year, I'd be working right now. God, work was my *break*.' She makes a face. 'Well, it was until they started running me ragged on a skeleton staff. I was almost happy to go, but I tell you, if someone offered me a job right now, I'd jump at it.'

Charlotte meets the gaze of these two women, realising that they are even more like her than she thought. 'I just . . .' She pauses, trying to figure out what to say. 'I just need something different from all of this.' She gestures to the hall of crazy kids. '*Besides* all of this,' she adds, so she doesn't offend anyone. Not that she would offend Jemma and Jo, now that she knows how they feel.

'Well, I can certainly understand that,' Jemma says, hitching the baby up on her shoulder and placing a pristine muslin under her head. 'Have you started looking yet? Any success?'

Charlotte shakes her head, a sigh escaping at the thought of how dismal it's been. 'I've sent out loads of CVs, but nothing. I've been out of work so long that no one seems to want to take a chance on me. No one but my old company, anyway, offering me a role I pretty much started in ten years ago.'

Both Jo and Jemma shoot her sympathetic looks. 'It sucks, doesn't it?' Jo says. 'I've gone to a few interviews, but as soon as I say I have a three year old, I keep getting asked when the next one's coming along. As if the state of my womb is any of their business. No one seems to believe me when I say I've closed up shop.'

'If I were you, I'd take that job at your old company,' Jemma advises. 'Just get your feet back on the rungs, get back in the game and up to snuff again. And you know what they say: it's much easier to get a job once you're already employed.'

'Wouldn't that be going backwards, though?' Charlotte bites her lip.

'Well, yes,' Jemma says practically. 'But the sad truth is that taking three years off might as well be ten – at least in finance, anyway. I don't know what it's like in your industry.'

'Probably the same,' Charlotte says, a heaviness settling over her. *God*. If only she'd known. Had she even paused to think what giving up her career would mean? Until experiencing it herself, she'd never once thought about the difficulty women face getting back into work – or tried to help them, she realises again. She'd just carried blithely on, so certain of her own trajectory.

'But the good news is that once you get back in the door, I'm sure you'll work your way up quickly. If not at your old company, then a new one,' Jemma says. 'If you're really ready to go back, don't wait around for the perfect offer, because it's never going to come. Just get back in there.'

Charlotte smiles at Jemma. 'Thank you.'

'No problem. Keep me posted!' She looks at her watch. 'Now, ladies, it's time to round up Layla and make a run for home again. I need to get some . . .' And she's off again, busily organising her life for the next one hundred years.

Charlotte scans the room, raking her eyes over the toys and children for Anabelle. It's like trying to find a needle in a haystack. Where on earth is she? She moves her gaze methodically up and down the hall, trying to ignore the small knot of panic inside when her daughter doesn't appear after ten minutes of searching. She must be here somewhere; of course she must. Charlotte would have seen her if she'd tried to leave the hall, right? But then . . . she'd been busy talking to Jo and Jemma.

She gets to her feet and takes a few steps forward, as if that will help her see better. She's being ridiculous, she knows, but she can't stop the horrible pictures tumbling into her head . . . of Anabelle crying, alone and afraid, without her. Where the hell *is* she?

'Anabelle!' Charlotte shouts, a strident edge of fear in her voice.

Jo touches her arm. 'What wrong?'

'I can't find Anabelle,' Charlotte says in a shaky tone. 'I don't see her anywhere. I know she must be here, but . . .'

'Right.' Jo beckons Jemma forward. 'Let's each take a section of the hall, and I'm sure we'll find her. Layla can watch our lot in the meantime.'

Jemma gives a curt nod, and Charlotte feels a rush of gratitude that these women aren't just telling her she's being silly and irrational. They each stride off, Charlotte's heart pounding and her mouth dry at the thought of losing her daughter. *Losing her daughter!* It's unthinkable. Her panic grows into terror as more minutes pass without Anabelle.

'Over here!' Jo waves an arm from the far side of the hall and Charlotte flies over, moving faster than she can ever remember.

'She was just having a little rest.' Jo gestures into the nylon tunnel where Anabelle's lying on her tummy, chin on her hands, gazing up at them with a mischievous glint in her eyes.

'Anabelle!' Charlotte swoops down on her daughter, wedging herself as far as she can into the tunnel. Her arse is on show for everyone to see, but she doesn't care. Her little girl is safe, and that's all that matters. God, for a second there . . . She takes a deep breath. She hadn't known it was possible to feel such a potent combination of fear, panic and guilt, then such a rush of relief and . . . love? If this is even an iota of what she felt after Anabelle's birth, then she can understand why she changed her life – why *she* changed so much. How could you not?

'Can I get out now, Mummy?' Anabelle shuffles forward on her tummy, and Charlotte can't help laughing through the anger now coursing through her. She'd been so worried, and her daughter had been having a rest in the tunnel!

'Sure,' she says, easing herself out. Please God, may she not be stuck in here. That's the last thing she needs after all this excitement. 'But Anabelle, you need to stay in a place where I can see you. No more hiding. Okay?'

'Okay!' Anabelle runs off again and Charlotte sags against a column, trying to calm down.

'I think I need a stiff drink,' she says, glancing up at Jemma and Jo. 'Thanks for your help.'

'No worries. I lost one of mine once in Boots,' Jemma says. 'Can't even remember which kid it was now, but I do remember the absolute terror. Your mind goes straight to the worst-case scenario, doesn't it?' She shrugs. 'That's what us mums do best.'

Charlotte nods. *Us mums.* For the first time, she feels like she's not just acting like one; that she really is one – a mum . . . a mum who couldn't bear to even think of losing her child. She's never experienced fear like that before, and if she had her way, she'd never let her daughter out of her sight again. Except . . . she swallows down the conflicting emotion. That's not exactly true, is it? She *does* want to go back to work, right?

Of course I do, she tells herself. She keeps her eyes trained on Anabelle, following her daughter's movements across the hall. She seems so independent – she'll be more than fine when Charlotte finds a job, and Charlotte will be, too. They may have got used to being together 24/7, but it's time now to loosen the apron strings. And maybe Jemma's right. Maybe she should take up Ed's offer and head back to the office. Although every little bit of her quivers at the thought of having him as her boss in such a familiar environment, it won't be long before she can move on to a more senior position – back to the place of authority she used to have.

She'll make the phone call as soon as they're home.

CHAPTER THIRTY-NINE

12 October

Wow, it's been so long since I've written . . . almost a year, in fact. That must show everything's bumping along fine! Anabelle will be two soon, and she's happy and healthy. I'm happy and healthy, David's healthy (I'm not sure about 'happy', since our conversation rarely strays past 'good night', but he seems content enough), and this past year as a dedicated stay-at-home mum – and I say that with pride now – has flown by.

Anabelle is a treasure, full of unexpected surprises to unwrap every day. She's talking now, and although much of it resembles a foreign language, I love hearing the new words she masters. Other than the usual sniffles and sore throats, she hasn't been seriously ill since her pneumonia, and she's passed all her heart check-ups with flying colours. I couldn't be prouder: of both me and her. We are a team, and I love her more than I ever thought possible.

Sometimes, it's hard to believe I've become one of those smug mums I used to avoid like the plague. Actually, I've more than just become one: I happily seek them out now, hitting up playgroups and baby classes daily. Despite my initial resistance, the women I meet there now form the foundation of my new life, and I couldn't be more grateful for their tips and advice on how to nail this mothering gig.

Popular topics include how all food must be organic or you risk poisoning your child; how to find the best photographer to ensure you don't miss capturing a second of your child's life as they grow and change; how you need to stretch your child's mind by taking them to music classes, to movement classes, to the excruciating Mummy and Baby Yoga from which my hamstrings still haven't recovered . . . how the day should be filled with valuable interaction, how the tablet is the source of all evil and TV something Satan created to liquefy children's brains.

In my previous life, I'm sure I would have sniggered – or, at the very least, rolled my eyes – at how obsessed these women are with their children. Now, I try to memorise everything, thinking how to apply it myself. Now, I understand. When you're a mother, it's not enough to be obsessed – and it's not a job. It's your life. It's *you*.

The unofficial leader of this tribe is a scarily efficient woman called Jemma, who has a daughter Anabelle's age, a newborn, and is planning a third. She seems to know everyone – and everything. She even knows what schools her kids will go to, something I hadn't even begun thinking about; but apparently we're already too late for some places. Just hearing that made me feel like I'd already failed my daughter. I went straight home and phoned all the private schools within a one-mile radius, getting Anabelle on to every waiting list I could . . . even though we'd struggle with the fees on just David's salary. I researched our local state schools, which were sadly lacking, before hitting on the idea of Anabelle attending the school close to Miriam's house. Miriam is always going on about how outstanding it is, and I'm sure she'd let us use her address to apply from.

Or maybe . . . maybe she'd even let us move in? She's constantly saying she's too old for such a big house and that she doesn't feel safe, but she just can't picture selling it. This could be the ideal solution for everyone! Imagine all the space Anabelle would have to run around in, not to mention her own room. It'd mean a longer commute for David, but we barely see him anyway. And it'd mean leaving Chelsea, but truth be told, I'm ready to go. I'm ready to start afresh, in a place with no bad memories.

I'm finally getting there; finally feeling like a great mum. I make organic food for my family, ignoring David's grimace at kale and quinoa. I organise biannual photo shoots for my family to document Anabelle's every growth stage, and I dutifully display them in our lounge. I take away the tablet and set strict limits on any television time. I've enrolled my daughter in every toddler class going, even if it does mean we're dashing around Chelsea like headless chickens most days. I've even used the last of my savings to buy a second-hand car so we can get to all our classes that much faster.

And by the end of the day, I collapse. Motherhood may not be mentally draining, but wow, is it *physical*. There is nothing left of me once Anabelle's in bed; I can't even rouse myself when David comes through the door. My determination to do everything I can to give my daughter a solid start overrides everything else.

Anabelle is my life, and I'm loving it.

I am.

CHAPTER FORTY

Charlotte stands in front of the mirror, examining her reflection. *Not too bad*, she decides, tugging her trousers up over the roll of fat ringing her waistline. She's managed to lose some of the excess weight through her daily races with Anabelle – that girl has definitely inherited Charlotte's competitive spirit; her hair is freshly cut and coloured and her suit is elegant. And if you don't look too closely, you might not spot the three and a half years since she's left Cellbril on her face.

God, three and a half years. She sinks down on the bed, trying to identify the emotions swirling inside. She's excited to get back out to the wonderful world of work; to show everyone how much she hasn't forgotten and that she can still sign clients with the best of them. Hell, she can sign *better* than the best of them.

But . . . there's something else there, too, a sadness tinging the anticipation. Because although she may look like the same woman who secured the company's biggest account, she's not. Pancake-making and watercolour skills aside, she actually feels like a mother now – a mother who's still learning every day, but a mother who loves her child. It's a love gained from the hours of care and attention, an emotion that's grown and almost snuck up on her, culminating in that moment when she thought she'd lost Anabelle last week. And while she knows beyond a doubt that she needs to work, the thought of leaving her daughter behind each day tugs at her heart.

Ed had been a little shocked when she'd called to say she'd take him up on his job offer, but he'd quickly recovered and transferred her straight through to HR. The same dozy woman from Charlotte's days still worked there. Since she remembered Charlotte, there was no need to complete any new paperwork beside the contract, which Ed had had couriered over the next day. Charlotte had admired his efficiency; maybe they *could* actually work together. Although – she grimaces – he's already scheduled her in for training sessions to learn his 'certifiably successful pitch techniques' for 'the newbies'. As if she's a newbie!

'All set?' David gives her a rare smile, and Charlotte nods. He'd been so pleased when she'd told him she'd found work; she'd longed to throw herself into his arms then crack open a bottle of champagne to celebrate, like they used to. She'd had to remind herself that his happiness was probably because he could now leave with slightly less guilt.

'I think so. Your mother's going to be here until you get home from work, right? I'm not sure what time I'll be back.' *Hopefully not too late*, she thinks. It *is* her first day. Anabelle will need to see a familiar face after the change of routine, and—

Charlotte stops herself from going any further. Anabelle will be fine; she'll have David. Charlotte needs to focus on proving herself.

'Mama!' Anabelle runs in from the lounge, where she's been finishing her breakfast, her face covered with milk and cereal. Charlotte takes a step back, only just managing to get herself out of harm's way. She bends down to Anabelle's level, her trousers biting into the tops of her thighs.

'Hi, honey.' She smooths her daughter's hair, thinking how much she's going to miss their daily adventures – although she won't miss the whining and the tears, that's for sure. 'You set for a good day with Granny?' Thankfully Miriam has jumped at the chance to be with Anabelle, even if it does mean a long drive every day . . . until they move, anyway.

Charlotte had been hesitant to tell Miriam of her decision to return to the office, but her mother-in-law's response came as a surprise . . . and unnerved her. Instead of the haranguing Charlotte had anticipated, Miriam had patted her arm.

'I'm happy to help out as much as you need me,' she'd said. 'I know the past few weeks have been trying, but you are such a good mother to Anabelle. That won't change just because you go back to work – Anabelle will always be the most important thing in your life. It's just part and parcel of being a mother.' She'd smiled, and Charlotte had forced a smile in return as uneasiness gripped her gut. *Could* she still be a good mother to her daughter? She'd need to put in long hours for the next few months, at the very least. And what would happen when she made it to a position where she'd need to travel and be away from home for a week here, a week there, then back in the office for hours on end?

That won't mean Anabelle isn't important, though – or that I'm a bad mother, she'd reassured herself through the pangs of guilt. After all, her mother had worked like a demon and Charlotte had never doubted her love. Charlotte might be a different kind of mother to the one she'd been before – and the one she couldn't remember – but Anabelle would know she loved her, just as Charlotte had with her mum.

Predictably Charlotte's mother had been overjoyed to hear her daughter would be working again. She was furious that she'd accepted a junior position, but she believed just as strongly that Charlotte would climb back to where she had been before – and rise even higher. The only one who was really upset about her return to the office was Lily, who Charlotte dropped round to see on her last free day. Lily had stared at her as if she didn't know her; as if she'd morphed into someone unrecognisable.

'But you always said you'd never go back!' Lily cried, once she'd closed her gaping mouth. 'Won't you miss Anabelle dreadfully? Won't *she* miss you? You've been practically glued to each other since she was born. It's going to be a huge adjustment for you both.'

Charlotte had kept a smile nailed on, even though every word was like a boot to the gut, punching holes where guilt poured in. It *would* be a huge adjustment, and of course they'd miss each other. But how could she explain to a new mother completely besotted with her baby that it wasn't enough for her?

Give her time, Charlotte had told herself. Liam was only a few months old. Maybe after a while, Lily would feel the pull of her old self again, too . . . or maybe not. As her mother had said, people changed. Charlotte wasn't going to judge her friend any more than she would judge herself. Every mother *does* need to make her own way through the minefield of competing needs to strike a balance that works best for her.

'You'd better get going if you don't want to be late,' David says, shaking her out of her reverie. 'I'll wait here until Mum comes.'

Charlotte nods and leans down to scoop Anabelle into her arms, not caring now about the cereal and milk combo. She bites her lip, remembering Jemma's nightmare goodbye scenario with Felicity. *Please God may Anabelle not be the same.*

'Bye bye, sweetheart. Be good!' Her gut tugs and she steels herself for Anabelle's tears and heartbreak. Instead, though, her daughter gives her a quick cuddle then scoots away.

Right, then. Charlotte stands still for a second, feeling curiously let down for some reason. She laughs and shakes her head as she walks down the stairs and out into the busy street. What, does she want Anabelle to kick off each time she leaves? She should be proud that her daughter is so secure. She breathes in the air, savouring the mix of diesel and flowers from the hanging pot on the lamppost above her. Then she strides towards the bus stop, eager to jumpstart her career, but still thinking of the little girl she's left behind.

CHAPTER FORTY-ONE

22 June

Lily is pregnant! After years of trying and I don't even know how many rounds of IVF, my best friend is going to have a baby. I couldn't be happier for her, and I can't wait to share everything I've learned over the past two and a half years. This is our chance to really connect again . . . not in the same way as before, of course, but as mothers.

We met up last night in our old haunt in Shepherd Market, and I couldn't help thinking back to the time when I'd told her, just tables from where we were now sitting, that *I* was pregnant. A rogue wave of guilt washed over me at the memory of my pregnancy, but I pushed it away. I'm not that person who put her daughter at risk, thank goodness. Not any more, and never again.

It was so strange being out late at night. Well, when I say 'late', I mean past eight. That would have been early back before I had Anabelle, but now I'm usually tucked up in front of Netflix or reading about potty training as my eyes sag closed, before I drag myself into the bedroom to sink into oblivion around nine. It sounds so dull, but I actually want my evenings to be like that. I couldn't bear a repeat of what happened last month on a 'girls' night out' – more like 'mothers on a binge'. God, I feel sick just thinking about it.

David was late coming back from work, and I'd somehow been roped into organising a night out for the playgroup mums. The very last thing I wanted was an evening out, let alone planning it, but Jo had begged and pleaded, saying she was going to kill herself if she didn't drink something other than Ribena. Even Jemma had joined in for once, saying she could do with a dinner that didn't involve clients or husbands. I'd stayed silent, thinking how I didn't really have anything to complain about, telling myself over and over how lucky I was to be able to stay at home with my daughter. It really was a privilege.

Somehow, my silence nominated me as the person in charge of choosing the restaurant, making the reservation and organising RSVPs in our newly minted 'Night Out!' WhatsApp group. Judging by the number of yeses flying in, these women were ravenous for the outside world . . . or alcohol. I really didn't want to leave my daughter, but David had agreed to be home by half six and I'd put Anabelle to sleep before I left. She wouldn't even know I was gone.

I spent ages cobbling together an outfit, feeling ill at ease in my too-tight jeans and clompy high heels. The minutes ticked by as I waited for David to come home. I sat on the sofa trying not to mess up my hair, the jeans cutting into my waist, fielding messages from the women who were now minutes from the restaurant – and from emptying the place of its booze.

Even though I hadn't been keen to go, the later David was, the more upset I became. Why wasn't he here? I never asked for his help. I'd given up everything to take care of our daughter . . . because I wanted to, yes – but still. Surely the least he could do was make it home at a reasonable hour one night?

When he responded at last to my increasingly furious texts, saying Miriam would come and babysit since he'd be late, I was practically shaking with anger. The intensity of it unnerved me, and took me by surprise.

By the time I was sitting at the restaurant table, I was gagging for a drink – for something to quell the storm inside me. I gulped my wine as the other women competed over who'd had the worst day, complaining about how relentless being a mother is, how thankless it is, how tiring. Their children were diabolical, their husbands were useless, and they didn't know how they'd make it through the next ten years without losing it. They couldn't wait to go back to work – at least they'd get to use the bathroom in peace.

I sat there and drank, their voices only feeding my anger. The more they spoke, the more I couldn't bear it. Their words were like hot pokers, stirring the flames inside me into a full-blown fire. I tried to block them out by drinking more. Another glass, and then another, repeating under my breath how I should – how I *do* – appreciate every minute with my child. I wasn't like these ungrateful women. I *wasn't*.

Suddenly I couldn't sit there any longer. I grabbed my handbag and pushed blindly between the tables and the chairs, my eyes focused on the door as if it was an escape hatch. I rushed back up the street and towards my daughter, desperate now to burrow into her and breathe her scent, to drown out those voices still ringing in my ears.

'Oh!' Miriam said as I entered, both she and David looking up from the TV blaring out the news. 'Is everything all right?'

'Char, I'm sorry,' David said, getting to his feet and running a hand through his hair. 'I got tied up in a meeting, and I couldn't get away.'

I stared at their faces like they were strangers, unable to take them in. There was just one person I needed to see. Without responding, I rushed into the bedroom and over to the cot. I knelt down beside my daughter and grasped the bars, my heartbeat slowing and anger fading as I took in her sleeping form under the soft blankets.

I was safe. Safe from what, I didn't know, but nothing could touch me now.

When Lily told me she was having a baby, she took my hand and said she hoped she'd be as good a mother as I am – that she wants to be as patient, as dedicated, as happy as me. She looked at me full of hope, love and joy about her future, and my insides ached with a mixture of pride and regret. I finally believe that I am a wonderful mother. I've come such a long way, and I'm proud of what I've become. But at the same time, part of me longs to go backwards, to urge my former self to enjoy my pregnancy, as Lily is clearly enjoying hers. To look forward to having a baby, not as a project that needs to be managed, but as a human to love and cherish.

I can't change the past, though. All I can do is keep moving forward. I *am* happy with this life, and nothing – least of all a group of drunken women – will convince me otherwise.

CHAPTER FORTY-TWO

Although she only remembers being gone for a couple of months, when Charlotte enters the office, her colleagues greet her as if she's been away for aeons. Some of the team have moved to rival companies, but many familiar faces smile and wave a greeting from behind computer screens. The office hasn't changed: flickering lights that never get fixed, grey cubicle walls and stained beige carpet. Even the air smells the same, dust mixed with the faint scent of someone's bacon sandwich.

God, it's good to be back.

'Charlotte!' A heavy-set man with jet-black hair and swarthy skin appears from Vivek's office, and Charlotte blinks. This must be Ed – she'd have met him before going on mat leave, but she doesn't remember him at all. *Maybe that's a good thing*, she thinks as he flashes her a cheesy grin.

'You're looking well. So pleased you decided to join us, after all. It's good to see you again.' He gives her a swift once-over that makes her feel like she's being assessed for fitness to work. 'How's the kiddie?'

Kiddie? Charlotte grits her teeth. 'Her name's Anabelle. She's great, thanks.'

She glances at the clock, hoping Miriam will remember to give Anabelle her mid-morning snack in a bit. Anabelle gets so cranky if she doesn't eat regularly . . . kind of like her mother. Charlotte's stomach grumbles and she remembers that between getting Anabelle and herself dressed, she didn't eat breakfast. She never used to have anything but coffee, but in the past couple of months she's got used to having a bowl of cereal.

'Come on, let me show you where you're sitting.' Ed takes off so quickly that she has no choice but to trot after him, nearly tripping in her unfamiliar high heels.

'Right, here you are.' He gestures towards a bank of computers in the corner, squeezed together so closely it'd be a miracle if she doesn't jab her neighbour with an elbow. Her heart sinks as she remembers her roomy cubicle, complete with her very own potted plant and view of the car park. That seems downright luxurious now.

You won't be here long, she reminds herself. *Do what needs to be done, and move up – or on.*

'Right, let me introduce you to everyone – well, you know most of the team, I think. Then I'll give you a chance to settle in. I've booked you a session this afternoon with one of your fellow team members to refamiliarise you with everything and get you up to date on all the accounts.'

He leads her on a speedy handshake with the rest of the team before depositing her back in front of her desk. Charlotte slides into the chair and faces the computer. She closes her eyes for a second, savouring the moment. Then she flicks on the switch, takes a deep breath and prepares to plunge in.

The next few weeks pass in a torturous haze. It may be the same office with many of the same people, but everything has changed, from the top accounts to the pitch presentation template she'd so carefully created. Even the timesheet system is different. Her position in the company couldn't be further from where it had been, and she'd be lying if she said she found it easy to bear. Instead of being the shit-hot star practically guaranteed to be the next VP, she's the mum who's taken time off to be with her daughter and, in the process, has seemingly been rendered brain-dead . . . at least if the constant mansplaining is anything to go by.

As the sole woman in the team, it's getting harder and harder to grin and bear the constant jokes about clients' 'fuckability factor' and the laddish antics on her colleagues' big Friday nights out – Friday nights she has every intention of avoiding after going along to the first one and getting beer poured all over her. Vivek – although not exactly a paragon of feminist virtues – would never have allowed such talk in the office, but Ed seems to be encouraging it.

It's just for a few months has become her mantra, and often she catches herself sitting at her desk in the midst of updating client data for the rest of the team, wondering what Anabelle and Miriam are up to. Sometimes she even steals away from her desk to the storeroom for a quick call to check in. Anabelle has adjusted well to Charlotte's return to work, loving her action-packed days with Miriam, who has taken her to almost every museum within the M25. And David's usually able to be home by Anabelle's bedtime, taking over from Miriam and putting their child to sleep. Sometimes, Charlotte's only interaction with their daughter is over breakfast, often while she's flying through the lounge with her coffee on the way to the door.

This is exactly the life she would have been living if Anabelle hadn't been born with a heart condition: with a busy job, a husband helping out and a daughter who doesn't disturb her working routine. But it's not *really* the life she'd be living, is it? Because she'd have been VP by now, not toiling away in a position she would have held ten years earlier. She'd have been happy at work, not chomping at the bit to do something – anything – to move up a rung. She'd have been dreadfully busy, yes, but she'd have had more control over her time, instead of taking orders from a man who should be *her* junior. And she'd have had a partner to share her life with, not a stranger who's just biding his time until he can leave.

Would all that have made up for practically missing out on her daughter's childhood? Or would she still have felt the same tug at her gut every morning as she kissed Anabelle goodbye, knowing she wouldn't be home again until her daughter was fast asleep?

The only way to find out is to get back to where I left off, Charlotte tells herself as the bus lurches towards the office in the 7 a.m. gloom. What other choice does she have? She can't stay in this position for much longer without self-combusting, and she can't stay at home, either. All she can do is to keep moving, keeping hauling herself up a jagged cliff, keeping fighting the feelings of guilt and sadness and keep praying that soon, it will be worth it.

Charlotte steps off the bus and on to the busy pavement, her pace quickening as an idea hits. There's a big pitch coming up next week in Berlin for a potentially massive account – a company she's worked with in the past. She volunteered to help out during the last team meeting, but Ed had ignored her, as usual, assigning the presentation to a 'very sexy' colleague from their Birmingham office. But maybe . . . maybe if she puts together her own presentation, based on her experience, she can show them she should be on the pitching team, too. It's not much, but it's a step in the right direction.

She nods at the receptionist and slides into her chair, her brain ticking over as she pulls up the bid information on the computer. *Bingo!* Excitement rises as she realises the project manager at Freen, the German company, is someone she knows quite well; they've even gone out for drinks together several times after meetings. She *should* be pitching for this project . . . or, at the very least, she should be included in the meeting. If Ed has half a brain, he'll have to recognise that.

Right, that settles it: this is her chance to leapfrog forward – to show she's in top form, that her mind is still sharp and that her industry experience and connections are still relevant. She'll prepare the best pitch presentation known to humankind and make a case so solid for her presence in Berlin that even Ed can't deny it. Her heart sinks when she realises that, on top of all her other work, she'll need to burn the midnight oil, as well as work all weekend. She's promised Anabelle a ride on the carousel on the South Bank, then hot dogs and ice cream afterwards. Charlotte's been looking forward to it almost as much as her daughter.

But this is too good an opportunity to pass up. There will be other weekends, and David will find something fun to do with Anabelle. Charlotte leans back in her chair, resolve flooding through her. She's found a foothold on that jagged cliff now, and she's going to pull herself up as high as she can.

CHAPTER FORTY-THREE

13 December

I'm shaking. I'm shaking with excitement, with potential, with a new idea that's entered my mind, stemming from the unlikeliest conversation. *A baby.* A new baby, to add to our family. It's funny I hadn't thought of it until now, but I suppose that's how it goes when your first child has had such a difficult start and you're just focused on getting her through the hours.

Today started off as one of those days that inevitably crop up, despite my relentless upbeat thinking: a day where everything seems so complicated and takes so much time. Anabelle's three now, but sometimes, instead of getting easier, it seems . . . a little trying. I love that she's so chatty, but I'm tired of talking, explaining, convincing. I'm fed up with asking her not to chase the poor pigeons, of telling her to be careful not to get her feet wet in puddles, of trying to grasp her little hand before she wriggles away. I'm exhausted from the constant nonsensical negotiations (no, you can't have another scoop of ice cream because your favourite colour is blue. What the—?).

None of this means I don't count myself lucky every day, of course. None of this means I'm not super-grateful – not like the mums I went out with that night; the mums whose complaints scorched my ears. None of this means I'd change any little bit of it.

Anabelle woke up early and David had to duck out for a meeting, which meant I didn't have a chance to take a shower. And let me tell you, with the state my hair was in, I was in desperate need of one. I tried to slick my strands back into a ponytail but, even so, they looked greasy and unkempt.

Anabelle refused to eat her cereal then spilled it on the floor; I managed to kneel in half of it when I was trying to clean it up. Staying inside with her being so grumpy was a non-starter and today was a rare day without any playgroups, so I bundled her into a coat and wellies and dragged her the short distance to the park. While there, she managed to fall into some mud, get sand in her hair, and somehow – I still don't know how – lose a welly.

I was in the process of half-carrying, half-dragging her across the King's Road back home when I heard someone calling my name. I swung around, nearly knocking over a passer-by with Anabelle in my arms, and met the gaze of a blonde woman in a red coat.

'Charlotte! How are you?'

I blinked, trying to place her; then suddenly it came to me. This immaculate, polished woman had been an intern at Cellbril around the time I'd been promoted to senior account director. I hadn't worked with her much; I'd been too busy running the team, but I'd seen her in meetings and been impressed with her drive and efficiency. My mind whirled as I tried to remember her name, but with Anabelle struggling in my arms, I hadn't a hope in hell of doing so.

'Good to see you,' I said. 'How have you been?' I let Anabelle slide down to balance on my feet, conscious that my hair had escaped from my ponytail, I had mud on my trousers from Anabelle's one welly, and that my daughter resembled an urchin more than a Chelsea child. I tried not to notice how the woman – God, I wished I could remember her name – took a step back from us. Not that I blamed her.

'Great.' She smiled, and I could see that she really meant it. 'I'm just down in London for the day, doing some shopping and visiting friends. Cellbril hired me full-time a couple of years ago, and I'm now an account manager in the Birmingham office . . . working my way up to director, like you did. I love it. And you? What have you been up to?'

I met her eyes, wondering what to say. Could she believe that the woman she'd known – the one who'd worked every night until late – was now happy staying at home? That the person who'd poured all her energy into securing multimillion-pound contracts spent her time potty training and reciting lines from *Peppa Pig* episodes?

No. Of course she couldn't. And the truth is, the person she had known – the old me – *wouldn't* have been happy staying at home. I would have wanted more.

But I wasn't that person now.

I lifted my chin. 'It's been a wonderful three years with this one.' I tried not to flinch as Anabelle jumped up and down, crushing my toes.

'You're not working?' The woman – *Lucy*, her name finally popped into my mind – gave a fixed smile, but I could see the horror in her eyes.

'Nope!' I grinned back at her. 'I've been home with my daughter and really enjoying it. In fact, we're thinking of having another one. Another baby! The more the merrier!' My eyebrows shot up as the words left my mouth. Where had that come from?

'Oh, fabulous.' I could see Lucy didn't mean it, though. I knew exactly what she was thinking: *rather you than me*. I'd have thought the same in her position. I *had* thought the same in her position.

She said goodbye and I scooped up Anabelle, mulling over our exchange. Did I really want another child, or was it just to show Lucy that I had changed; that all thoughts of work had gone from me now, and I was fine with that – more than fine, actually: brilliant?

I shook my head. I *was* fine, of course. I didn't need to say I wanted another child to prove it. And so . . . I must have really meant it. I couldn't help but smile as the realisation sank in. It made perfect sense. Sure, the odd day here and there with Anabelle could be challenging, but I'd mastered life as a mother of one. Why not have another? Wasn't that what stay-at-home mums did: have more children so the siblings could play together? I'd heard it countless times in playgroups, but I guess I hadn't been ready. Anabelle took up all of me. But I've expanded into this role, and I can handle more. I *want* to handle more.

And there's no reason why we shouldn't have another. Anabelle's condition is something that just happened, a random mutation . . . a simple birth defect, like David had said. We'll keep close tabs as our baby develops, of course, but I'm certain everything will be fine. I'll take every possible precaution to protect my child. I know that I can trust myself to do so.

Lily's face, full of hope and joy when she told me she was pregnant, flashed into my mind, and I recalled my longing to turn back the clock – my regret that I hadn't treasured that time. I grinned. I might not be able to change the past, but I can control the future. And this time, it *will* be different. Like my friend, I'll blossom as the months go on. I'll bask in Baby, knowing that I can handle anything now.

I'll need to talk to David, of course, but he shouldn't have any objections. We've been managing fine on his salary; we already own all the baby gear, and once we move into Miriam's, we'll have tons of space. Maybe I'll even try co-sleeping. Isn't that supposed to make breastfeeding easier? Because I'll definitely breastfeed this next time around.

Another baby. Another *life* to take care of. It'll be insanely busy, and I'll be exhausted. But this is my chance to do things right, and I'm going to grab hold of it with everything I have.

CHAPTER FORTY-FOUR

Charlotte's eyes snap open, her brain instantly alert. Today is the day she's going to show Ed the pitch presentation she's slaved over, and she absolutely cannot wait – especially to witness the expression on his face when he sees how airtight, how professional and how bloody brilliant it is. It's the best piece of work she's done in . . . well, maybe ever. After creating this masterpiece, she's sure he'll find a role for her on the pitching team. With her experience, he'd be stupid not to.

Berlin, here she comes.

Charlotte crawls from the covers and pads over to Anabelle's bed in the corner. Her daughter looks so peaceful, curled up with Zebby and her thumb stuck in her mouth. Charlotte reaches down to smooth back a lock of hair from her forehead, the now-familiar combination of sadness and guilt mingling inside. Apart from the day when she discovered Zebby in her handbag and rushed home to return him before bedtime, she's hardly seen her daughter in the past week or so, and – all things going well – she'll be off to Berlin in a couple of days. It's just a quick trip, but still . . .

If they win the account, Ed will have no choice but to promote her. The client wouldn't like someone with such a junior title working on their account. It'll be yet more work, but at least she'll be doing a job she's proud of instead of toiling away entering data for hours on end.

That'll go some way towards easing the pain of leaving her daughter . . . hopefully.

Charlotte swallows, heading over to her wardrobe, where her carefully chosen suit is waiting. In the few weeks since she's been back at work, she's already dropped almost ten pounds, mostly down to forgetting to eat lunch and being too busy to snack. Her old wardrobe would fit again – if only she could figure out where she put it! The mounds of *stuff* crammed into their cluttered and disorganised flat defeated her few attempts to find it, and it was easier to give up and buy more clothes than sift through piles of God knows what.

'Anabelle's still sleeping,' she says to David as she eases out of the bedroom. 'I'll see you later tonight.'

As she catches the bus to the office, she thinks how strange it is that David knows nothing about this big pitch – she'd only told him she had extra work at the office – or about the potential trip to Berlin and the chance to move forward. Back in the day, he knew everything about her workplace. She'd even rehearse her pitches with him, playing a game where they'd gulp wine for each PowerPoint slide. Eventually she wouldn't be able to focus any longer and they'd end up in a sweaty heap on the bed after making love. God, she misses him – even though he hasn't gone yet, it feels like he's already vanished from her life . . . just as he becomes more visible in Anabelle's. They'll both feel his absence, even if he's adamant they won't. She sighs, wondering for the millionth time how he can even contemplate leaving.

Two hours later, she's standing outside Ed's office door. He beckons her in and hangs up the phone, smiling his 'what can I do for you?' grin as she sits down. 'Hi there. How's the kiddie today?'

Charlotte forces a smile. No matter how many times she tells him Anabelle's name, he seems incapable of remembering it – or anything else about Charlotte other than the fact she has a child. 'She's fine, thanks.'

'How are you settling in?' he asks. 'I can appreciate it's probably not been easy adjusting to the workplace environment again and familiarising yourself with all the new procedures, especially after not working for so long. You seem to be doing all right, though.' He nods approvingly at her, and she almost feels like she should pant and roll over for her tummy to be rubbed. God, how patronising.

'Thank you,' she says through gritted teeth. 'And it hasn't been difficult at all, actually. I'm really enjoying it. I've been working harder than ever, and I wanted to show you this.' She cracks open her laptop and turns the screen towards him, her heart pounding with excitement.

'It's a presentation for the Berlin meeting with Freen on Friday,' she says, when Ed doesn't react to the material on the screen. 'I know the Birmingham office has pulled something together, but perhaps they might add this material to it?' She tries to keep her voice level as Ed flicks through her slides. 'You may not know that I've worked with the project manager, Ute, quite closely before – on another trial. But I know what's important to Freen and exactly what they're looking for.' Ed's eyes flicker when she says this, but his neutral expression stays unchanged. 'I've tailored this exactly to their needs. I can run through it now with you, if you like.'

'No, no, that's fine.' Ed waves a hand, his eyes still glued to the screen. 'Lucy and I will go over this later. She's here for a few days so that we can review everything before we fly over.' He meets her eyes. 'Thanks for this, Charlotte. I'm impressed.' He smiles distractedly then glances towards the door, indicating that her time is up.

But she's not moving. She can't move. She spent hours on this, and that's it? He's *impressed*? She'll be damned if this Lucy character is going to take her hard work and run with it. This presentation is one of the best she's ever done, and if this doesn't boost her forward, nothing will.

Charlotte swallows. 'It goes without saying that I'd be happy to accompany the team to Berlin,' she says, forcing her voice to be strong yet not overpowering, which would be sure to get Ed's back up. 'Given

I have such a great history with Freen and a very solid relationship with Ute.' She hasn't spoken to Ute in years, but nothing helps women bond better than (several) vodka Martinis.

'Hmm . . .' Ed leans back in his chair, tapping on his desk. 'It *would* do us good to have someone with previous experience with Freen. Ute can be a tough nut to crack, and between you and me, I think Lucy's a little scared of her. Perhaps you can do a slide or two. Let me call Lucy in and we'll have a chat.'

Charlotte barely refrains from punching the air as they wait for their colleague from Birmingham to appear. A chance to get back out there and pitch again! God, how she's missed it. 'Perfect. Just let me know what you'd like me to do, and please do let me know if you think we should add my material to what Lucy has—' She comes to a stop as Ed lifts a hand in the air.

'Ah, here she is now,' Ed says, gesturing Lucy in. 'Have you two met?'

Charlotte turns to see a woman come into the office, and her mouth drops open. *Lucy* . . . an intern, from several years ago. Lucy had been eager to gain work experience before starting her masters, and Charlotte had been impressed with her ambition and drive. In fact, she'd reminded Charlotte of herself when she'd first started out.

So Lucy had managed to get a job here, then. Good for her! It's bizarre to be working alongside a former intern, but . . . Charlotte shakes her head. She'd thought she'd be walking back into the world she'd left. Like everything else, though, it's changed.

'Charlotte, hello.' Lucy smiles and holds out a hand. 'I heard you were back. It's so good to see you again.'

'Charlotte's been kind enough to develop her own presentation for Freen,' Ed says, and Charlotte can't help noticing how Lucy's face hardens. He swivels the laptop towards the former intern. 'Have a look; there's some solid material here. And since Charlotte has previous experience working with Ute, I think it's a good idea to let her present some slides.'

'Really? I don't.' Lucy's blunt words make Charlotte's eyes pop in surprise, and Ed's brow furrows.

'Why not?' he asks.

'Well, we don't know how long Charlotte's going to be with us, do we?' Lucy says sweetly. 'We don't want to put her in front of Freen only to have to tell them she's left us.'

What the hell? Charlotte freezes. Had Lucy somehow uncovered her plan to stay only a few months before moving on to something better – if she can't boost herself up here, of course?

'What do you mean?' she manages to say. She meets Lucy's glittering eyes and nailed-on smile, realising that this woman might not be very happy at the sudden reappearance of her former boss. *She* certainly wouldn't be, in Lucy's place.

'Well, when I ran into you on the street a few months back, you said you were thinking of having another baby. You made it sound quite imminent, actually.' She stares pointedly at Charlotte's midsection as if she is carrying a child right this second. Ed looks, too, and Charlotte fights the urge to tug her suit jacket closed. 'I have to admit, I was rather surprised when I heard you'd returned to work.'

'Oh, goodness.' Charlotte waves a hand in the air like Lucy's words are nothing, but she wants to kill the woman for landing her in it in front of Ed. 'You must have misunderstood me. I said we *weren't* thinking of having another. No way.' She smiles, but anger churns inside. So what if she *was*? She still has the experience and the connections needed for this pitch. She should hardly be punished for procreation.

'Okay.' Lucy shrugs, but from the way Ed is eyeing her, Charlotte can tell he's still not one hundred per cent convinced.

'Right, well . . .' Ed shifts in his chair. 'Perhaps it's best if we stick to our original plan, Charlotte. The last thing we want is to put you front and centre if, er . . .'

'*No.*' Even Charlotte is surprised at the vehemence in her voice. 'I am *not* going to have another child. I am one thousand per cent dedicated to this job, and—'

The tinny tune of 'Baby Shark' fills the room, and Charlotte freezes in horror as she realises it's coming from her mobile phone – she's changed the ringtone to Anabelle's favourite song. Her cheeks redden at Ed and Lucy's bemused expressions.

'Should you get that?' Lucy asks pointedly. 'Might be your daughter or something. You'd better make sure she's okay.' It's as if she's trying to drive the point home that Charlotte can never be one thousand per cent dedicated, as she's just promised.

'Three year olds can't dial mobiles,' Charlotte mutters before putting the phone on silent. Shit, it's Miriam. *Is* everything all right? She takes a deep breath and tries to refocus.

'I want to do those slides,' she says firmly. 'It's the best thing for this pitch, and I promise that if we win the account, I won't be going anywhere.' *If* Ed gives her a senior role, but she'll cross that bridge when she comes to it. 'I know Freen, I know Ute, and I know they'll listen to what I have to say.'

Ed tilts his head. 'Okay,' he says finally. 'But I'm trusting you, Charlotte. Don't let me down.'

Charlotte can sense Lucy radiating anger, and she barely resists shooting her colleague a triumphant grin. Instead she nods, excitement circling through her stomach. She did it! She's taken a giant step towards where she used to be. There's still a long way to go, but the clifftop is getting closer.

First things first, though: she needs to call Miriam.

CHAPTER FORTY-FIVE

14 January

I don't know what I'm doing. I can barely focus on this page. My hands are trembling so much that I can't even form these letters. I can't believe what's happened. I can't believe what David just told me. Hell, I can't believe he only told me now, after all these years! Three *fucking* years.

Calm down. I need to calm down or my head will explode – like my heart already has. It's been smashed to bits, lodging sharp splinters into every part of me.

Okay. I'll write this down from the beginning, to try to get a grip. To help me try to understand, if that's even possible.

Lily called me this morning, inviting us over later to meet her brand-new baby. She'd had her beautiful boy last week in a perfect, calm home birth. I thought she was crazy to have the baby at home – too many things could go wrong, and after what happened with Anabelle, I wouldn't take any chances. But everything went fine. According to her husband, Lily was a star, delivering in a serene, Madonna-like way without any painkillers.

David was working, but he agreed to swing by Lily's on his lunch break and meet Anabelle and me there. I was bursting with excitement – I'd managed the Herculean feat of waiting until now to talk to him about having another child, confident that seeing a newborn would sway him in my favour. Who could resist a tiny, perfect infant? In the few weeks since I'd had the idea, my desire to have a baby had ballooned so much it felt almost visible, like my womb was wearing a 'vacancy' sign.

My head was filled with visions of how wonderful my pregnancy would be this time around: how I'd glow, not with worry and stress but with love for our unborn child. How those early days would be filled not with adrenaline and fear but with peace and calm. How David and I would work together, instead of me shouldering everything to allay my guilt.

I dressed carefully, pulling on a bright red top Miriam had given me ages ago but I hadn't yet worn – my usual wardrobe consisted of washed-out greys and blacks that wouldn't show the dirt. I wanted to start our next baby's journey on a bright and cheerful note . . . unlike Anabelle's, which hadn't even been planned.

I ushered Anabelle inside Lily's flat, expecting a chaotic place crammed full of dirty laundry and dishes like ours had been. Instead, the flat was spotless, and Lily looked as rested as I'd ever seen her. Her son, Liam, was sleeping peacefully in a Moses basket, and my heart picked up pace. This beautiful scene could be my reality in nine months' time.

David arrived, his eyes softening as he stroked Liam's head. Lily raised her eyebrows pointedly at me when we clocked David's expression: something like longing streamed from him so potently it almost coloured the air. Was it possible we were actually on the same page – that he'd been thinking the time was right for another child, too? Fizzing inside, I pulled him into the kitchen to talk. I wrapped my arms around him, ignoring how he stiffened in surprise. Not that I could blame him – it's been ages since we touched.

'What do you think about another?' I asked. I couldn't stop myself from grinning. It'd been a while since I'd felt so alive, so full of possibility.

David's brow furrowed. 'Another what?'

'Baby!' The word burst out of me, and I shook my head, laughing. My husband could be so dense sometimes.

I waited for him to nod, to smile, to pull me close . . . something. Instead, he said nothing, his muscles tensing under my fingers.

'What?' I moved back, scanning his face. His lips were pinched together in that way I hated – a way I hadn't seen before having Anabelle. 'You don't . . . you don't want more children?' That couldn't be it. We'd never discussed it, but I was sure he'd have told me if that was the case. So what was he thinking?

I held his gaze, my mind ticking through any possible objections. We'd already agreed to move, so it couldn't be a space issue. As for money, we could manage. Could it be something related to Anabelle's traumatic start? Maybe . . . maybe it had affected him more than he let on?

I took a deep breath, desperate to reassure him. 'If you're worried about our next child having the same thing as Anabelle, I want you to know that I'll take every precaution. I'm not working. I don't run. I barely even drink. Hell, I'll sit on a chair with my feet up the whole time if I need to, ramming Brussel sprouts down my throat. We can have extra scans, extra tests, whatever's required to make sure everything's fine.'

But David shook his head. 'You could do all that and more, but it wouldn't matter.'

I froze. What did he mean, 'it wouldn't matter'? I reached out to take his arm, but he moved away from me, bracing himself on the counter.

'Charlotte . . .' I couldn't see his face, but his voice was strained. 'It's genetic. Anabelle's heart condition is genetic.'

'Genetic?' I repeated, trying to understand. 'No one in my family has heart problems.'

'But they do in mine.' His words cut through my confusion, and he swung around to meet my stare. I stepped back, stunned by the hurt and pain I saw there. 'After the nurse took our family history, I asked my mum if there are any heart problems in our family. Mum told me no . . . but she phoned later, after remembering that my father had a brother who'd died as an infant because his heart hadn't developed properly.' David let out a shuddery sigh. 'They didn't know exactly what was wrong – obviously medicine wasn't as advanced back then. Mum remembers my father saying there was another relative with heart problems, too – a cousin, she thinks. I tried to get in touch with him for more information, but no one knows how to track him down.'

I tried to answer, to scrabble at something to say, but I couldn't. I couldn't take this in.

'I've done a lot of research, and with my family history, there's a chance that if we have another child, she or he might have the same heart problem. A small chance, but still.' He shook his head. 'I can't go through that again. I can't face almost losing a baby again. I *can't*.'

I stared at my husband, at his mouth moving, feeling like the world had shifted. Like the world I'd poured everything into – the world I wanted more of – had tilted, leaving me unsteady.

Threatening to topple me over.

'But . . . you've known this since Anabelle was born? That her condition is genetic?' My voice emerged reedy, like it was swimming up from the depths of me. 'Why didn't you tell me? Why didn't you say something?'

'I should have. I know I should have.' David ran a hand over his face. 'But God, I couldn't get the words out, Charlotte. I was utterly destroyed that our child had to go through this because of *me*. Had I known – had we known – this was running in the family, then maybe . . . maybe we could have prepared for it better . . . or something. I don't know.' He reached out for me, but I still couldn't move. 'And then as the years went on, and Anabelle was all right, well . . . You were so caught up with her, another baby never came up, and it . . . it was easier to put it all behind me. Behind us.'

The words swirled around me, a flurry of sounds. A door had been slammed in my face, and I couldn't even lift a foot to try to kick it open. Silence stretched between us.

'Charlotte?' David's face was creased with pain. 'Please, say something. I'm sorry. I'm sorry.'

I met my husband's eyes, but I was numb to his agony. If anyone could have understood how he was feeling – how he had felt – these past few years, it was me. I knew only too well the horror of lugging around the weight of guilt and blame. But the difference is that David's life has carried on, while mine . . .

Mine is unrecognisable. *I'm* unrecognisable. I had to change. I wanted to change, and I did: I became all mother. And I want even more of it. I *need* even more of it. I need to keep moving forward, diving deeper and deeper. I feel that with an intensity like no other.

But I can't, because David's words have stopped me short. I'll never have the chance to cherish a pregnancy, or to live through those first few months with my baby minus the cloak of guilt. I'll never be able to show that now, I can finally give all my care, attention and love to my child as it grows and develops inside me. I'm stalled here, continuously trying to right a wrong, without being able to do anything differently.

Hot lava seared my insides, bubbling up into my throat. I let out a cry, then spun around and into the lounge. Somehow, I managed to say goodbye to Lily and wrestle Anabelle into her coat, down the stairs and into the car. I barely saw her, though. I barely heard her voice.

I drove blindly through the streets, some part of me navigating my way back home. I went up the stairs, unlocked the door and shoved the tablet at my daughter. My mobile rang again and again as David tried to reach me, but I didn't answer it. I grabbed this diary and tried to grasp it all.

I can't stay here. I can't stay still; I can't let this volcano engulf me. I need to keep moving. I'll drop off Anabelle at Miriam's, and then . . . I haven't a clue.

How can I know which way to go when the only road I need to travel is now closed to me forever?

CHAPTER FORTY-SIX

'What story are we going to read tonight?' Charlotte ruffles her daughter's hair, happiness flooding through her that she actually managed to make it home in time for Anabelle's bedtime. The team leave for Berlin tomorrow morning, and Charlotte has spent the past couple of days and nights holed up in the office with Ed and Lucy, finessing their presentation until it's a work of art. They couldn't be any better prepared. Even so, Lucy and Ed had raised their eyebrows when she'd crept out of the office at five-thirty.

'I want Daddy.' Anabelle's lower lip juts out, and Charlotte's heart sinks. 'Daddy reads bedtime stories the best.'

David darts a glance at Charlotte. 'Honey, Mummy's going away for the next few days and she really wants to read tonight. Okay? I'll do it tomorrow.'

'No.' Anabelle shakes her head. 'Daddy. Daddy Daddy *Daddy*.'

'Go ahead.' Charlotte sighs. She goes back to the lounge and sinks down on to the sofa. She knows she shouldn't take it personally – that children are creatures of routine, and Anabelle's got used to David doing her story – but she can't help feeling like something is slipping away from her. She listens to their laughter and David patiently answering Anabelle's endless questions, hoping her daughter will cope all right when he takes off. All this time he's spending with her now certainly isn't going to make that any easier.

A few minutes later, David closes the bedroom door softly. 'She's asleep. Look . . . can we talk?' He sits down next to her, and Charlotte's gut squeezes. This is it. He's going to tell her that he's leaving. Terrible timing – the night before her big pitch – but it's not like he cares any more about her world, is it? Hurt shoots through her and she forces it away.

'Okay.' She stares straight ahead, steeling herself.

'I've turned down the job in Exeter,' he says, and Charlotte's head snaps towards him. *What?* He's not leaving, after all? She draws in a breath, trying to get her mind around it. It's a good thing, of course. She'd just been wondering how Anabelle would cope. But what does this mean for their family . . . for *them*?

'Since you started looking for your job, I've spent a lot more time with Anabelle . . . time I didn't feel I could ask you for before. Time I didn't feel I deserved.' Guilt flashes across his face, and he ducks his head. 'And, well . . . it's an understatement to say that I've enjoyed it. I've loved it, and I think she has, too.'

Charlotte nods. It's more than obvious how well the two of them get on.

'I thought getting out of the way was the best thing for us all,' David continues. 'But I've realised that it's not the best thing for *her*. She needs a father in her life – she shouldn't miss out on having a dad. I know what that feels like all too well.' He meets her gaze with a determined expression. 'And if you do remember everything, well . . . I'm not going to step aside this time. I'm ready to be a father now. I *need* to be a father now.'

Charlotte nods again, unable to speak through the emotions swirling inside. She's thrilled for Anabelle and delighted that David has been able to lift himself from the pit of blame to be the father he always wanted to be . . . even if it means turning down an important job. Maybe her husband hasn't become the complete stranger she'd thought he had. But she can't help noticing that he hasn't said a word about their relationship – about wanting to stay because of her, too. Does she feature in his decision at all? If he's able to get past his guilt to be with Anabelle, does that mean he might be able to get past his guilt to be a husband again, too?

Or are they too far beyond that now?

She's desperate to ask, but she's not sure she wants to know the answer. What if he tells her it really is over? And if there is still some small hope for them, how long will it be before some semblance of their former closeness returns? Living this way is torturous, and she doesn't know how much more she can take.

'I'll make sure I'm home to put Anabelle to bed,' David says, 'and I'm not going to work any more weekends. I'll stay here in the morning, too, so you can get off to work quickly. You won't need to worry about anything when you're off on your trip. Mum and I have it covered.'

'Okay. Thanks.' She swallows back the questions, telling herself that, no matter what happens between them, she should be relieved – her husband has just handed her carte blanche to pursue her career with the 'thousand per cent dedication' she'd pledged. Instead, though, she can't help feeling like the circle surrounding her daughter is closing without her . . . as if she'll be on the outside looking in. Was that what her mum had felt like sometimes? Had she ever minded that Charlotte turned to others before going to her – and that she still did?

'I'd better get to bed,' Charlotte says, unable even to think of anything else to say, let alone form the words. Too late, she notices David's face drop, and she wonders if he was hoping for a more enthusiastic response. She *is* happy he's staying, but how can she show that when he didn't even mention her?

The next morning passes in a blur of travel and rehearsals, and at last the team is sitting around a table in a bland boardroom in Berlin, ready to deliver their pitch. Charlotte is practically vibrating with excitement. She loves this moment: standing up in front of the challenging gaze of professionals and showing them that not only does she understand their business, she can also uncover angles they might not have thought of themselves. Ute had given her a huge hug on seeing her, and Charlotte had noticed Ed watching their exchange with satisfaction. The stage is perfectly set for her to deliver and move forward.

One hour later, Charlotte's cheeks are flushed with success. Her part of the presentation has gone off without a hitch, and she's answered every question with confidence and knowledge, even rescuing a floundering Lucy when she couldn't respond to a particularly difficult question.

'One more question,' Ute says, 'and then we'll have a quick break. Who is going to be working on this account? Is this team finalised or will there be some changes later on?'

Charlotte suppresses a gleeful grin. Ed will have to name her to the account now, won't he? Especially given her strong performance and her relationship with Ute.

'We're very pleased to confirm that Lucy here will continue to liaise with you until the project is up and running. You'll have Gamal on project management, Chris on medical, and—'

The thumping in Charlotte's ears drowns out Ed's voice. Lucy? Instead of her? She has three times Lucy's expertise, and she's proven it in spades in this meeting. She sits in silence, unable to lift her gaze from the table for fear the rage on her face will show. Ed gets up to leave the room and Charlotte edges out after him.

'Ed,' she calls as he rushes away, probably in an attempt to escape from her. '*Ed!*'

'Not now, Charlotte.' He doesn't even turn around, just lifts a hand in the air. The fury she's been trying to contain spills over, and she races down the corridor until she's right beside him.

'Why didn't you name me to the account?' she asks, her voice shaking. 'You know I'm the best person for it. Not only do I have the experience, but I also have a great working relationship with Ute.'

Ed sighs. 'Can we talk about this when we get back to the office? Mid-pitch is not the place for hysterics.'

Hysterics? Charlotte is even more livid now. Just because she's standing up for herself, she's being accused of hysterics? 'No,' she says, not caring that her voice is echoing down the corridor. 'No, we cannot. I deserve an answer.'

'All right then.' Ed turns to face her. 'You may have the experience, but I'm just not sure you have the right attitude.'

Her mouth drops open. 'Right attitude? I've *slaved* over this presentation.' He can't deny that.

'Yes, you have worked hard. But what about sustaining that effort long term?' he asks.

Charlotte huffs in frustration. Is this about having a baby again? 'I told you, I won't be leaving anytime soon.'

'It's not about leaving. It's about your commitment now. Making personal phone calls at the office? Leaving early when we have crucial work to cover?'

Shit. Her hearts drops. She'd thought no one had noticed her nipping into the storeroom with her phone. As for leaving early . . . that was just one day, when Anabelle needed Zebby. And heading out the other night at five-thirty was hardly slacking; the pitch had been more than ready. None of those actions had affected her work. For God's sake, it wasn't as if she was going out and getting drunk every night, like half the team!

Charlotte holds Ed's gaze, her brain ticking over. She could win multiple accounts time and again, but the second she needs to leave early, Ed will challenge her commitment. It's nothing to do with her attitude or dedication, she realises in a rush. It's to do with her being a mother, with all the emotional attachment and responsibility that go along with it.

And she's not going to apologise for that. She's not going to try to hide it any longer. She doesn't *want* to try to hide it.

'If you really want to advance,' Ed continues, 'there's no room for anything else. We need all of you – body and soul.' He thumps his heart and Charlotte barely refrains from rolling her eyes. 'I demand nothing less. Maybe if you can show me that, eventually – and I'm talking *eventually* – we can speak about moving forward.'

Charlotte shakes her head, knowing instantly she can't give that. She *won't* give that. Maybe she could have before, but she's not that person any longer. She has a child – a child she loves, and a child she wants to be with. Yes, she still needs to work, but she refuses to stay in a place that belittles her skills and experience . . . in a place that is forcing her to negate an important part of her. No job is worth that.

'I quit,' she says, and the look of surprise on Ed's face is worth the drudgery of the past few weeks. 'Give Ute my best.'

And with that, she walks away.

Towards her home.

Towards her daughter.

CHAPTER FORTY-SEVEN

It's just after midnight when Charlotte reaches her flat. She stares up at the hideous blackout curtains, remembering the first time she saw them after the accident. Although she still hates them just as much, she's not the same woman who looks at them in dread, terrified of the life that lay behind them. The notion of being a mother doesn't scare her any longer. In fact, after what just happened with Ed, she knows now that she wants to embrace it. It's a part of her, just as much as wanting a fulfilling career is.

Charlotte creeps up the stairs and turns the key in the flat door. It's dark and silent inside, and she gently pushes the bedroom door open. Taking advantage of her absence, David is sprawled on the bed, hogging the duvet like he always used to. Anabelle is lying flat on her back, her little rosebud mouth open and closing with every breath. Her dark hair fans out on the pillow, and Zebby is tucked under her arm. She looks so defenceless and delicate, and . . . Charlotte freezes as an avalanche of images tumbles into her brain.

Anabelle as an infant, her lips blue and her breathing laboured.

The huge bandage swamping her chest after the operation.

Bringing her baby home, and the terror and fug of fear that clogged her every thought process, colouring each move with uncertainty and worry.

And . . . a heavy sense of *guilt*, lying across her body like a block of cement, cutting into her skin every time she squirms under its weight.

Suddenly it feels like she's not here, by this bed, in her home. She's somewhere else, in a dark, dark place, gazing down at her daughter . . . her daughter, so small and pale, lying in a cot with tubes coming out of her nose. And Charlotte is vibrating with terror and love that fills every pore of her, so much that it spills over, engulfing her in a cloud that changes how she sees the world around her – a cloud that changes everything.

The cloud of motherhood.

Her heart is beating so fast now that she can practically feel the blood rushing through her body, carrying a tidal wave of emotions with it. She struggles to stand but suddenly feels light-headed and sinks back on to the bed. With every pulse, a wave of love, of fear, then love again breaks inside her, battering her soul.

Charlotte tries to catch her breath and process what she's seen; what she felt. Terror and fear she can understand – she had a tiny taste of that when she thought Anabelle was lost. But guilt? Why would she feel guilty? She did everything she could to be with Anabelle, managing to become a 'wonderful mother', by all accounts. She tries to grasp the end of the yarn of memory to unravel it further. There was something . . . something she was supposed to do . . .

The knowledge hits her like a hammer. The ultrasound. The one that might have spotted Anabelle's condition . . . the one that might have made those first few weeks less traumatic for everyone.

The one she'd never completed because she'd rushed back to work.

Oh, God.

She gets to her feet and staggers to the window, buckling under the weight of the memories now rushing into her. She pushes aside the curtains and stares at the street, struggling to make sense of it all, twisting and turning each new piece of knowledge to fit into the framework of her former life . . . a life she thought she'd known, but hadn't at all.

Because her life as a new mum wasn't what she'd envisioned: a jolly place full of joy and light. It was a place that was shrouded, most of all, in guilt. Guilt that seeped out of every pore; guilt and blame that guided her choices.

She understands now why she didn't go back to work, even if she'd been ready after that first traumatic year. It wasn't because she didn't want to, but because she'd believed her drive and ambition might lead her astray once more. And the only way she could live her new life was to shut down her old self for good . . . or try to, anyway.

She longs to reach back through the years and give herself a huge hug; to say that even though she'd made a careless decision by rushing back to work instead of completing the scan, she couldn't have begun to grasp the consequences – she'd had no idea exactly how much she was risking. And while Charlotte can understand the crushing sense of guilt, the distance she's gained helps her realise that even if she had rescheduled, her daughter's condition might not have been spotted. The outcome might have been the same.

She could have done things differently. She *should* have done things differently, there's no doubt about that. She'd known that, and she'd tried to change herself because of it. But now, Charlotte can see that, despite all her efforts, she hadn't completely changed. She'd still loved David but she'd shoved him away, unable to succumb to his comfort . . . never knowing he felt as guilty as she did. She'd wanted to work but was too worried it might suck her back in. She'd longed to run when he'd given her the trainers, and she'd fled the women's negativity on that night out as if she might crack and join in. She'd even convinced herself she wanted another baby, in a desperate attempt to prove that she was all right with her life.

No wonder she'd been so angry when David had told her his secret. She'd forced her whole identity into the role of mother, only to be told she could never really atone.

Charlotte breathes in a long, shuddery sigh. She *has* changed since becoming a mother, there's no doubt about that. How can you not, when you have a child; when you're responsible for another being . . . a being you love with an intensity like no other? But ever since the accident, she's struggled to understand how motherhood seemed to have transformed her into a completely different person. It hadn't, though: that woman wasn't completely a stranger – not how she'd believed. She'd tried to deny it, but she'd wanted all the things Charlotte wants now: a job where she's valued, a piece of her heart that belongs just to her . . . and love. Love for her husband, and a marriage that works.

A marriage that's not torn apart by guilt and blame.

Charlotte turns from the window towards the bed, taking in her husband's sleeping form. Is it any surprise they'd been so far apart? They'd both wrapped their secrets and guilt around themselves like shields, each believing they were responsible for their daughter's suffering, unable to let the other in. If only they'd been able to *talk*, they might have been able to come together. Instead, they'd let the space between them grow and grow, to the point where David had actually thought he'd be better off leaving. Only Anabelle had stopped him from going.

Charlotte sits down beside her husband, his warmth seeping through the duvet. David is ready now to be a father, and she's more than ready to be a mother. But are they ready once again to be husband and wife? Can they fight their way out of the tangle of secrets that has held them back and have a marriage once again? David did say he still loved her, but . . .

'Charlotte?' David's eyes open and he gazes sleepily up at her. 'Is that you? What are you doing here?'

'Hey.' She smiles, her lips trembling. 'I came back early.'

David sits up, scanning her face. 'Is everything okay?'

'David . . .' Charlotte pauses, garnering every last bit of strength and courage to tell him she remembers the past. To tell him about the ultrasound, about the one thing she could have done to protect their daughter – and didn't.

To tell him the real reason she wanted more of motherhood and the truth about why she pushed him away.

To start to untangle the web of secrets and see if they might have a future.

'David, I remember.' The words fall from her mouth and David's face hardens. 'I remember what happened before the accident, and Anabelle's birth, and . . .'

David's already out of bed and gathering up the clothes he left in a heap on the floor. 'I'll go,' he says quietly, not even looking at her. 'I'll sleep on the sofa tonight and I'll head to Mum's tomorrow.'

'Wait!' she hisses, trying not to wake Anabelle. 'You don't need to go. I don't want you to go. Just sit *down* for a sec.'

He sinks on to the bed without answering, his eyes locked on her. Charlotte takes a deep breath. Then, with their daughter fast asleep just inches away, she starts talking.

David is quiet while she speaks, his steady gaze not faltering even when she tells him of the ultrasound. She works her way through the past three years, and when her voice fades away, the room is silent but for the breathing of their daughter.

In and out. In and out. In and out.

Charlotte fills her ears with that precious sound, her heart pounding as she awaits David's reaction. After what feels like a lifetime, he folds her into his arms . . . and for the first time in years, she can sense he's giving her all of him. She lays her head on his chest and breathes in his familiar scent. There's no need for more words – no explanations, no apologies. There's just the two of them, battered and bruised, yet still together.

No, Charlotte thinks with a small smile: not just the two of them. It'll never be just the two of them again, and that's okay.

More than okay, actually.

Because finally, they're a family.

CHAPTER FORTY-EIGHT

Two months later

The leaves glow yellow in the autumn sunshine. Charlotte's legs churn out a rhythm as she puffs along the pavement, her breath coming in neat, controlled breaths. This is her first race since before she got pregnant with Anabelle. Training has been a challenge amid taking care of Anabelle and her busy work schedule, but thanks to David and Miriam's help, she's managed to fit in all her runs, growing in confidence as well as strength.

She'd found a pair of brand-new trainers in the dark depths under the bed, of all places. Even though it had been ages, she hadn't been able to resist putting them on and struggling into her running gear. David grinned when he saw her, rolling his eyes when she said her legs looked like overstuffed sausages in Spandex. Starting again was a challenge. Her legs ached and her lungs burned, but she kept going, covering more miles every day. Her body's different since giving birth – her stomach muscles have never returned to where they used to be – but overall, she's stronger than ever.

Finding a job that suits her experience has made her more confident, too – able to actually enjoy working again, without the stress and strain of constantly trying to prove herself. She smiles, remembering the email from Ute that pinged into her personal mailbox a few weeks ago. Ute was starting up her own consultancy, and said she'd love to have Charlotte on board as a UK-based consultant. Not as an employee, but as a freelancer, taking on contracts as needed. She didn't know if Charlotte was keen to stay put at Cellbril, but given the management's seeming inability to value employees' experience, she wondered if Charlotte might consider a move. She could work from home and manage her own schedule – Ute had had enough of managing employees. What did she think?

Although she'd had a few irons in the workplace fire, this had sounded like the perfect opportunity – and Charlotte was pleased someone had recognised how Ed had pushed her aside. She'd jumped at the chance, and she's been busy working ever since. At her own pace, as her own boss, getting the credit she deserves . . . it's been wonderful. Working from home is a challenge some days, but right now, she wouldn't trade it for anything. Anabelle has settled into nursery well and already has four 'best friends'. Miriam is only too happy to help out when needed, and with Charlotte doing pick-ups while David does drop-offs, it's all worked out brilliantly. With things going so well, they've decided to hold off on the move to Miriam's, eager to give themselves a chance to learn how to be a family first.

There are days, of course, when Charlotte wants to tear her hair out – when she needs more hours to work and Anabelle has to be picked up. There are times when she longs to cuddle her daughter just that bit longer before sending her off to nursery or disappearing on a week-long business trip. Life will never be as uncomplicated as it was before Anabelle came along, but Charlotte's learning to love the messy motherhood mix of frustration, fear . . . and love. Because above everything – even in that first year when she could barely blink without feeling guilt – it was love for her daughter that pulled her through; love that brought Charlotte back to her family after the accident.

And love that connected her and David once again after years of blame. Warmth rushes through her at the thought of her husband.

Learning to let go of their past mistakes and give themselves permission to be a couple again isn't always easy, but they're working on it . . . together. And if the night before last's lovemaking session is anything to go by, then practice is definitely on its way to making perfect.

Accommodating all the roles that make up who she is – mother, wife, worker, a person in her own right – may never be easy. They may push and strain and sometimes collide, one overtaking the other when the need is greater. But as long as Charlotte holds them all close to her heart, she needn't worry about losing any of them. They are written into her soul, the very fabric of her, and she can no more erase them than she can change the colour of her eyes. God knows, she's learned that by now.

Her heart leaps as she spots Anabelle, David and Miriam at the final bend before the finishing line. They jump and cheer when they see her, their voices so loud they cut through the cacophony of the crowd. Charlotte waves and gives them a huge smile, every inch of her glowing despite the fatigue of her body.

She focuses on the finishing line looming up ahead, getting closer and closer with every step. And she knows that, in life, she still has a long way to go – that in motherhood, there is no finishing line. There will always be new worries and new fears. There will always be obstacles to face, and new challenges as she tries to keep it all together.

But there will also be new hopes and dreams.

There will be laughter and light.

As the finishing line draws nearer, everything else drops away . . . everything but herself, pushing forward, pushing on.

Her legs churn faster and faster; her grin grows wider.

And she feels like she's flying.

ACKNOWLEDGMENTS

A huge thanks to the people who read this book in its early stages and gave me such support and encouragement: India Drummond, Glynis Smy, Mel Sherratt and my wonderful agent, Madeleine Milburn. A big thank you to the team at Amazon Publishing, especially Victoria Pepe, who has been such a pleasure to work with. Thanks, also, to my editor Sophie Wilson, who never fails to amaze me with her thoughtful input and ideas.

Finally, thank you to my husband for always being there to discuss complicated plotlines, and to my son, who teaches me something new about motherhood every day.